# A SHRED OF HONOUR

*By the same author*

THE HUNTING SEASON
WOLF'S HEAD
CRY HAVOC

# A SHRED
# OF HONOUR

## J K Mayo

**HARVILL**
*An Imprint of* HarperCollins*Publishers*

First published in 1993 by Harvill
an imprint of HarperCollins*Publishers*,
77–85 Fulham Palace Road
Hammersmith, London W6 8JB

9 8 7 6 5 4 3 2 1

©J K Mayo 1993

The moral right of the author has been asserted

BRITISH LIBRARY CATALOGUING IN PUBLICATION DATA

A CIP catalogue record for this book
is available from the British Library

ISBN 0 00 271136 2 paperback
0 00 271855 3 hardback

Typeset in Linotron Bembo by
Rowland Phototypesetting Ltd, Bury St Edmunds, Suffolk

Printed and bound in Great Britain by
HarperCollinsManufacturing, Glasgow

Put me in the Kalahari
Leave me on the sand
Give me only Mata Hari
And a small string band

# 1

The shadows of the three men, who were standing fifty paces or so apart from one another, sketched a line that made a shallow V with the front of the wood to which the field rose gently before them. The wood was mixed, mainly of oak and beech and sycamore and ash, whose remaining leaves were paled now from their first autumnal splendour, though here and there Scotch and Corsican pine struck patches of dark against the thinning foliage.

At the lower end of the field, where two keepers waited behind the three men, mist had begun to form, and in the upper air the setting sun filtered through the moistness of the ending day to throw, upon the meadow and the trees, a purely English radiance which would have brought Constable to his easel.

From the dusk that edged the strip of wood a covey of pheasants burst upward, as if the stillness of the waiting men had broken their nerve. Five barrels flared, the explosions whacked the air, and four birds fell. In the instant of silence before the dogs ran forward a woodcock took wing from the undergrowth and, with a fast and unpredictable jinking flight, made first for the sun and then turned, dropping, back to the cover of the wood.

At the western extremity of the line the sixth barrel fired and the bird was tossed, a brief memorial of loose feathers drifting after it, to the foot of the trees.

"Well done, sir!" the man on his right called out, but the executant of the brilliant shot lay on his back cursing, apparently unable to get himself to his feet.

Two men, who had been lying prone in the middle of the strip of wood, came stumbling out, and from the south side of the field ran another handful of men. A woman followed them, not running, but walking briskly.

A helicopter whisked up from the east and hovered, clattering, overhead. Two Land Rovers appeared at opposite corners of the field, and men debouched from them.

The two from the wood stood close, in front and behind, the man who had shouted out his congratulations to the fallen gun.

"I wish you would get down, sir," the man in front said.

"Oh, rubbish," was the answer. "I'm sure it's nothing; just that tin leg of his gave way. Let's go and see."

The third gun, however, had waved the nearest Land Rover in, and set it to passage between the group and the wood as they went to succour the fallen.

They arrived to hear the stricken man excoriate the party from the south, who had got there first. "Don't just stand there like a collection of half-shut knives," he said. "Help me up, for God's sake!"

Two men bent towards him.

"No," the woman said, arriving. "Leave him alone. He must do it himself."

"Damn your black soul to hell," the man on the ground said. "You're fired."

"I doubt it," the woman said, and smiled; and if she had been beautiful before, at the smile a thousand ships would have leapt into the water. "Come on, you gutless wonder, do your stuff," she said, and kicked him gently with the toe of her boot.

A frisson of dismay ran through those grouped about him, as if a courtier had spat on the throne.

"Oh, very well," the gutless wonder said. "But get that damned helicopter out of here. I'm not going to be photographed doing this."

At this exchange the man who had been the middle gun masked his expression and turned his face up to the sky. The third gun put his head in at the window of the Land Rover and spoke briefly, and the helicopter swept off out of sight and then out of earshot.

The fallen man grasped his prosthetic leg with both hands and revolved onto his stomach, put both hands on the ground, and came up to kneel on the knee of his real leg.

"Shooting-stick," he said, flourishing an irritable hand.

One of the keepers pushed forward and put the stick into his hand. "Can you manage, Sir John?" he asked.

"I can, thank you," Sir John said. "I have to, with that termagant watching." He planted the stick in front of him, put both hands on it, and by walking the real leg and shuffling the other towards this prop, which wobbled precariously under the stress put on it, he came to his feet.

"Aha!" he said, his face reddened with effort and filled with triumph. He put an arm across the woman's shoulder, but in affection, not for support. "What about that woodcock, then?"

"Yes, indeed," she said. "How's the stump?"

"Nothing much wrong with it," he said, "that you can't make better."

"Don't show off," she said, but when he took the arm off her shoulder, she held him by it lightly with both hands as they set off for the car that had parked itself at the field gate. They moved together like lovers, but their appearance made such an idea extraordinary.

He might have been seventy. He carried himself like a survivor of ancient wars, confident of outlasting those to come. Like a Frenchman of the Third Empire, he wore a long moustache, and this was piebald, the left side black and the other white. It grew under a nose which thrust like an eagle's beak from his florid countenance. The mouth below it – even now, when it was smiling wide, when he was in his good humour, when its self-indulgent fleshiness suggested the well-lived life of a fortunate man – had a cruel turn to it; and behind the bright-blue glitter of the eyes hardness lay, like ice under a sunlit sea.

The woman who walked beside this vigorous monument and held his arm was in her early twenties. She was wearing an open thorn-proof jacket, an Aran sweater and cords, and hiking boots. Despite the slow pace they kept, a natural bounce in her walk suggested a hopeful and vivacious nature. Within her loose and heavy clothes, the motion of her body bespoke the rounded excellence of a Venus, deep-bosomed and small-hipped.

Beneath the dark and tousled hair, her brown eyes sparkled with a delight (in what? – in life, in the day, in the old man at her side?) that animated the whole expression of her face. It was that face of

9

a lovely Jewess which has large eyes, arched eyebrows, a broad and intelligent forehead, dimpled cheeks, a retroussé nose, and a generous and kindly mouth; but in her incarnation these elements united to compose one of those declarations of beauty with which life transcends the imagination.

They reached the car.

A pall of cloud cheated the sunset of its last moment and freezing rain began to fall. A man in a mackintosh that was rusting with age, and with a wide-brimmed leather hat on his head, held open a door of the Jaguar.

"God, you're a rotten dresser, Maxton," Arkley said. "Leap aboard, Anna."

"Handsome is as handsome does, Sir John," Maxton said, regarding his boss with a bland eye.

"Don't be insolent," Arkley said, "or you'll be out on your ear and back to bouncing drunks out of nightclubs."

"That wasn't insolent, for one thing," Maxton said, "and for the other: roll on the day."

"Do we just go?" Anna said. "What about the Foreign Secretary?"

"We just go," Arkley said. "I'm not having protocol on a shoot. That's his car there, and it's my house, and I want my bath and my whisky. Let's get on with it."

As the car went slowly down the cart track to the road, Arkley said: "What did you make of that security response, Maxton?"

"What can I tell you?" Maxton said. "Too little, too late."

"They seemed pretty quick to me," Anna said.

"Ten years too late," Maxton said. "If the Army had been let loose on the IRA the way they wanted, that's one war that would be over by now."

"You can't say things like that out loud, for God's sake." Arkley said. "What do you think, Preston?"

"What he said about the IRA?" the driver said. "Fucking right."

"You've got the instincts of gangsters, you two," Arkley said.

"I should hope so," Maxton said.

Arkley, who clearly felt himself to have been stroked by this frank and free exchange of views, became refulgent, and silent.

"I covet the hat," Anna said.

"I'd give you anything," Maxton said, "but not the hat. This is my lucky hat. All my luck is in this hat."

"All of it?" Anna said. "That's risky, to put all your luck in one hat."

"Life is risk," Maxton said.

Anna brushed some mud off the stout cheviot cloth which clad Arkley's legs, the real leg and the artificial replacement for the one that had been shot off last year. She remembered the wild and cunning flight of the woodcock in front of the trees before it fell to Arkley's gun.

She looked out into the rain, and after a while, so long a while that Maxton did not at first realize that she was responding to him, she said: "Yes, life is risk."

Those who had been the three guns were now three English gentlemen after dinner. Since it was an informal evening at the end of a day's sport, they had not dressed for dinner. They were wearing between five and ten thousand pounds' worth of quite ordinary, but decent, suits, shirts, shoes, and so forth.

"The Third World," the Foreign Secretary said, and stretched out in his chair and sighed. "The problems it gives us."

"Have you formed a view?" Arkley said.

"Yes," Lander said. "We are going to do nothing."

"Nothing," Arkley said. He looked into the fire, which looked back at him and, with the shifting of a log, flared up, putting a weird and evil light into his eyes.

The third man, who was a soldier, mistook Arkley's repetition of the word for a question and a complaint.

"We cannot, for example, put the SAS in," he said. "You don't give us enough to go on. You don't give us a target, Arkley."

"I don't give you a target?" Arkley said. "You people enlarge this blight upon the world and then tell me I don't give you a target."

"It is true," the Foreign Secretary said comfortably, "that in one sense 'we people' have enlarged this blight upon the world, but you seek to make us responsible for it in a very old-fashioned sense, Arkley. I take you to mean, in the first place, that the

Defence Secretary must take responsibility for what goes on in his Ministry; and in the second place that, according to the doctrine of collective responsibility, the whole Cabinet must share responsibility for a blunder made under the aegis of one of its members, and therefore it is the British Government that has unleashed this menace."

He made those slight motions with his hand that set the cognac swirling in the glass; put the glass to his nose, and then to his mouth.

"I do like this brandy, Arkley," he said.

"It's nothing very special," Arkley said without courtesy. "Good enough for a plain meal after a day in the fresh air."

The words might have described the room they sat in. Everything in it was old and comfortable to look upon. Worn leather chairs, faded rugs, pools of light from table lamps, the log fire glowing and hissing and sparking, the old labrador at Arkley's feet, and the bitch – one of the old one's offspring, herself due to whelp in three days – lying on the cool oak planks near the door: all this had more to do with fresh air and plain meals than with international power politics.

"Where was I?" Lander said. "Yes: your statement that 'we people' are to blame. That opinion of yours requires the idea of collective responsibility to bear an interpretation far wide of the way in which it is understood by this Cabinet. We understand it to mean something quite different, no more than that we are honour-bound – if honour is not too strong a word – to have it seem to the public that we are all agreed on every policy and every action framed or executed by the Government of which we are a part. That is what we mean by collective responsibility."

"Honour," said Arkley, "is indeed too strong a word."

"That goes beyond the bounds, Arkley," Lander said.

"Much I care if it does," Arkley said. "Bounds, what bounds? We three are met in my house because you dare not have us meet either in your house or at the Foreign Office; because you dare not trust any of your officials, any more than General Tinsley dare trust his officials, or even his officers, at the Ministry of Defence, with the knowledge of this imperial fuck-up that you people—" and he paused to emphasize his repetition of that phrase, "—that

12

you people have made. And in my house, Mr Secretary, it is I who set the bounds."

Arkley smiled with pleasure, because he meant with great sincerity what he said about his house. He did not know how he looked or sounded when he said it; possibly absurd. But saying it, he felt like some feudal baron or Renaissance prince, sitting within his massy castle with his men at call, or like some Mafia chief in his stronghold: felt like them because he was secure against all opposition that fell short of assassination. There were a good few who would assassinate John Arkley if they could, but he did not number Lander or Tinsley among them.

The Foreign Secretary was one of those small but strong-built Celtic men that come out of Britain's once industrial cities, the natural mobility of whose dark and fiercely marked countenance had been trained into a professional mask, giving the effect of a volcanically formed landscape whose convulsive origins had been long forgotten.

"Arkley," he said now. "What are you on your high horse about?"

"Let me ask Tinsley a question," Arkley said, "and then you shall have your answer from me. Tinsley," he said, "if I gave you a target and if you were to put the SAS in, with no identification on them of any kind; say there were casualties: could you guarantee they would not become known as ours?"

"A target would presumably be some kind of military base," the General said. "No matter what African state, it would be a fortified target. We would have a probability of casualties and fatalities, a probability of not being able to get them all out. One way or the other, they would become known to be ours."

"In that case," the Foreign Secretary said, "it is out of the question. In itself it would be a published act of war."

"Are you telling me," Arkley said, "that even if I know the target, we can do nothing?"

"I'm telling you no such thing," Lander said. "We can't do nothing. These bestial devices are British, for pity's sake. God knows where they'll end up, who plans to use them and on whom. Is it not plain that if they are used against certain states and their origin becomes known – and it might be politic to either the aggressor or the victim of aggression to let their origin become known – is it not plain that appalling consequences may flow?"

"The chief of which, in your mind, is I suppose that it might bring down the Government," Arkley said. "It would hardly be enough," the smile under his long parti-coloured moustache was nothing less than ribald, "for the Defence Secretary alone to resign."

"I happen to believe," Lander said, "that a change of government would be the worst thing that could happen to this country."

"It is a great creed," Arkley said, "that marches with self-interest."

"Damn your eyes, Arkley." The choler filled out the Foreign Secretary's face and neck with red. "You're ten times dirtier a street-fighter than I am. Don't throw that high-flown stuff at me."

"You go too far, Arkley," General Tinsley said.

"You're not a law unto yourself, you know. You're a servant of the Government," Lander said.

"Do you truly believe so?" Arkley said. "Let's get something out of the way first. This business came to my attention when a man from another intelligence agency defected because of what he felt to be the horror of a consignment of chemical and/or biological weaponry being on its way to an end-user somewhere in Africa. He went to a man called Mullen at MI5, whom he had met in the way of business.

"I pass this information to your Secretary of State, to Tinsley, and to the Foreign Office. The next thing I know is that an inner committee of the Cabinet . . ."

"How the hell do you know that?" Lander asked.

Arkley just looked at him.

". . . of the Cabinet has met, and I am told that no one in my Department, outside those who already know, must be made aware of this dread secret. Which is asinine, since of those who already know, some are low-level. Nevertheless, I conform, sending the most low-level of those who know to staff the safe house where the defector is to be held, and where at least they will talk only to each other.

"I am then told that, whatever action I may be called upon to take, I alone must know the whole picture. The separate actions of those taking part must be compartmentalized, so that each individual or group knows only what that separate individual or group needs to know.

"Well, I know where that came from. That did not come from four Cabinet Ministers meeting alone. That kind of theoretical rubbish was drafted to order by a civil servant who knew damn well it meant nothing, and would certainly mean nothing to me. What's more, I'll bet he, or she, told you so to your faces."

At this, General Tinsley let discipline go altogether and laughed. He left his chair and began to walk about the room, moving with a contained restlessness, as if this talk of Cabinets and civil servants had evoked in him the frustrations that political constraint imposed on direct military action.

Tinsley was a tall man, and seemed by nature calm. His smooth face looked ten years younger than a lieutenant-general's should. You found this man in his eyes, which gave you a candid stare, but were of a cold and pallid blue that let him think anything he liked behind their honest curtain.

"I wouldn't wonder, Arkley," Tinsley said, "if that bitch isn't going to have her pups tonight."

Arkley looked round and saw her biting at herself in what certainly looked like pre-natal agitation. "I think you're right," he said. "I'll have Maxton put her out in the kennel tonight. She's been making a secret nest, of course, up in the garden. Yes, it's time to have her in the kennel."

He nudged the old dog with his toe. "What do you think, Top?" Top shifted his chin from one forepaw to the other.

Arkley grinned to himself and rubbed his hand down his moustache and mouth and chin: might as well ask guidance from Lander and his fellows.

"I'm tired of all this," Arkley said. "That's why I got up on my high horse. We all know that I'm the only one who can do anything about this, and we all know the Cabinet doesn't want to sanction the way I'll do it, or even hear about it afterwards. Honour," he said, "the word sticks in my throat. I have not understood it since I left school and I do not miss it. I dare say Tinsley has some: it's part of his profession."

He lifted a hand to cut the Foreign Secretary off. "Do you need to wave your rank at me? We all know you're the top man here, in certain terms. We know you're a Minister of the Crown. Let's leave *amour propre* out of it. Let us talk simply as men, for God's sake, and get it done with."

He waited, insisting on a response.

"Go ahead," Lander said crossly. "But before you do, Arkley – and don't get up, I can help myself—"

Arkley came to his feet. "I'm not a cripple. I can stand up," he said, taking Lander's glass. "And I can do what you, Foreign Secretary, and you, General Tinsley, cannot: I can fight wars where I choose. And I have begun this one."

At this piece of braggadocio the Foreign Secretary's colour fired up again, but he kept his temper this time and took the glass from Arkley's hand. "Thank you," he said. "What have you done," he asked, "by way of beginning this war of yours?"

"I have hired my army," Arkley said.

Tinsley came to a stand by the drinks table, gave himself some brandy, and sat down again.

"This council of war is over, isn't it?" Tinsley said.

Arkley inclined his head.

"It never was a council of war, to you," Tinsley said.

"No," Arkley said. "I did not ask for this meeting."

"We know that," Lander said. "I called it. The Cabinet needs to know what's being done."

"When we went to war in the Gulf," Arkley said, in a reminiscential tone, "some mini-committee of damn fools, acting on a level of authority that had either been delegated to them when no one was looking, or descended upon them from above and alighted long enough to endorse their judgement, decided to send this materiel out so that the enemy would know it was there; so that the enemy would know we had on the ground the capacity to retaliate in kind if he used his own chemical or biological weapons.

"Not that we would ever use them," Arkley went on. "Tsk-tsk! Certainly not. And now they have been stolen and sold on. I don't suppose they were that easy to steal; on the other hand, I recall how after Iraq's surrender, our tanks – which had done rather better than anyone else's – were left to rot, whereas the Americans immediately serviced theirs and covered everything with oil, or

16

whatever one does to keep tanks serviceable, so that they'd be ready for action again at once."

He smiled at Tinsley, who stared grimly back at him.

"When I consider that fact," Arkley said, "I suppose that a dozen or so green packing-cases looking like ammunition could easily lose their labels saying fragile, treat with care, this end up – or whatever was felt to be the appropriate top-security measure – and could easily be lost sight of in the euphoria of the idea that the war was won and we could all go home now."

Behind him the black labrador bitch heaved herself around restlessly. He turned to look, and then cast his eye at the clock on the mantelpiece.

"Time for bed," he said. "I shall do all that is needed, but I value myself rather more than if I were a green packing-case, Lander, and so you will have no report from me until the thing is done. As it is, Tinsley's intelligence colleagues were alert to this before the Cabinet's, ah, particular proprietorial anxiety became known. Tinsley: your man Seddall, what is he doing?"

Tinsley turned his eyes downward and smiled, then looked up at Arkley. "Harry Seddall keeps his own counsel. He's a bit like you in that respect. Do you want to hear from him?"

"I've thought of it," Arkley said, "but no. He's old enough to look after himself. Two heads may just be better than one, if they're kept separate."

The Foreign Secretary stood up. "That is absurd, Arkley. It is obviously essential that you and Seddall communicate with each other on a regular basis till this is finished with. I'll want my car ready in five minutes."

Arkley stood up, too, and Top struggled to his feet in the hope of an evening stroll before turning in.

"Communicate? We've been communicating all evening, and a fat lot of good it's done." He leaned forward on his stick; malice and venom in his eyes. "You people have fouled up. Let people like Seddall and myself handle the dirty work."

He limped to the door and opened it, and the second door, for the room was, in this eighteenth-century way, draught- and sound-proofed.

"Maxton," he said into the hall, "we must put Snowdrop into

her kennel now, it looks as if she may whelp tonight. Oh, and tell the Foreign Secretary's staff that he is leaving. Come on, Top, let's walk round the garden."

He went off, leaving the Minister with his rage, and the general with his fortitude.

Maxton had helped Arkley into his coat. "Let me borrow that lucky leather hat of yours, Maxton," Arkley said, "just for ten minutes while I walk in the night air. I think I might need some of that luck."

# 2

After she had been a week in her mother's house, Toko M'pofu left the village and set off into the Kalahari.

"How long will you be gone?" her mother said.

"Till I come back," Toko said.

"How far are you going to go?"

"As far as till I turn round," Toko said.

"Don't be smart with me," her mother said. She looked at Toko in her shorts and T-shirt with the bag slung over her shoulder; it was an old white hunter's game bag that her husband, Toko's dead father, had come by. "I worry about you."

"You should have worried about me long ago, when I was a little girl," Toko said. "Do you think I don't know I'm crazy? I'm crazy and I'm unhappy. Now I'm going. Let me be. I'm going and I'll be back. There's nothing out there going to hurt me."

"You don't know what's out there. There are lions up north." She stood in the doorway of the hut in her cotton dress and jerked her head towards the river. "Take your father's rifle with you."

"When did you last see a lion round here?" Toko said. "Anyway, those cartridges are twenty years old. If I tried to use that rusted-out rifle, either it wouldn't fire at all or it would blow up in my face."

"I'm not talking about round here," her mother said. She looked at the sky. "It's a man, isn't it? You're unhappy about a man."

"I've been unhappy all my life, except once," Toko said. "I'm going now."

"You be careful at the river. Don't you swim that river. You know there are crocodiles here," her mother said.

"They won't touch me. I'm Bakwena," Toko said. She meant: the crocodile is the totem of the Bakwena tribe.

"You're not Bakwena," her mother said. "I'm Bakwena. You're Zulu, like your father was. And I don't swim that river."

Toko let go of the evil in her and her white teeth flashed in the sun as she laughed and laughed. "I'd like to see you swim," she said. "Oh, God, I'd like to see you swim right into a crocodile. What a meal he'd get out of you."

Her mother stood and put her arms out and shimmied. "He could feed off me for a month," she said, "if I let him." Her breasts swung like pumpkins under the cotton frock. She moved from the hut towards her daughter. "Can I hug you?" she said.

When Toko emerged from all that flesh, she leaned her forearms on her mother's shoulders and said: "I'm not going to get dead. I'm going into the bush to get my life back for myself."

"You try it, child," her mother said. "You do it, if you can."


At noon, Toko went to rest in a thicket of shrub acacia, taking not too many scratches as she made her way to the heart of it. She did not know how far she had come, perhaps twenty kilometres, perhaps fifteen, but in any case that was not how she measured distance when she was covering country on foot like this.

She knew how far she went in a day when she was fit (and she was always fit), and that was the measure she used: a day's journey. It was natural to her; what she had grown up with. The ancient Greeks, when they were on campaign, had measured distance in the same way, according to Dujardin. They had a word for it: a parasang, a day's march. Dujardin was the most professional soldier she had met, and she had met a few in her line of business, in one of her lines of business; well, in one line of business more than the other. God, he had been a good man to know. She did not think of it as love. She thought of it as passion. She did not think of herself as missing him. She wanted him.

"I want you, Dujardin, you bastard. Where are you, man? What's happened to you?" It had been most of a year now. He used to turn up at unpredictable intervals, after a month, after three months; but this one was too long. There was something

20

wrong about this one. If he'd wanted to quit her for good, he'd have told her straight. Something was wrong. "Don't be dead, Commandant Dujardin," she said. "I want you living, man."

She'd been with her mother three weeks now. When she emerged from the bush she'd go to Paris, and perhaps find word from him at home. Or he'd be there one night when she was performing.

She shut her eyes and saw him, then went to sleep, and dreamed.


When she woke, she felt freed from something. She extricated herself from the acacia and sat with her hands round her knees. She felt the heat of the ground on her bottom. She felt Africa. She smelled Africa. She wondered if Dujardin would live with her in Africa, and she laughed.

"Dujardin isn't going to live with anyone, anywhere," she said. "Get going, woman. Get up and go."

She put herself to running along the edge of the track, the red-brown dust kicking up from her feet. The Kalahari stretched away from her, a wilderness of thorn and scrub. She saw kudu and duiker, and twice, in the distance, great clouds of dust rising into the bright sky as herds of springbok or wildebeest moved across the plain. Yellow flowers flashed on her eye.

She heard a truck come up behind her. When it reached her, it slowed. "We give you a ride, girl," a voice called.

"*Merde*," Toko said, and stopped running.

The truck stopped too, and its dust settled round it. It was a pedlar's truck with two men in the cab and one on top of the load. The driver was a big Bantu man with a cheerful smile. The man beside him leaned forward to see her. His smile was not so good. The one squatting on top just looked at her and lifted a hand.

They were looking her body over: a lithe and sweating woman with her shorts and T-shirt sticking to her. She was used to this, used to men looking her over when she was singing at the bar in Paris, wearing less than this.

That was work though. In Paris, singing in her bare skin was her own aggression against men. This was not work, and the aggression now was not hers.

21

She stepped back from the truck and pulled the strap of the bag over her head and put it on the ground. The flap fell open, but she ignored that. She wiped the sweat off her face and ran her hands through her hair.

"Thanks," she said. "I don't need a ride."

The driver had the door open, and he stood on the step and looked along the track, before and behind. "Maybe I need a ride," he said, and jumped down.

"Oh, fuck," Toko said, and stepped one pace back. She blinked against the sun, looking up at him. "Leave me alone, man," she said. God, he was big.

A glimmer of blue and lilac flew between them and a small bird settled on the cab of the truck.

"I want you," the man said simply, and reached for her.

She took another pace back. "I don't want you, man," she said. "Don't bother me."

His eyes went dull and she knew words were not going to do it for her. He came on at her like a bull coming on to rut. She was going to have to work, after all.

She wiped the sweat out of her eyes again and moved in, her hundred and twenty pounds against his two hundred and more. She jabbed two fingers into his eyes and two into his solar plexus, and kicked him in the balls. He bent over a little towards her and howled. One eye was out, hanging on his cheek, and the other was a mess of blood and tissue.

She gave a moment to the truck. The man on top was still sitting there, staring with his mouth open. The other man was coming across the cab.

She hit the howling man twice, fast and hard on the back of the neck, and when he fell, his head hit a stone. She grabbed his hair and whacked his head on the stone and left him.

Still down there, she jumped from her knees towards the open bag, and as the man came out of the cab at her she took the Auto-Mag from the bag and shot him twice in the face. Some of his head flew onto the roof of the cab and the pretty bird, which had flown away when the pistol fired, came back and pecked at it and began to feed.

The man on top of the load proved himself smarter than the

other two. He jumped off on the far side and ran for the bush.

Toko cleared the front of the truck, brought the long barrel of the Auto-Mag down and fired one, two, three, and saw the hit of a bullet make him leap in his flight. The .44 in this pistol was a pretty hot cartridge. She fired again, and he ran a few more steps and fell. Toko went up to him, and was about to give him the *coup de grâce* when he lifted once and died.

"You shouldn't have been here," she told the corpse. "You had bad luck," she told the flying spirit. "You should have had good luck. Have good luck now."

She ran back to the truck, and that goddamn bird was still eating brains on the cab roof. The driver, the man who had been the driver, was on his back now lamenting his pain and blindness to the sky; a strange, sad sound of groans and sighs.

She took the knife from her bag and put it in his heart, leaving the weapon in him to keep the blood-spill down. She put the pistol in her bag and threw the bag into the cab.

The big man was a hell of a weight, so instead of hoisting him and the man whose brain-pan was feeding that goddamn swallow-tailed roller into the truck, she took some of the cord that lashed the load, tied them together and hitched them to the tailboard. Then she got in and drove over to the last of her dead, and him she lifted into the cab beside her, because he was a light and skinny lad, no more than a boy.

She drove off into the bush, singing in her sweet voice – she had quite a repertoire of voices to choose from; the sweet voice was the one she felt like using. She sang:

> *Plaisir d'amour*
> *ne dure q'un moment.*
> *Chagrin d'amour*
> *dure toute la vie.*

It was true. It was true. She'd had a bad life, and she was an unhappy woman, but tough, tough, tough. So she sang and laughed. She'd rather have cried, but the tears were so far inside her that she just laughed up here instead. There was no one in the world she trusted enough to cry on, and she was not going to cry alone.

She drove up to a sand ridge, going slowly. She stopped the truck and got out to see what was beyond the ridge, and found that it rose from a long shallow salt pan about fifty feet below her. The pan had a floor of white clay and looked as if it ran for miles. She walked the ridge until she found the place that would do for what she wanted: a place where she could start the truck down and be sure it would go all the way.

She wanted a good-looking accident. These guys were full of wounds or bullets, but a good-looking accident, a burnt-out truck and bodies, would be enough to stop anyone in this country getting interested.

She brought the truck along. She ran her eye over the bodies that she'd towed through the scrub. M'pofu, she said, you've turned these men into raw meat; they're just raw meat now. There was a lot of blood on them.

She stripped herself bare.

"Hell," she said, and laughed aloud. That old knife was still there, sticking into the big bull's heart.

She pulled a shirt out of a bundle on the truck and folded it around the top of the knife, gripped the haft of it and pulled. The corpse's chest lifted. She shook her head and let go. She took another shirt from the bundle and made a pad with it on the big bull's chest: she put a foot on the pad, and took hold of the knife again and worked at it until it came away from the bone and sinew.

Good old knife. She wiped it on the bundle of shirts and put it with the clothes in her bag, which she tossed well clear of the truck.

It took her long enough to get the two corpses up and into the cab. The rope helped, but they were as good as naked from their ride over the rough ground. By the time she'd done with them, her body was bloodied from its intimacies with the dead.

After she had finished this, she would run till she found water. She would shoot something good with that long-range pistol, and when she had found water, she would bathe. Then she would feast herself before she slept. She knew she would be hungry. She liked to gorge herself after killing, and she had killed three this time.

24

Toko started the engine of the truck, took the petrol can from the back, and splashed half of the fuel in it over the inside of the cab, bodies and upholstery alike. She soaked another of those cotton shirts in petrol, tied it to the handle on the outside of the door, and led it over the sill of the window down into the can.

She had the can jammed between the door and the big man's feet. He was lying across the floor with his head on his buddy's chest and his knees bent; pushing at the can with his feet, being useful. The boy was lying along the seat, face down, with that hole in his back where the bullet had gone in.

Toko had no idea what state of mind she was in by this time. It was weird: she could say that about it. She knew she was a ruthless girl and she had dealt with corpses before, but this was turning into the roughest disposal job she could remember. She was getting too involved with these dead men; she was wearing too much of their blood on her skin, and more to come.

Well, to hell with that. Get it done.

She'd got matches from the pedlar's stock in the back of the truck, but because she was doing this job naked, she had nowhere to stash them. She put the box of matches between her teeth, gripped the edge of the cab roof and swung herself through the window. She sat herself, bare-assed as she was, on the shoulders of the dead boy and found herself shaking her head. But what else could she do? She had to get the truck started.

For a moment she looked straight out of the windscreen at the sky: beautiful now, lemon-coloured as the sun went down. This day had done something wrong to her. She had done something wrong to herself.

She put the gear lever in first and pulled out the choke until it was edging the truck forward. She wriggled herself onto the sill of the window, clung to the roof while she got her legs out, and jumped to the ground. The truck was moving at walking pace and she walked with it, taking a clump of matches out of the box as she went. The truck reached the ridge where the plain fell away to the salt flat below. Toko struck the matches. She touched the flame to the petrol-soaked cotton fuse, stopped for a foolish second to watch it burn, and then, as the truck's nose tipped down, ran back from the edge and threw herself to the ground.

Lying there with her nose on the red earth, it came to her that if she'd had the sense she was born with she would have set light to the petrol tank. And, dammit, she was shaking. If she'd been on the job she would have been thinking straight. But this had been a private fight. Why should that throw her? Fuck these guys.

A solid thump hit the air behind her, muted by the fall of the land. She stood up and found her bag, and went to look.

When she reached the ridge, the truck was just finishing its run down the slope, burning with a thick orange flame and far too much black smoke. Still, it would be dark soon, the fire would not last long, and by morning the smoke would be finished. The petrol tank had gone up all right. The truck had stopped now and was being consumed by fire.

She slid and jumped down the side of the salt pan and made her assessment. She could wait till the flames were finished and make sure they had eaten up the bodies so that there was no trace of how the three men had died. Or she could rely on what she saw before her now: that the whole truck was a funeral pyre and the cab itself raging like a furnace.

She walked close enough to feel the heat on her body and watched the fire burn, but she had already made up her mind. She brushed the sand and the red earth from her body, and felt that smile, her own smile for herself, come onto her face as the stroking of her hands slowed and turned to caresses, and her eyes went with them.

It was, she was, a sweet long-legged body, her thighs lean and beautiful, her bottom high and round with those dimples above it that Dujardin loved, or had loved: had once loved, perhaps still loved if ever he remembered them. He was not a loving man, but perhaps he was better than that, for her.

He loved her body, as she did, and as she loved his. She was not a loving woman, except to herself. She had grown into her passion for Dujardin, but she would care for no one as she cared for herself. She held her breasts gently, and then clutched them to pain, and then opened her eyes wide in self-mockery. "You're too small," she said to them affectionately, and for the thousandth time. But small breasts were good for running, and she had some running to do now.

"Come on, sweetheart," she said to herself. "Let's get away from here."

She put the strap of the bag over her head and slung it from her left shoulder across her body, so that it hung at her right hip. She took out the pistol and inserted a new clip, and put it back in the bag.

She gave the burning truck one last look. Her face became grim, but then there was one more flicker of that smile she smiled for herself.

"Well, *ma chère*," she said, "at least you didn't get raped." She longed for a shower and for avocado soap to wash the blood and dirt off her hide.

She ran north, naked, lithe as a panther, towards the night that waited behind the sun to sweep over the Kalahari.

# *3*

Two thousand miles to the north, four camels, three of them ridden and the fourth carrying food, walked over a drought-stricken land. Here the acacias had died. The travellers had camped in wadis where the arak trees had shrivelled and turned grey, and they had crossed miles of dead grass where, within the decade, there had been grazing for camel herds and flocks of goats and sheep.

The life that used to exist in the desert had died. For two weeks, passing across this desolation, they had seen no living soul, neither man nor beast. Now, as they left the dune-sea and entered a wilderness of rock that closed round them in cliffs of shattered granite, broken and shaped by extremes of temperature and by the scouring wind, the lead rider held up a hand and pulled his camel round.

"Soldiers," he said, his rifle, the old Lee-Enfield, already in his hand.

"Military out here? The devil!" The speaker, from the height of his huge arabi camel, looked down on the old man, who had turned his racing dromedary on the spot as if it were a circus pony. "Are they those we seek?"

"Theirs are not the tracks we follow," the old man said, nodding his head down to the tyre tracks in the cream-coloured sand. "There are only a couple of armoured cars. Let us kill them, by God!"

The old man's face had set long ago in harsh and cruel lines, and behind the glow in his grey eyes was a hard and fixed will for battle. He wore the shirt and baggy breeches of the nomad, and his headcloth proclaimed that his was the Bedayatt tribe, famous

28

as bandits and camel-thieves in the days before the desert life began to end.

"Let us think about it first," said the other man, who was dressed also as a man of the Bedayatt. He crouched his camel and came off the high saddle. "Those armoured cars, what were they doing?"

"They were making tea," the old man said. "We could charge down and kill them all."

The man on the third camel, who was no more than twenty, said: "Are they government cars, or rebel?"

"Politics! Grandson, be quiet," the old man said.

"Taif," the other man said to the young man, "take this beast into the shade. I shall inspect these cars. Dear God, the heat!"

"Ingleez!" the Bedayatt said scornfully, implying both weakness under the scorching sun and cowardice in the Englishman's refusal to fall headlong upon the armoured-car patrol.

Yet neither in the Bedayatt's vocabulary nor the Englishman's own did weakness and cowardice describe the man to whom they were addressed. What assailed him was more mysterious than either of these. It had arisen in him over the past two weeks, and the Bedayatt knew it. He had seen it in the Englishman's eyes during the day and heard it in his troubled dreams at night.

To the Englishman, these two weeks had been as the onset of madness. For into them had come images from the weeks that had gone before. During each day's travel across this endless desert and in the dreams that came with sleep, images of what he had seen moved perpetually within him.

These images that beset him were of starvation and death. They had been formed in the first stage of the journey, as they passed through a land devastated by famine. At first they met those who had survived the long trek from the arid hinterland. They met them in their thousands, but that meant nothing to him at the time. To him they were merely refugees. It was later, well into the desert, that they came on the worst of it.

The worst of it was families in groups, the straggling survivors of nomadic tribes, who had made their final encampment. Who had left behind them the last of the grazing land, withered by drought, that had once nourished their flocks, and the thorn trees that had fed their camels. Who had killed the last of their goats or cattle or sheep, and finally the last of their camels, and walked now, perishing on their feet from lack of food and water, carrying their dying, and sometimes their dead, children.

The three men and their laden pack-camel trotted through them, giving nothing of their store and yielding no kindness. The iron face of Ibrahim led the way; Taif followed, sometimes weeping openly at what he saw, sometimes turned in on himself; and the Englishman came last, a hard and oblivious man, no sharer of the suffering of others.

The very worst of it, after that time, was families on their own: sometimes two parents, sometimes one, and always the children. That was the very worst, because so far into the desert all those they met would die before they could hope to reach such succour as the refugee camps and the cities – always supposing they were let near the cities – might offer them.

After that they met the dead. The dead were sometimes alone, often an infant or a child, left where they had died, or when a mother had acknowledged, at last, that she must leave the body she had been carrying if she was to go further herself. Sometimes they came on families, all of them dead, groups of three or four or five, as if the parents had recognized the futility of trying to keep on, and had chosen to make the dying of the family an act they would perform together.

There had been nothing, after that, but the desert, a desert of pebbles or sand, or dead grass and dead bush and trees. It was then, and not until then, that the images came to him. He could remember nothing like this happening to him in his life before.

At first he put it down to the heat. It was only three years since he had been in Africa, and even at that the Sahara was new to him. The sun burned with a ferocity that belonged to the summer, although summer was months away. The sun made its own seasons, Ibrahim said. It was true that he had never known it hotter, but this was the desert: there was no reason why it might not grow hotter yet. By now it no longer mattered to him what part the heat had played in bringing these appalling images to his days and to his dreams.

This man was a soldier. He knew himself for a particularly

hard-edged kind of soldier, and for a particularly ruthless specimen of that kind of soldier. He had learned, by his way of it, to be tough enough to expect nightmares from some of the things he had done, and to accept himself as the man who had done them. He had been a man with no illusions about himself: or so he had thought. For that simple equilibrium had now left him. He was disintegrating from within, and that brought with it an inexorable sense of doom. To him it had become as if he had been bitten by a rabid dog, and was awaiting madness and death. He was lucid enough to see an irony in this. If he was going to be driven mad (so he told himself) then it should be by nightmares about the things *he* had done, about the people *he* had killed, and about the things he had done to some of them before they died.

In those images that haunted him of the dead and dying he had seen on his desert journey, so many were children. So many children! Almost always children. Why should they dog his days and come to him in his dreams? He had never laid a hand on a child in all his life. He could not. Why so many children? Why must he sorrow for them? Be persecuted by them?

His nerve was gone. It was as if his will – and he knew it was strength of will that had made him what he was – was crumbling. It took every effort of this will to deal with the contempt now being offered to him by the old Bedayatt.

"You're feeling the sun yourself, Ibrahim Awdi," the Englishman said. He walked up to the muzzle of the rifle. "If you don't put the safety on that weapon we'll have a nasty accident. One shot and it will be those armoured cars of yours that come charging down on us, and we'll all be dried meat by nightfall." He tugged at the hairs on the dromedary's neck, which were the colour of bleached linen. The animal snarled. "So why," he said, "don't you get this pretty creature out of the way and find yourself a good spot to cover me, in case I come running back with these soldiers after my hide."

Watching the change in the old warrior's grey eyes, the Englishman, despite the furious heat, felt a chill touch his neck and run up the back of his head. Something inside the old bastard was actually urging him to pull the trigger and blow the Englishman's head off.

He yielded briefly to the unreality of the picture before him: the rim of the rifle barrel not two feet away, above it the cruel wild face of the Arab, and beyond, the fierce blue of the sky. It seemed to him that if this was to be his last sight in life it was excessively stark.

"'Whatever happens,'" he heard himself quoting to this madness, "'we have got the Maxim gun, and they have not'."

"The Maxim gun?" Ibrahim leaned down at him, intent and apparently deeply curious. It was as if some memory of race warfare had been awakened.

"It may have been a Gatling," the Englishman said. "I can't be sure it was a Maxim." The arc of tension between them had broken, and he felt his shoulders ease. He set off on the soft sand, walking close to the wall of rock that towered overhead.

He felt weak and light in the head. If it hadn't been for that old fool he would have remembered to take a mouthful or two of water from the goatskin on his saddle.

As he went, he freed the Beretta from his clothing. He thought of unfolding the stock, and then thought better of it: leave it folded. His thinking about these alternatives became more complicated. If by mischance the patrol saw him spying on them and opened fire reflexively – and with a civil war going on, though it was true the main fighting was a long way to the south and east, either a government or a rebel patrol out here in the middle of nowhere was likely to be quick on the trigger – then his best course was to let off a deterrent burst from his 30-shot magazine and scoot. He would not be hanging about to aim, so he would not need to unfold the stock. That was the short-term tactical view.

At this point he asked himself whether he was being intelligent or simple-minded. Was he in the habit of working things out in this rather laborious way, or did he just go in and do it? Was this part of the madness? Beside him the grotesque shapes of the rock wall, from which the heat sprang as if from the side of an oven, gave sympathy to the idea of madness.

So where had he got to? – Yes, the skirmisher's exchange of fire and the fast but orderly fall-back on the main body. This led to the strategic, or larger view, which was that if everything went wrong and the armoured cars came after him in an aggressive and hostile manner, the main body on which he would be falling back consisted of one demented old twit with a Second World War rifle, and a lad with a shotgun. Thus he had, in effect, nowhere to run to. Should war break out, his best hope would therefore be to pick off as many men as he could before they made it to their armoured cars.

"So what? So what? So what?" he said to himself. "What is all this about, Nick?"

Mind going. If he had to aim his shots it meant he must unfold the stock of the Beretta. He knew what it was all about. He was out here like that idiot hero in *The Four Feathers* to redeem himself. What a lunatic that laddie had been, resigning his commission before the Kitchener campaign – and his father a general, for God's sake.

Catch me throwing away a career like that, he thought. The sort of thing Seddall would do. Seddall's father had been a general, and Harry had some kind of grudge against the old man. So he put all generals in the same bag. Nothing quixotic about Seddall, though. Or was there? Nothing quixotic about young Nick, anyway.

To this puny figure, dwarfed by the rock wall on one side and by the immensity of desert and sky on the other, wrestling with his dilapidated state and putting one metaphorical foot, as well as a real one, in front of the other, by nothing but the exercise of will, since he was on his last legs in each of these worlds, everything happened at once.

Before him, in a shallow cavern at the foot of the rock wall, lay the bodies of a Sudanese woman and three children. He took them for dead, but found that this time he could not pass on. He stooped into the cavern. There was no smell or sign of corruption on their bodies. They were all dead, but it had not been long since they died.

There was a shelf of rock to sit on in there, out of the sun. He sat in the shade that had drawn the woman and her son and daughters. The youngest was a girl of about six. He thought there were few creatures more lifting to the spirits than a girl of six being happy, and few more terrible to see than the same girl unhappy.

33

He was quite unused to this kind of thought. The child's face was rested into death. He did not think this was any kind of blessing; only that she ought not to have died. None of this was what her small life was for.

He was not weeping, but tears kept coming up in his eyes and falling down his cheeks.

After a while he said to her: "Doesn't do you any good, does it, love, me sitting here crying away."

He was emerging, bent over, from the cavern when he heard the engine. One of the armoured cars was running along towards him, about twenty metres out from the wall of rock; or not so much towards him – its course would take it past him – but towards the two Arabs he had left with the camels.

In the blink of an eye, he was transformed into the military man. Soviet recce vehicle: BRDM-2 scout vehicle, quite good for the desert – land navigation system and a pair of retractable belly wheels each side which might help in soft dune sand. Moving slow, but could do up to 50 m.p.h. on this ground, and with armour probably 10mm thick – rather too thick for the Beretta. And then there were the guns in that turret, rather too much to think about really: the 14.5mm with the co-axial 7.62, two for the price of one. The car was most likely Khartoum's, but could have been taken by the rebels.

As soon as Ancient Ibrahim heard them coming he would do his death or glory bit, and the old twit and his grandson would be goners. Which would mean there was a good chance that the patrol would find the papers in his saddle-bag. Any chance at all of an alternative result was the thing to go for.

Good news, in fact. Time to do the gallant thing, which was also the right thing. He felt free, wonderful, about fifteen years old: that great freshness and ease in doing.

"See you soon, sweetheart," he said to the six-year-old girl. He was pleased to know that he had said it with love, without bravado, and that he meant it.

He walked out from the rock wall and took his stance. He stuck a spare clip inside each of his baggy boots. He unfolded the butt of the sub-machine-gun, aimed and began firing. Even as he sighted and fired, he thought that, ridiculous as it seemed, this fight might not be a foregone conclusion. There was one man standing waist-high out of a hatch, and another sitting on the back end of the car – presumably on a folded blanket, or he'd be getting his ass scorched. The driver's hatch was open. He'd bet his own ass there was no one down inside there except the driver. In this heat, in the back of beyond, not expecting trouble? You'd have to be crazy to sit inside.

Short bursts, very short. At the third burst the man sitting on the back fell off. Whether he'd been hit, or was just getting the hell out of it, there was no way to know. He gave the rest of the magazine to the driver's hatch and got the car's commander instead. The man's upper body fell back and then sprawled over the side of the car.

He jettisoned the empty clip and grabbed the spare out of his right boot and felt it go sweetly in. Breath-bating moment, this. Was there a gunner in there, whom failing, would the driver close his hatch and stop the car and get into the gun turret; or would he be so baffled he'd do something strange and foolish?

He did. He turned the car in towards the rock wall, a turn perhaps quite involuntary, and gave the back of his head to the Englishman and his attention to the dead or wounded officer.

A burst from the Beretta took the head away.

The man who had fallen off earlier was up and running south with the speed of a saluki. The Englishman tracked him with the Beretta, aimed, squeezed the trigger – and then everything went to hell.

The Englishman did not live to see much of it. He saw the turret of the armoured car turn and the guns elevate. He saw the second armoured car come fast round the end of the rock wall. The next instant he was dying, destroyed, carcase thrown back onto the bodies of the woman and children in their open tomb. On the way, he had a glimpse of sky. From where he lay, he saw a leg of his lying two yards in front of him, gushing blood onto the sand. He saw Ancient Ibrahim gallop by on his dromedary, with the rifle to his shoulder, and heard his demented war cry.

Into his head came the war cry of some savage tribe – "Sons of the hound come here and get flesh" – he reached a hand for the child he had given his love to, and laughed up blood, and died in it.

35

# 4

Mullen was much taken with the thick white French china with that fresh blue edge on all the rims. Everything was there: dinner plates, eight-sided coffee cups big and small; egg cups, even.

He pulled a ham knife from its slot in a wooden block and brushed a thumb across the edge. The thumb bled. He sucked it and looked at it. It went on bleeding. He wiped the blade, with care, on the inside of his wrist, and slid the knife back into its place.

"I've cut my thumb," he said to the woman behind the counter.

"You poor thing," she said. "There's a chemist across the road. You could get some Elastoplast."

She was a woman, not a girl. Her face was pretty and intelligent, and at the moment, witty. Her hair was gilded by the sun. He wished he knew her, and on one of his better days he might have done something about this. He knew that today was not going to be one of his better days.

"Terrific shop," he said, winding a handkerchief round the thumb.

Her face acknowledged this, a little.

They were surrounded by china, by pots and pans, cauldrons and fish kettles; by knives, skewers, ladles, and outsize forks and spoons. Copper and stainless steel rose on shelves up all the walls; and in the windows, to his right and her left, metallic tiers and high white glazes gleamed in the bright September day.

"You looked as if you liked the Apilco," she said.

"That stuff with the blue on it?" he said. "You know what it does to me? It makes me want to get a cottage in the country. It has that kind of feel."

A current passed through the air above the counter. When she felt it, her chin moved towards her shoulder for a moment, and back again, while her grey Nordic eyes watched him. He was two or three inches taller than she was, nearly six feet, and he was about five years younger, nudging thirty. She could see him as if he was still at school, enough of that was left there still: belting into the other team with the ball under his arm and wiring through them with violence and cunning. He had tow-coloured hair lying anyhow, and a big sexy mouth, and charm and aggression and confidence.

"Get the cottage," she said, "then we can talk business."

"About the nice china?" he said, moving it forward.

"You might want a fish kettle," she said. "Take it from me, poaching salmon is the only way to cook it."

"You'd have to show me how," he said.

"First catch your fish," she said.

He smiled as if he was the best friend she'd ever have. "See you later," he said, and went out. He came back in again.

"Wish me luck," he said.

"All right," she said. "Good luck."

"Thanks," he said.

In Westbourne Grove he turned right. He walked past a few shops, picked up *The Times* at a newsagent, and turned into a cafe. He chose a table and ordered breakfast: two eggs, bacon, fried bread and tomato, and coffee to have a cigarette with while all this was cooking.

"All that cholesterol," the waitress said. "What happened to the orange juice and toast regime?"

"I'm having a day in the country," he said. "I'm having a difficult day in the country. I'm going to need sustaining."

"A day in the country," she said. "Some people."

"All the luck," he said, meaning not a word of it.

He glanced round the cafe. It was a big place and, at ten-thirty in the morning, almost empty. He opened the paper at the middle and let it lie. He looked at the people in the street and the traffic. He wondered who had decided to toss the poor bugger in the safe house out into the world. He wondered if the poor bugger had eaten a hearty breakfast, or if he'd gotten one of those inklings that everything was about to go wrong for him.

It's a dirty job, he said to himself, and it's me that has to do it. I'm in a dirty business. I wonder if it's what I do best? Perhaps I don't dislike them enough, days like this.

The waitress arrived: "There you are, then," she said. He moved the newspaper and she put his breakfast on the table.

A big man with a red face and white hair sat down across from him. A knobbly white scar ran over the right cheek from the edge of his mouth. "Robert Mullen," the big man said. "Am I right?"

"You're wrong," the man with the breakfast said, "and you're early. The name's Roberto. We'll talk after I eat."

"Bobsie to the girls, they tell me," the big man said. "Bobsie Mullen." He smiled with tarry teeth and a nasty sort of pleasure. "They call me Starker," he said.

"You invented that," Mullen said.

"Course I did, when I was a lad with the Krays – the Kray Brothers?" the big man said.

"And now you're down to being a leg-breaker for the bookies," Mullen said. "Go for a walk, why don't you, and come back in ten minutes. So that I can eat my breakfast."

"Don't hold your breath," the man called Starker said. "You got no salt," he said. He leaned over to the table behind him and took the salt cellar from the hand of a young man about to season an egg roll. "Thanks, sonny," he said, and he sprinkled salt, delicately enough, over Mullen's breakfast.

He put out an arm to stop the waitress as she went by. "I'll have a cuppa, darling," he said.

"One cuppa for you, Scarface," she said, leaning her waist against his arm; lightly, it was true, but not in a hostile way either.

If Mullen was surprised that the big man took no offence at being named for the ugly scar, he was amazed that the girl seemed to like the rotten old bastard. He must be forty and more years older than she was, for God's sake. Old enough to be her grandfather. She could see he was a bad man: the face was heavy with it, the eyes were bright and hard and wicked, and she was looking right at them.

The fried bread, which was perfect – crisp without and moist within – turned to ashes in his mouth. The girl had been working here for three weeks now. She was a delight, with that lovely body inside the short bell–skirt and sweater, and a face that would grow into actual beauty soon; but she was a child, a schoolgirl working her holidays, and even Mullen's imagination had shied away from having any, well, ideas.

And now here she was, this infant, obviously taken with that ancient personification of evil sitting opposite. Mullen swallowed the fried bread and attempted the necessary intervention. "How did you come by the scar, Starker?" he said, and he got some bacon and egg in after that. Starker wouldn't last two rounds if he actually had to talk about himself.

"Oh, that was just in fun. I got that in Brighton, before I went into business. I was a Rocker then. We 'ad a fixture with the Mods. Before your time, darling." Saying this, Starker held her now on his arm.

"What kind of fixture?" she asked. Her eyes were intent, and the intentness was without innocence.

"What about my cuppa?" the big man said, watching her, knowing what he was doing.

Just what he knew he was doing, Mullen didn't like to think. He settled down to polish off the breakfast and tried to screen out his reaction to this conversation.

"What kind of fixture? What kind of fun?" she said.

"That was a bike chain," Starker said, touching the scar with his free hand, stroking it in time with the hand that was stroking the girl's back. "We used to go down to Brighton and fight on the beach or the sea front. We had bike chains and we had flat 'ats with razor blades in the brim and we 'ad these," and the hand dropped from his face, and all in the same second went inside his jacket and came out with a flick knife that flew open as it cleared his lapel.

"That was fun?" she said, but she was listening to the idea, not asking the question. Gently she brushed away the knife, not as if it was a threat, but as if it was being too familiar, was too close to her breast, and eased through his arm; which Starker pulled away with a gesture of curious grace, like a sweet lover allowing ease; even as the other hand closed the knife and spirited it from sight.

"I'll get your cuppa," she said.

39

Mullen finished gobbling down his breakfast and swallowed some coffee. "Whatever happened to feminism?" he said, a little wildly.

"What d'you mean, feminism?" Starker said. "The girl's entitled, ain't she? That's feminism." The cuppa came. "Thanks, love," Starker said, without looking up, and the girl went away.

"Mr Simpson wants his money, Bobsie," he said. "If he doesn't have it midnight Saturday, he'll 'ave your fucking legs broken and your fuckin' face too. He's very cross, Bobsie," he said, and slurped half the tea down at a gulp. "I'm to tell the boys to pop an eye out. They've been boxers, they know how it's done. Now that's heavy, Bobsie, poppin' an eye out. That's really heavy. Sell the house, sell anything, that's my advice. Not a very nice cuppa," he said. "Not very nice meeting you, either. I don't like the vibes I been gettin' from you, Bobsie. I might be there myself, midnight plus one, Saturday. Four thousand and seven hundred pounds. You'll never make it." He stood up with the cup still in his hand. He might be old, but he was big, and he looked very tough.

Mullen thought what a lousy day he was having, and how much lousier it was going to get, and set himself.

Starker put the cup to his mouth and slurped at the rest of the tea. His Adam's apple moved as he began to swallow, and Mullen's left fist hooked up from beside the table leg and belted the bastard in the gut. It went in with a thud and he felt it hard, right up to the shoulder. He thought he might have sprained his wrist.

Starker folded and went down choking. First he knelt, and then he rolled on his side and lay there, a bent foetus with the eyes shut and the face all wrinkled up, and tea dribbling from the mouth.

Mullen reached into the jacket and found the knife, and slid it into a side pocket of his suit. He sat up again, and sat still. He looked round the cafe. The boy who had surrendered the salt to Starker was gone. Some heads had turned, not all. Down by the door, the woman who owned the place was looking at him. The girl was nearer, staring with her head on one side and her black hair a glossy flow over that shoulder.

Two tables away a man eating a chip buttie said to the man across from him, "I never seen that before."

Both of them were watching Mullen, one facing him and the

40

other twisted round in his seat. That one said: "Seen what?"

"A man sitting in his chair, there," and he nodded at Mullen, as if in acknowledgement, as if including him in the reply, "a man sitting in his chair punch a man down. Never seen that before."

Starker's face was less red than it had been; it was pale. Mullen hoped the old bastard wasn't going to pop his clogs. The high colour he'd come in with might be bad blood pressure. Mullen hoped for the best.

He stepped over Starker, whose hard and wicked eyes were still shut, and went down towards the till.

"What he do to you?" the commentator who had never seen a sitting man floor another man with a punch said, as Mullen passed him. "What did he say?"

Mullen smiled, about to move on and pass, next, the young, young waitress. "Lover's quarrel," he said, and let her have the smile, watching her face change as he went on by.

"Mrs Minter," he said to the woman behind the till. "Will I be allowed back?"

"Is he all right?" she said.

"I bloody well hope so," Mullen said, "or I'll be sending out from Wandsworth for my meals. I think he'll be all right. He's a tough old bugger."

"Don't swear so much. And don't tell stories like that to Sandra." She took the fiver. "I'll never like these," she said. "The Queen looks awful, and the man on the other side is a real sour-puss. If that's the best the great minds who run the Bank of England can come up with, Heaven help us. He's standing up," she said, and gave Mullen his change. "He's a bad one, I can tell. You can come back. Don't fight too often. And don't tell lies to the girl: she's at the impressionable age. Lover's quarrel, for pity's sake!"

Mullen said, "Thanks, Mrs Minter."

He turned to see Starker, who was not yet able to stand up straight and held himself in a stoop, but with his head back to look at Mullen; to look at Mullen past Sandra, whose head turned from one of them to the other, as if she were a child being asked to choose between parents, Mullen thought oddly, for he knew she was expressing no more than bewilderment.

41

Starker did a terrible thing then, and the sight of it recurred to Mullen for days, it was so ugly and so abandoned to malice. He stared at Mullen and lifted both hands, and jabbed the thumbs, first one and then the other, at the side of each eye socket in turn. As a next act in the dumb show, he mimed clutching at something that might be lying on his right cheek and pulled at it and threw it away, and then did the same with the other cheek.

For this, he was saying, I'll have both your eyes.

It was an appalling threat, but it was not the threat itself that got to Mullen, it was the way in which that clumsy, goblinesque rage bared the fouled spirit in Starker.

He put fifty pence in front of Mrs Minter. "That's for his tea," he said.

When he reached the girl, he held her hand and took her back to the cash desk. Then he went up the cafe again.

"We're leaving," he said, and without looking at Starker's face, went a little behind and took him by the shoulders, and walked him slowly for the door. Starker said nothing.

The man who had been so pleased to see him floor Starker met his eye like one betrayed. He kept his eyes on Mullens' and said to his mate: "You can never tell now, can you?"

"For Christ's sake!" Mullen said, and stopped beside them and steadied Starker. He held up his middle finger to the man who had spoken. "Spin on that," he said, and was gratified beyond any expectation by the response. The man flung up his hands before his face as if to hide. "Don't do that," he said. "I can't stand that."

Out on Westbourne Grove, Mullen saw a taxi and hailed it. He opened the door and put the silent Starker inside.

"Well, where's he going?" the taxi driver said.

"Belsize Park," Mullen said, since it seemed so unlikely an address for Starker.

The taxi drove off.

Mullen stood in the sun and brushed the touch of Starker off his sleeves. He was wearing The Suit. It was the only good suit he had, and therefore the only suit. He seldom wore it, and after seven years the pleasure of its cloth was still fresh to him. It was almost invisibly two-coloured, one colour just less than navy blue and the other just more, in stripes about a centimetre wide. You did not see the stripes unless you looked close. He had had the waistcoat made extra long, so that he could have two buttons undone without showing the waistband. He did not think he was a dandy, but he'd got them to make that suit how he wanted it.

He was wearing the suit out of respect for the man in the safe house, because he knew that when he told Frankl he was being thrown out into the world, he would be taking him his death warrant – barring a few miracles, and Roberto Mullen hadn't seen any of those lately.

He looked at his watch. Just past eleven.

Another taxi came, and he got into it and went on his way.

# 5

Sorrel was at the back of the room drinking a dry martini, one of those cold-as-sin, old-fashioned "just give the gin a sniff of the cork" dry martinis. She had taken her first swallow and could feel it, right this minute, putting a chill on her liver. It felt wonderful.

Sorrel was a big, beautiful girl with short yellow curls and eyes of deep blue. She was wearing Wrangler jeans and a cashmere sweatshirt. And she was getting a bit of a once-over from the men in suits, which – since she was in a good mood – felt quite friendly for her.

She was in a restaurant with big shop-front windows looking out at White Horse Street, which was basking in a bright Indian summer autumn day. She watched Joanna Harvey come slanting across the road in the sunshine and into the restaurant. Joanna was wearing white leggings with a black horizontal stripe, and a black woolly sweater with white shirt-tails coming out from it, and carrying a black leather jacket.

"You're looking gorgeous," Sorrel said. "Are you going to tell me who it is?"

This estimate of Joanna was general. The business suits, Sorrel had observed, eyed the movement of the fine Harvey body on the fine, long, springy Harvey legs with varying degrees of frankness and evasion as Joanna strode into the room. Joanna put her jacket on the waiter's arm and sat down, and the watchers went back to whoever they were with.

"Why can't it just be me?" she said. "Being gorgeous all on my own?"

"Have some gin," Sorrel said, and Joanna knocked back some of the freezing elixir and shuddered. "And don't piss about,"

Sorrel said. "You're having a wonderful time with a new bloke and it shows, you know it does."

"Hmmm. Yes, I am," Joanna said, and speculated at Sorrel. "I don't know . . ."

"Lord, am I being quizzy?" Sorrel said.

"It's not that, you dim bunny." Joanna leaned forward and put her elbows on the table and tossed her glossy dark hair off her eyes. "Are you secure?"

"Of course I'm secure," Sorrel said. "Oh, I see. Cross my heart and hope to die."

Joanna smiled a wide and radiant smile. "It's Roberto Mullen," she said.

"Wow!" Sorrel said.

"Yeah, I know," Joanna said. "The dreaded Mullen. The guy can't stick with the same woman more than three months on the trot; but I'm no great settler-down myself. What the hell, Sorrel, it's happening and I feel great. Roberto *per se* is not the problem. It's Duncanson: he has this absolute thing about staff in the department not shagging each other."

"I like shagging," Sorrel said. "I mean, I like the word. That is, I like doing it . . . Where was I?"

"In the first place, you're halfway through this cocktail shaker and you've got a head start on me," Joanna said. She filled her own glass again. "The rest is ice," she said, "so we'll be running even. You were liking shagging, that's where you were."

"Yes, I've got it now," Sorrel said. "It's just that it's not a word I can imagine Duncanson would use."

"Of course he doesn't," Joanna said. "His memo said that members of the department must not involve themselves in personal relationships on pain of, etc."

"My goodness," Sorrel said. "I knew he was a piece of cheese, but I didn't know he was as full of holes as that. One chews the lip then, I take it."

"A piece of cheese is right," Joanna said. "He took over in the spring and he's behaved like the Sirdar of all the Egypts ever since. In fact, I really truly actually don't give a shit if I do get sacked. A girl has to get out into the world and start doing things for herself sometime, and I'm about ready. It might be the best thing for Roberto too, in the long run; only he doesn't know he thinks that yet."

"Goodness," Sorrel said, "if you're thinking for two, we'd better eat something."

They ordered food and beer.

"Spice," Joanna said, starting to eat. "Duncanson's interdict adds spice. It's absurdly exciting, keeping it dark from the Department, and all that. It's like having an affair at school."

"Well, quite," Sorrel said. "But how do you manage the keeping it dark?"

"We use my place mostly," Joanna said. "But anyway, Roberto says he can run rings round anything they can come up with, as far as that goes."

"He certainly likes himself," Sorrel said.

"He knows what he's good at." Joanna lifted her chin and gave Sorrel a strong clear look as she said this. "I go for that in a man. He's daft in some ways, but he's tops at the trade."

They bounced hostile looks off each other. Joanna emptied her glass, handed the hair off her face again, and kept her eyes straitly on Sorrel.

"All right?" Joanna said.

"Dammit, Joanna, there's a lot I like about Roberto Mullen," Sorrel said.

"And?" Joanna said.

"And that's all," Sorrel said. Then she said: "No, it's not all. Mullen's always had a self-destructive streak in him, but now it's a yard wide. I know you can see that. I just want you to look out for yourself."

Joanna's face remained vibrant, but its vitality now showed as intelligence, which was one of her strengths. "You're not wrong," she said. "I know quite a lot about him now. Roberto tests himself too much, and he does it in a really wild way. He tests himself against anarchy: that's what I make of it. He brings chaos into his life and challenges it to put the boot in. When you just like the guy, it's rather fun to watch; but when you love him and get to learn him, it's bloody worrying.

"In fact, I'm worried about him today. He's wearing a suit, and

46

he was very grim, and at the same time he's all wired up about something."

"A suit?" Sorrel said.

"He only has one," Joanna said, "and he hardly ever wears it. It's a good suit," she said, as if her lover was an artist and she was defending his work. Joanna was a pretty tough article, and this readiness to be vulnerable on Mullen's behalf made her seem, paradoxically, even tougher.

"He's just not a suit man," Joanna said. "Least of all to go into the country. It felt like an omen. A real one. An ominous omen."

Sorrel assumed that Joanna knew what she was talking about, but she couldn't fathom this suit business. There must have been more to it: the vibes Mullen was giving off, the atmosphere in which he and Joanna had parted this morning, all that sort of thing.

"I think I'm out of my depth, darling," she said.

"Such a great day to go into the country," Joanna said with indignant spirit. "I thought he could wangle me going with him, but he's off to a high-level meeting over some guy in a safe house. I think that's what he was exercised about. Well, who, actually: the guy."

"If the shit hits the fan, sweetie, I'm in your corner," Sorrel said. "I'm glad we got our little spat over."

Joanna flashed her a brilliant smile. "We can be friends and have rows, for heaven's sake," she said. "It's what friends are for. How are things with your bloke, anyway?"

Sorrel burst out laughing. "Do you really want this to turn into one of those Fifth Avenue lunches where the women meet to discuss their love life? Have a heart."

"You're right," Joanna said. "How awful. Talk about something else, quickly. How's your boss behaving?"

"Harry's on terrific form," Sorrel said. "He's moved house."

"I heard that. I thought he was in Phillimore Gardens for life. Why'd he move?"

"Because of the great shoot-out that happened there," Sorrel said. "Olivia's not prissy by any means, but she drew the line at starting life with a man in a house that had been knee-deep in assassins' corpses. Well, there was an awful lot of blood and bits.

47

Harry was using the Browning. The stairs were like a charnel-house. Anyway, now he's in Sumner Place. I think he likes it . . . Your face has gone all befuddled. What's up?"

Joanna was staring at Sorrel, but it was as if she was looking at something, or someone, else. "I dunno about this," she said, "but I don't think I've got a choice. I told Roberto I was lunching with you, and last thing before he went off this morning he said would I give a message to you for Harry Seddall. But you're not to pass it on till this evening."

"I can't do that," Sorrel said, "not if it's in the line of business. I'd have to give it him at once."

"Yes," Joanna said, and impatiently batted the long hair back behind her shoulders. "Roberto said you'd probably take that line. In that case, I've got to phone Seddall at nine o'clock."

"Joanna," Sorrel said. "What is this garbage?"

Joanna fired up at once. "It's not garbage," she said. "Roberto was in a real state, as if he's feeling guilty about something. I think he's trying to square himself with himself. That's what the message seems like to me. I think the timing is part of that. I promised him, Sorrel, so that's that. Has Harry taken the same phone number to Sumner Place? And what if he's out to dinner or something? Damn it!"

The girl was anxious, and Sorrel went in for reassurance. "Yes, he has kept his phone number," she said, "and he's not out to dinner. But, far better, ring me at nine o'clock and I'll deal with it. I know you're not going to give the message away, but can you tell me how important it sounds to you?"

"On a scale of one to ten?" Joanna said. "Not easy. More than three, I'd say, judging from the words, which mean not a lot to me. But from the way Roberto was going on, anything up to ten."

Later, in Piccadilly, when Joanna had gone on her way to Cork Street, Sorrel made the premonitory phone call to Harry Seddall.

# 6

At Mill Hill East station, where the London Underground's Northern Line has been running in the open air for some time and runs, at last, out of steam, Mullen said to himself, "End of track," and got off the train.

He thought of waiting for a bus, but set off up the hill towards the edge of London with the sense that to make the climb on foot would be to acquire virtue. Something over a mile, by George. Joy through strength; strength through joy: one or the other.

The day was fine. There were trees and, as he reached the Ridgeway, there were playing fields. The sky was blue and decorated with white clouds. Neither blackbird nor thrush was silent, and flights of swallows gathered into flocks, settled and rose again, discussing whether to leave for the south today or tomorrow.

He wondered if there might be something awry with the Mullen personality, that he should experience the pleasures of this benign day while his own life was in a bad place and he was on his way – mutinously, against his expressed will, but under orders nevertheless – to deprive a man of the security, and probably the life, which Mullen had promised him.

Nobody's perfect, he told himself, and at the silent fall of those disingenuous words felt the touch of darkness within.

In this ambiguous mode, then, while the last of the late beneficence began to fade and the bile in his spirit to expand, he came in sight of the pub called the Three Hammers and saw at once that they had sent the wrong car.

He went back down the hill until he found a call box, and dialled the Cork Street number.

When he was through to the office and asked for Duncanson, Joanna Harvey said: "Hold."

When she came back to him, she said: "His message to you is as follows: I am in conference and not to be disturbed. What's your message to him?"

Mullen said: "Tell him if he doesn't talk to me before this ten-pence piece stops working, I'm going to come back there and catch up on my paperwork."

"But Roberto," she said, "you're in the field, on a mission. Could you endure the contempt of your fellow officers? Do not take this reckless step."

"By Christ, Harvey," he said, "can't you tell that I'm being serious? One more crack out of you and I'll throttle you when I get back there. Just tell the bloody man if he doesn't talk to me the mission's fucked. And I mean it, I'll be in the first taxi back to base."

"We must talk more of this throttling," she said. "I've heard it adds zest. I'll coax the boss to the phone."

After a pause, "Speak," Duncanson's voice said.

"That car," Mullen said, "where did it come from this morning, and by what route did it get here?"

You could say what you liked about Duncanson, but at least he was quick on the uptake. "Hell and devils," he said. "Which car is it?"

"It's the silver grey Volvo 760," Mullen said. "The driver looks about eleven years old. I mean, if he didn't join yesterday it must have been the day before. It's a garage car, and I'll bet you it's come straight from the car pool by the most direct route. I have been at great pains to come here by devious ways to make sure I am clean, since I am going to Safe House Six, and we don't actually want to blow Safe House Six; for all I know, it's quite possible that we don't even want to blow the occupant of Safe House Six, because we want him to lead us to certain people, rather than lead certain people to him. Were it to transpire, therefore, that the car-pool watchers have been energetic today and trailed the Volvo out here, who knows what unlooked-for misfortunes might not occur were I to get sedately into the back and let the eleven-year-old drive me to my secret destination?"

"That's a lot of rhetoric for a man who's down to his last ten pence for the phone," Duncanson's voice said. "What a balls-up.

I'll have Edward Raleigh's guts for garters, but we'll do the post-mortem later. First: have you been spotted? Second: have you spotted anyone?"

"To the second, no; to the first, probably not," Mullen said. "I came away as soon as I perceived the debacle and headed back down the hill, a full furlong to this phonecard box."

"I knew it was a phonecard call, Mullen," Duncanson said. "I knew that crap about your last ten pence was a metaphor. What do you propose?"

"I'm going to have to do some fast driving," Mullen said, "and I need every second I can get. Someone intelligent – which excludes Raleigh – must phone the child in the Volvo, and tell him to leave the keys in the ignition and the door lying ajar, stroll into the pub for a long lunch and then get the bus home."

"I'll get Joanna to do it," Duncanson said. "How long do you need to get back up there?"

"Give me quarter of an hour," Mullen said.

"I'll give you twenty minutes," Duncanson said. "I've seen your medical."

Mullen let the receiver settle gently onto its rest and crossed the road before he set off up the hill again. He had no time now for birds or trees or sky. His eyes were everywhere on this suburban road. They marked everyone he passed: all vehicles, a pair of cyclists, a woman being pulled along by a Bedlington terrier, a man and a woman jogging. He kept straight on past the pub, across the road from him this time on his left, without looking at it, but he knew there was nothing wrong there.

He looked at his watch, and it was time. He re-crossed the road and began the return move, began the action. When he rounded the corner, and the pub and the car came into his view for the second time, Mullen took off like a sprinter from the blocks. He slid into the seat, started her up, got off to a flying start and kept his foot down.

He felt his eyes stretch wide with alarm when the Volvo 760 Turbo leapt to the bottom of Hammers Lane as if it thought it was on the Cresta Run. He eased off a bit to take the long bend, gulped in a few litres of breath, and relaxed into some serious driving.

As he ran the Volvo along the edge of Hendon Golf Course he recalled that after Voisin had beaten Bugatti to win the first Le Mans Grand Prix, Bugatti had been asked: "Why do your cars not have front-wheel brakes like M. Voisin's?"

"Because," Bugatti had replied, "my cars are made to go, not to stop."

Mullen had always thought this joke banal, but today it made him laugh. You've had your bit of fun, he told himself, but remember the object of the exercise, which is to make sure there's no one on your tail. He lit a cigarette and kept his eye on the mirror.

Christ! this was a rotten errand.

What kind of honour do you pretend to have, Mullen, that prides itself on not using the brakes on a car going too fast down Hammers Lane, and will break its word to a man who's staked his life on it?

He threw the car onto the motorway and drove north as if the hounds of hell were in winter's traces, or whatever it was the poet said.


The letters on the bronze plates on each of the red–brick pillars said: SHINING LIGHT MISSION. CONFERENCE CENTRE. STRICTLY PRIVATE.

The gates that hung from the pillars were open, and Mullen passed the lodge and put the Volvo up the drive. A rising wind whirled the fallen leaves about and tossed more down from the trees. He reckoned he had covered three furlongs when he reached the next set of gates, which were shut. Like the gates at the foot of the drive, they were ironwork of some elegance, set in a high wall of weathered brick.

Through them, Mullen saw the house called the Old Rectory, where Georg Frankl had been living these past weeks, wrapped in a state that was about to be demonstrated to him as one of false security. The house itself, for all that to Frankl it was only a way station on his journey into a new life, would have added its own layer of illusion to this sense of security.

It was a considerable Queen Anne mansion: something more than a rectory, even of the largest size. Through the fanlight in the pillared porch he saw the lights of a chandelier, but the other windows were curtained against the imminence of night. It was a warm and welcoming place for a journey's end on a cold autumn evening.

So thought Roberto Mullen, and then saw, above the roof, against a pale and azure sky, a sickle moon.

"Damn!" he said. He pulled a handful of change from his pocket and turned on the car's inside light and examined the money. One pound coin, three fifty-pence pieces, two tens, some fives, and some twos and ones. He extracted the coppers and, after debate, the pound coin as well. He dumped the rejects on the passenger seat and put the rest back in his pocket, then got out.

He walked round the Volvo, turning the silver in his pocket as he went. He had made one complete circuit when a voice spoke from the trees.

"Stop right there," it said.

Mullen said: "Just one moment, and then I'll be with you."

He went on walking anti-clockwise round the Volvo and turning the silver over in his pocket, and was completing the second circuit when one man came at him out of the bushes and another from the side gate beside the carriage entrance.

They were bundled up against the cold, with balaclavas and gloves; one in a flying jacket and the other in a down-filled gilet over a big woolly sweater. The one with the big woolly sweater had a tweed cap on top of the balaclava. He said, "When I say stop right there, I mean stop right there. That's better. Pat him down, MacFall."

MacFall did this. He found the pistol in the shoulder holster.

"Well, well," the man with the tweed cap said. "What have we here?"

"What we have here," Mullen said, "is the Volvo you know perfectly well you were expecting to be here, and me, R. Mullen, driving it. I am now going to dip my right hand into my inside

53

pocket and fish out my ID, and you are going to look at it. All right?"

"Not all right. Find it, MacFall."

MacFall found it and passed it over. The man held it down in front of the sidelights and studied it. He handed it to Mullen.

"All right," he said. "Get in the car and we'll open the gate."

"Pistol," Mullen said.

"When you're in the house and vouched for," the man said. "Get in the car."

"In a moment," Mullen said, and he moved MacFall gently aside and went one more time round the Volvo.

"What the hell do you think you're doing?" tweed cap said.

"I think he saw the new moon through glass," MacFall said.

"He's right," Mullen said. "If I'd been at home, I'd have walked widdershins three times round the house and turned the silver in my pocket. It's a nuisance at home, because it means walking three times round the block."

"Widdershins?" the man said.

"Counter-clockwise," MacFall said.

"Exactly," Mullen said. "It's hellish cold out here."

"You're telling us," the man said. "Do you want to get in the car now?"

The man was holding the door, looking down at him. He had pulled the balaclava and cap down off his head: the face was lean, the skin taut, and the features hard-edged. In the courtesy light from the car, the eyes glinted sharp and bright like that ice-chip of a moon.

"What's up?" the man said.

"Nothing," Mullen said. "I think too much."

"Are you an intellectual?" the man said.

"No," Mullen said. "Perhaps that would have been best. But no."

"I intensely dislike pitifulness," the man said.

On that remark, Mullen looked at him. Mullen thought each of them had the other sussed. "Drive on," the man said.

Mullen drove through the opening gates round to the back of the house, and parked beside all the other cars.

# 7

The new resident in Sumner Place was having a high old time. For one thing, the house was being redecorated; most of his furniture was in store, and he was living – camping, more like – in the kitchen and in the room that was to be his study. His study, save the mark!

He had never used a study in his life, but Olivia had views on the need for a man and woman to allow each other their own space, so that the relationship did not deteriorate under the stress of perpetual closeness. She, too, was to have a study, this being a sauce to be equally distributed between goose and gander. Indeed, she had presently decamped to her house in France, from which she had telephoned to say that she had it in mind to travel, perhaps to India, possibly to North Africa.

Seddall had not thought this was what it would be like if he took a woman into his life. He was well into his forties. It seemed to him that, at the time of his youthful and only marriage, the word "relationship", which was deployed so frequently by Olivia, had not been used to describe the connection between a man and woman who loved each other. There had been no intent discussion of the need for each of them to flourish independently within the relationship, of how the relationship would be strengthened by the fulfilment of these individual needs.

He had said if that was what it took, they were well placed. They would have his house in Sumner Place, her house near Compiègne, and the farmhouse in Somerset: it seemed almost sinfully propitious.

She had detected the drollery in this comment, and it had not been well received. She gazed at him from out of her beautiful brown eyes and said that what she was saying to him was important to her.

He had not the experience to understand in any depth what she was saying to him, and he had no wish to read books of psychological theory (an interest of Olivia's, but not of his) in a field – this field of relationships – where he had no experience. But he had got her drift, he was sympathetic to her idea, and anyway:

"*Quant à ça*," she had said, "you are very happy being with me, I know, but inside yourself you must be terrified at the change I make for your life. You must fear for your freedom."

When he said, "Rubbish," he got from the brown eyes the same look that had put paid to his attempts to cope with her extreme seriousness on this question: a *fin de non reçevoir*, as statesmen used to say on declining to receive a Note from another Power.

On this thought, he had told her she made it sound as if they were embarking on a lifelong negotiation.

"Lifelong?" she said. "Who knows? Negotiation, yes. *Tu commences à me comprendre.*"

"Sweet heaven!" he said. "Come to bed."

"Sweet heaven," she said. "Yes."

It was all working out rather well, so far. Here, camping in this house, he missed her, but he knew she was there, somewhere. He had what he felt as an extraordinary sense that he was more free than he had been before Olivia. Stirring the sauce for the fricassee, he was exhilarated.

The Brussels sprouts had begun to boil. In the oven the rabbit, cooked and keeping warm, awaited the sauce.

The rabbit, too, was a consequence of Olivia. He had not eaten rabbit for years, not since the myxomatosis, but at the farmhouse Olivia had said, watching one of the creatures eating the lettuces, "There is nothing wrong with him. See how fat he is."

"Plump," Seddall said. "We would say a rabbit is plump, not fat."

"Plump, then; but shoot him."

So Harry had got the .22 and shot the plump rabbit, and Olivia had skinned and butchered it for dinner, cooking it exactly (he hoped) as he was cooking this rabbit tonight.

When the sauce had thickened, he turned the gas low, put a

fork into one of the Brussels sprouts, and sat at the kitchen table with a cigarette and a glass of Scotch.

In the kitchen were the table, two wooden chairs, and a small equipment of pots, crockery, cutlery, and utensils.

He tilted his chair back and put a foot up on the table. His contentment was enormous.

The phone rang. It was on the wall, within reach of his hand. One thing about the Office, they got your phones in fast.

"Seddall," he said.

A young male voice, not quite accentless, spoke: "This is a good clear line," it said.

Seddall took the phone away from his ear and looked at it. He brought it back. "Well, yes," he said. The cat came into the room and sat down and stared at him. "Ah," he said into the phone. "Yes, I believe it may be a good clear line."

"Is belief synonymous with faith?" the voice enquired. "It could be argued. I have a message for you."

"I am all ears," Seddall said.

The voice smiled: "Believe this," it said. "You want this message. I can be at your house in ten minutes."

Seddall looked at the cat, and at the steam rising gently from the saucepan and energetically from the sprouts, and sniffed the rabbit in the oven.

"Ten minutes?" he said. "No longer?"

"No longer," the voice said.

"Come then," Seddall said, and put the receiver back on the wall.

"Bloody mysterious, Sacha," he said to the cat, and went over to consider the state of the sauce. He moved the saucepan so that only an edge of it was in the flame. He picked up the pan with the Brussels sprouts in it, then replaced it.

"First things first," he said.

He left the kitchen and ran upstairs to the prospective study, which just now was a bedsit. In addition to the bed, its chief furnishings were a comfortable armchair, a desk, a chest of drawers, a wardrobe, and a couple of rugs. He went to the chest of drawers and took a revolver from it, the short Smith & Wesson .38.

57

He spun the cylinder and hefted it, wondering where to stow it. He was wearing a sweater over a shirt, and ancient moleskin trousers. He took a jacket at random from the wardrobe and put the weapon in the right-hand pocket and ran back down to the kitchen.

He drained the sprouts in a colander. He opened the oven – how excellent the bouquet of that rabbit – and transferred the sprouts to the bowl waiting there.

The black cat, who was already keenly aware of the rabbit, had been drenched into a state of passion by its scent when the oven door opened. She masked this, when that door closed again, by jumping onto the window ledge and staring her rage into the night.

As suddenly, she jumped down again and left the kitchen, turning to the front of the house.

Seddall put his hand on the pistol in his pocket and followed her. He released the lock on the front door, which opened a fraction, and then he moved back and went into the darkness of what would eventually be the drawing room.

The doorbell rang.

He drew the pistol and called out: "Come in."

There was a hesitation, as of surprise, and then he heard footsteps on the wooden floor of the hall.

"Close the door, please," Seddall said. "Push it hard. I want to hear it shut."

He heard it shut.

Seddall said: "Now walk forward slowly, till I tell you to stop."

The figure that came into his view was of a young man, slight in build, wearing a black overcoat and carrying an attaché case.

"Stop there. Drop the case, please," Harry said. "Just let it fall on the floor."

The case thumped to the floor.

Seddall advanced towards the light, but not into it. "What's this message you have for me?" he said.

"It's in the case," the young man said.

"Very well," Seddall said, "but what is it?"

"It's Nick Churchyard's notebook."

Seddall was as perfectly astonished by this as he could remember

58

being in all his life. He stood in his silence and watched as the cat rubbed her shoulder and then the length of her body against the young man's leg. Sacha rarely offered this endorsement.

"A notebook?" Harry said. "And why would you have a notebook of Nick Churchyard's?"

"Nick's dead," the man said.

Harry, who had begun to trust this self-contained young man, found he had taken a step towards him and lined the pistol on his heart.

"What did he die of?" he said.

"He was machine-gunned by an armoured car," the man said. "I think he drew their fire on himself on purpose. To give me a chance to escape."

"And you took it?" Harry said.

"Certainly," the youth said.

There was no apology in this, no sense that an explanation was called for. The composure of voice, face and stance were perfectly undisturbed. The face was square and jutty-chinned, the hair black, short and curled. The eyes were black, aware and resolute together. For so calm and easy-mannered a young man, it was a tough face.

"Well then," Harry said. "Who the devil are you?"

"I am Taif Awdi. My grandfather and I were with Captain Churchyard in the desert."

"Is that so?" Harry said. "Is that so, indeed? But, d'you see, Churchyard said he was going into the desert with two bandits of the Bedayatt."

This brought him the smile he had heard on the telephone. "I am Bedayatt," Taif Awdi said, "and my grandfather was undoubtedly a bandit. He was killed, too. He made a camel-charge on the armoured cars."

"He sacrificed himself for you as well," Harry said drily.

An expression of distaste for this concept crossed young Awdi's face. "Not in the least. He did it because his blood was boiling. And because, Mr Seddall, the desert is finished. May I take off my coat and sit down? I've been travelling a good deal lately."

He shed the coat without waiting for an answer. "I am a desert Arab," he said, "but my father is a merchant. I studied politics and economics at Cairo. I do not dress like a bandit to come to Europe, or even in the office at home."

Seddall felt wonderfully instructed, but it was the edge of impatience behind the instruction that convinced him. He put away the pistol.

"Let me take your coat," he said. "Come through to the kitchen."

He stood aside to let Taif precede him. He shook his head. "A desert Arab," he said. "One of the notorious Bedayatt. What would the Orientalists at the Foreign Office make of you?"

Taif smiled at this. "I know what they make of me," he said. "Trade. But that's what I make of them too. What does it matter? It means only that we deal without respect, but we deal."

Harry looked at him. What a fellow this was.

He laid the coat with decent care over the back of one of the wooden chairs and draped his jacket on another. He went to the cooker and moved the spoon about in the sauce. "Seems all right," he said. "Have you eaten? Will you share my rabbit?"

"Yes, I will. And thank you," Taif said. "I came straight from the plane to my hotel, and from there to here. But do you have enough for two?"

"Three," Harry said. "We have to give a piece to the cat or there'll be mutiny. But there's plenty of bread and cheese. Make yourself at home while I fuss about."

Taif sat himself at the table.

He put some more milk in his precious sauce and stirred it in furiously, threw it over the rabbit, shut the oven door, turned the oven off, and splashed sherry into a glass.

"Need a little something after all these excitements," he said. "Will you have sherry?"

"I see Perrier there," Taif said, "may I have some of that?"

Seddall passed him the bottle and a glass, and sat across the table from him.

He did not at all fit Taif's idea of the English officer, which, since he had been Nick Churchyard's commander, he clearly was. Churchyard had been tall, lean, visibly confident, and in charge of what was going on; until, that was, he disintegrated; went mad.

Seddall was a bit more than middle height, and managed to

60

slouch, even in an upright wooden chair – to achieve which, he had tilted it back so that it seemed ready to fall over. He wore an almost pleasant, quizzical, slight smile on his loose-lipped mouth. His hair, nondescript brown and thinning rather, was all anyhow. He was a kind of human mess. There was a tough feel to him though, which Taif could not pin down. It was something to do with the shape of his head and the heavy look of his shoulders. There was a strong look to his neck too, of all things: perhaps it had to hold up a lot of brains.

Taif became aware then that this survey had been watched, and he found himself half-believing that it had been understood word for word as it moved inside his head. The eyes that met his were brown with a yellow gleam in them and from behind their surface he felt something much colder, as if he was being searched by a harsh intelligence working away at an agenda on which he himself was an exceedingly minor item.

"Time to eat," this suddenly alarming creature said, and let the front legs of his chair fall. "I'll bring on the food, such as it is. You'll find knives and forks in that box. That's right."

The sauce was not what it might have been, and the rabbit was a little dry, but the odd circumstances of the meal added an extra kind of salt to it.

"What did you make of Nick Churchyard?" Harry said. "Tell me the tale."

Taif told him in more detail how Nick had died.

"I admired him. He was very tough and determined. He knew he was losing his mind, not that he said so. He gave me your name when he began to . . . deteriorate," Taif said. "He started to go out of his mind once we were right into the desert. I thought it was the desert doing it to him, and the heat. My grandfather said he was going mad anyway, and the desert hurried it on for him."

"There was enough in him to drive him mad," Seddall said, and left it there. "How did you get out? It must have been a hard ride."

"Not that hard," Taif said. "The desert's a good place to be alone. It was long, but I knew where the wells were from my grandfather, and he'd taught me how to travel at night, how to choose a star to ride for. I had enough food for me and the camels."

"How did you get away in the first place?"

"I doubt if it occurred to the patrol that I was there at all," Taif said. "At the time, I had no way of knowing. I just went north as fast as I could. It was the only thing to do."

"You set off, and you've been travelling ever since, to get that notebook to me. Is that right?"

Taif said: "I went to Khartoum and then Cairo, saw my father, and flew in here tonight."

"Well," Harry said, "why did you do that? You could have posted the notebook. You didn't owe it to me to come here."

"There seemed to me to be an obligation," Taif said. "I read what Nick wrote in there." He nodded over at the attaché case, and then on the thought went over and opened it and took out a plain notebook, with cardboard covers, like a student's.

"I might have posted it," he said, "but it seemed to me I had to come and tell you myself what happened. Also," he said, in an offhand way that was the first appearance of self-consciousness Seddall had seen in him, "it felt wise to me to keep on the move. I don't know if the armoured cars were rebel or government, or where they came from. I don't know if they were there by chance, or if they were sent to sit across the trail of that camel train we were following."

Taif's eyes fell to the notebook, and Seddall put a hand with the fingers spread wide on its marbled surface. "You've read this? Did Churchyard have ideas about it?"

"He had ideas, all right," Taif said. "And I believe them." He got up and began to walk about. "There are times in the desert when you feel you are being watched," he said. He shrugged. "It may be a habit of the desert to make you feel that. There were times in Khartoum and Cairo when I felt I was being watched, and that may have been a hangover from being in the desert, but it felt different. I had read the notebook," he said again. "I thought it best to get here as fast as I could."

He sat on the edge of the table. He smiled, self-conscious again. "For what it's worth," he said, "I have a cover, if that's really what you people call it. I have some business to do here for the firm. For what it's worth. Maybe it's not worth much. I thought if I got the book to you, then the heat would be off me. Is that the phrase you use? The heat? Do you have a cigarette? I don't smoke, but I'd like one now."

"Your jargon's wonderful," Seddall said, "though it's from different kinds of movies." He drew a distressed packet of Gauloises and a lighter from his pocket. "Here," he said. "I'm trying to cut down and I must say you're no help. Now," he said, when they had both inhaled and breathed out smoke, "let's be done with all this displacement activity and get to it: what does Nick Churchyard say in there?"

Taif became brisk as if he was making a business report to that merchant father of his. "The cargo was put ashore in Egypt," he said. "A dhow came into the beach north of Halaib—"

"A dhow, for God's sake!"

"What's wrong with dhows?" Taif said.

"Dhows, camel trains. It's all too romantic," Seddall said.

Taif shrugged. "To you maybe, not to me." He went on: "It was night, of course. At the beach were the baggage camels. A lot of money was spent on this. Fifty men on riding camels, well armed with automatic rifles. They went south-west into the Nubian Desert, and we followed. Nick made us wait days before we followed. My grandfather said that would work. He was the best tracker in the desert and, unless he was unlucky with wind moving the sand, he said he could keep track of them. Much of the desert is pebbles, or has a thick crust on the top, you know, or dead grass, dead brush, all kinds of terrain. He could follow tracks on anything, except on soft sand covered over by the wind, and even then he would expect to be able to work out where they were going and find their trail again.

"Nick made us wait because he said if they had any sense, which they seemed to have, they would drop one or two men off to watch their rear, with orders to stay a day, two days, behind them."

"Knew his stuff," Seddall said.

"You're very cold about him," Taif said. "He died doing his duty, and he did it well."

Seddall stared at him and said: "I was cold about Nick when he was alive. I'm not going to start warming up now that he's dead. And I don't quite see that getting duffed by a couple of armoured cars when he had the whole fucking desert to choose from can be called doing his duty well."

"He thought," Taif said, "about what he was doing. That cargo was lost, hidden, right down the gulf, and he picked up its trail in the Hadramaut. Who else could have done that? It went in on one of the Yemeni-Iraqi joint fishing company boats to al-Shihr, and he was there to see it."

"And just how did he do that?" Seddall said.

"He heard about it from a Palestinian in Kuwait. They're treating the Palestinians like garbage there, you know that. He got among them until he found the right man, a man who had heard something from another man who had heard something from a man who knew."

"I'll make coffee," Seddall said, and got up to put the kettle on. "Go on," he said. "Don't stop now."

Taif saw that his face was closed. He had no interest now in his visitor, only in the story that was being told.

"So," Taif said, "when he heard that the cargo — whatever it was — he always referred to it as the materiel — was going to al-Shihr, he went to Saudi Arabia and hired a gang of cut-throats, then went down through the Empty Quarter. He crossed into South Yemen and became a Russian in al-Shihr. The Soviets have been involved in the South Yemen fishing industry, along with the Japanese, the Danes and, among others, the Kuwaitis. It was risky being a Russian because his Russian wasn't that good, but he brought it off, except that he had to stick a knife in one man who looked sideways at him. He said one sideways look was enough, he couldn't take chances."

"Well," Seddall said, "he was right. Coffee? I've got sugar somewhere. Here it is."

"At al-Shihr the cargo was loaded onto a big trading dhow. Twelve crates, with a full guard on them day and night so he couldn't get a look at them. The dhow had an owner-captain."

Taif swallowed coffee and said to Seddall, "What would you have done then, if you had been Nick?"

"Not what Nick did, I'll bet," Seddall said. "I'd have got next to the captain and bribed him to tell me where he was going to land the crates."

"Yes, well," Taif said. "Good coffee. Nick went one better than that. He got next to the captain, and was shown pictures of his beautiful young wife. The captain was mad about her, and as far as Nick was concerned that was it. The dhow's home port was Hodeida. Nick had a week in hand before the dhow was due to sail, so he sent some of his men to Hodeida and they kidnapped the wife and took her up into the mountains, and one of them came back to al-Shihr with a picture of her naked and a lock of her hair. Can I have more coffee?"

"Absolutely," Seddall said, and poured from the jug. "Then what?"

"Nick offered the captain his wife back in one piece, unharmed, and a thousand pounds to tell him where he was off-loading the cargo. So the captain told him. Told him the dhow was being met by a camel train, too."

"Of course he did," Seddall said. "I dare say Nick offered to cut his throat for him as well, if he didn't come good."

"Yes," Taif said, enigmatically. "So then Nick got himself to Egypt, and then Sudan, and hired my grandfather and therefore, as it happened, me, to get camels and water and provisions."

"How did he come across your grandfather?"

"He did the best thing," Taif said. "He went to Khartoum and flew to El Fasher, a desert town. He looked and asked, saying he wanted a guide to go into the desert. The drought has killed the desert. The nomadic life is dead, as you know. There has been an exodus from the desert. Many have died, there is famine, there is the war, there are those camps – and what sort of life is left, even for those that survive? What can it lead to? Some, like my grandfather, have gone to the towns. He met Nick at the market, which is where the idlers go, where you find news and rumours. My grandfather said they knew each other at once. He thought they were the same man inside, in some ways."

He pushed his cup across the table for more coffee, and helped himself to a cigarette, too absorbed in recollection to deal with social niceties. His narrative went on.

"We followed them from the coast, south-west, as I said. They split into three parties, travelling a day apart, and yes, they did put out men to watch their rear – Nick had been right about that – and my grandfather always knew how far behind them we were. It was the best we could do. I don't know if we were seen or not.

"We were on the Chad border, south of Geneina, when we ran into the armoured cars. The camel train had slowed in the last days, as if they were feeling their way down the border, perhaps to choose their crossing-point."

"And that's the story," Seddall said.

"That's the story," Taif sighed and stretched, a man relieved of a burden.

Sacha, who had gone off to wash herself after dinner, came into the kitchen and jumped onto the table. Seddall sat leaning on one arm and with the other rumpled his hair and rubbed the back of his neck. The cat watched him with cold, jade-like eyes.

Seddall stroked the cat, which lashed round and bit his hand, but slowed in the strike so that the bite was no more than a gesture, which she held for a moment before letting go.

Seddall sat up straighter. "You're a fiendish beast, Sacha," he said. "You told me Nick Churchyard had done some thinking," he said to Taif. "What did he think this was all about, dhows and camels and creeping down the Chad border?"

Seddall thought Taif's face was showing the strain. All at once it was tired, drawn-in and flabby at the same time.

"He thought the idea of using camels instead of vehicles was quite simple," Taif said. "That spy satellites, or the people who scrutinize their pictures, don't register camels crossing the desert."

"Not bad," Seddall said. "Same with the dhow, if you like."

"Yes," Taif said.

"What else?" Seddall said.

"Well, the crates they landed from the dhow were quite big, but what came out of them, after the packing – and there was a lot of packing – wasn't much. Six smaller boxes from each." Taif found that his eyes had become engaged with the cat's unwinking stare. "Nick thought," he said, "that they must contain something out of proportion to their size. He thought they must contain biological warfare materiel. They couldn't contain any other kind

66

of weaponry that would have been worth all the money spent on this.''

"Well, Nick was right," Seddall said. "I knew it, but I didn't want to hear it. A camel train of CBR wandering into the heart of Africa, to no one knows where."

Taif said: "CBR? What's that?"

"For God's sake, man!" Seddall shouted in a fit of astonished rage. "Don't you know anything? CBR: chemical, biological, radiological warfare. Warfare, forsooth! Be damned to that for warfare!"

"Well," Taif said mildly, "my English is not expert in your military terms," so that Seddall felt ashamed of his outburst.

He reached for the cigarettes and lit one.

Then he stood up and filled the electric kettle and switched it on, and drifted through the kitchen and out through the house into the dark and empty drawing room, where he stood with his back to the wall and faced, across the empty room, the night outside.

He saw cars pass under the streetlights and heard voices from passers-by, but he held out to them an illogical and unfair contempt, and in his mind saw Africa, places in Africa he had known, city and desert, farm and bush, river and lake and mountain; and remembered people he had met, people good or bad or indifferent.

The cigarette burned his fingers and he threw it into the hearth and went back to the kitchen. Sacha was still on the table, crouched now, with her front half claiming possession of the notebook. Taif was sitting as he had left him. The two men looked at each other in an oddly objective way that put Seddall's fit of temper behind them more effectively than any exchange of deprecating words or grimaces could have done.

"So then what?" Seddall said. "You followed these camels across the desert?"

"Yes," Taif said. "That's to say we followed the larger party."

"The larger party?"

"Yes," Taif said. "The party that kept the baggage camels, or most of them, at any rate."

"You're telling me they split into two groups," Seddall said.

"That's right," Taif said. "On the second night they made a

67

rendezvous with a dozen or so men who had ridden down from the north. My grandfather read this in the sand, afterwards. About a third of those we were following went back north with the new people."

"What did Nick do about that?" Seddall said. "It must have made him think a bit."

"It did. But he decided that the serious cargo, as he called it, must be the one going west. North meant Egypt, and he said if the Egyptians wanted these weapons they could manufacture them for themselves."

"Well," Seddall said, "I suppose so."

"Also, on the third night, when the main group had resumed their westward journey, my grandfather went into their camp and made sure that the boxes were still with them."

"Did he indeed?"

"My grandfather could do anything in the desert," Taif said.

"What did you make of the men from the north?"

"Just that there was some side-cargo – drugs, maybe, or something valuable, perhaps stolen, riding in the dhow." Taif shrugged. "Wherever there is movement of trade, on land or sea, across frontiers in particular, you will find criminals taking their own advantage of it."

"That's true enough," Seddall said.

"There was another thing," Taif said, "Nick says, in there," and he nodded to where the notebook lay under the cat's claws, "that the Palestinian who passed him the word about al-Shihr had quite a laugh over who was supposed to be the buyer of these secret super-weapons. That's how he thought of them, you understand, as some extraordinary bit of firepower, a rocket or something, not CBRs as you called them. He laughed because he thought they were going to a woman."

"A woman?" Seddall said. "Hard to believe, isn't it? A woman somewhere south and west of the Chad border who has a use for CBRs."

Taif shrugged. "There are women fighters in the PLO, of course, but in the Moslem world the idea of a woman war chief would surprise us."

The telephone rang.

"I have news," Sorrel said. "I'll be round in, oh, fifteen minutes."

"Right," he said. "Listen, I may be out, but if so I shan't keep you waiting long. Let yourself in."

He put the phone down.

"Taif," he said. "I'm going to walk you back to your hotel now. It's shockingly ungracious to push you out, after what you've done, but the less you know about all this the safer you'll be. Do you believe me or do you think I'm disingenuous?"

"Both," said Taif, "but I have no objection to either. I'm here for three days. Call me if you've anything to tell me: I have an interest in this. Or if you want to let me help. You don't have to walk me back there."

"Actually I don't think I do," Seddall said, "but I want to. Get your coat and we'll be off. I'll just put away the notebook."

The fact was that Harry did not seriously expect any attack on Taif. It simply seemed to him an essential courtesy, and an insufficient one at that.

It was therefore with surprise that he found himself obliged to say, as they reached the end of Sumner Place and turned into Brompton Road, "Taif, show no sign, but we're being followed by a very large man."

"I'm glad to hear it," Taif said. "My father insisted."

"Ah," Harry said, and under their talk his mind began to suggest questions about this father and son.

Taif said many interesting and apparently informed things about the business of the high-powered entrepreneur, but Harry began to wonder if he believed them.

At the Hotel Rembrandt they exchanged cordial goodnights, but about these there seemed to Harry something guarded running between him and Taif, as if the Egyptian (or was it Sudanese? Sudan-born, Egyptian passport: a question there, even) had sensed the reservation the Englishman had begun to hold about him. And was lightly amused by it.


Sorrel Blake was at the kitchen table reading Nick Churchyard's notebook. Her hand curled loosely round a glass with a pale drink in it, like a weak whisky and water, but some of her fingers trailed on the table top as if she had forgotten the glass was there.

She lifted her head and acknowledged Harry's return, and then went on reading. He poured himself a whisky as well, and went wandering with it round the empty house, standing by this window or that, staring into the night and thinking his thoughts.

When he went back to the kitchen, Sorrel said: "Nick's back?"

"No, no," he said. "How on earth did you find the notebook?"

"Sacha was scrabbling at the dog's basket when I came in," Sorrel said. "Was that your idea of hiding it? Quite hopeless."

"I was only going out for a few minutes," he said. "I was counting on Sacha to defend it."

"Sure," Sorrel said. "It's quite a story. Where's Nick now?"

"Nick's dead," Seddall said.

"I felt that was what it was," Sorrel said. "How did it happen?"

"Firefight in the desert," Seddall said.

"Best way for him," she said.

"I knew you'd say something like that," he said.

"Come on, Harry," she said. "He was a real shit. He was a sadist and a torturer. You should have got rid of him as soon as you knew that."

He sat down and looked across the table at her, all beautiful and young with her golden hair tumbled about her head, her face as clear as a goddess and her eyes implacable.

"He was a soldier," he said, and felt foolish with unconviction as he said it, "and he died well." Why was he doing this? When Taif told him Nick was dead he'd behaved pretty much as Sorrel had.

He said: "Why am I being such a hypocrite?"

"Who cares?" Sorrel said, "Just stop doing it. Old women and young children in cancer wards die well, and nobody plays the Dead March from Saul or parades with Colours dipped and arms reversed for them.

"Now: Joanna's message, which is the reason I'm here. Arkley is turning Georg Frankl out of the safe house tonight. Or telling Frankl tonight and turning him out soonest."

"What does this mean?" Seddall said to himself, and to Sorrel: "On what terms? That's what we ask ourselves. So this is Mullen's leak? Mullen's boss, the egregious Duncanson, promised Frankl some start money and the new identity routine. Will Arkley honour that?"

"No idea," Sorrel said. "That was all Joanna knew. Roberto seems to be trying to purge some guilt he has about Frankl. I don't know what he expects you to do about it though."

"I don't know what he expects me to do, either," Harry said. "I'll have to chew it over a bit. Let me tell you about the chap who brought Nick's notebook, and perhaps my enfeebled intellect will do some chewing on its own while I'm telling you."

"Why don't you just chew it over," Sorrel said, "and tell me the rest of it tomorrow. Because, unless you want some fast work done that needs me, I've got a supper date."

"Go to supper," Harry said. "What I really want to do is mooch around and think about these people and events in all directions in a vague sort of way. We'll talk tomorrow."

Sorrel shook her hair out and grinned. "The guru is about to transcend," she said.

"Mock on," Harry said. "But who knows? Who knows?"

After Sorrel had gone, he walked around the darkened house, lay on his back on the bed staring at the ceiling, sat in the cold in the back garden, and took a turn up and down the street, while the cat appeared and vanished and reappeared again, as elusive and tantalizing as the picture he was trying to compose from what fragments he had of the Frankl affair.

After about two hours of this, back at the kitchen table, he was staring at Sacha, who blinked back at him from Bayard's basket, when suddenly he said to her: "The monthly conference. Tomorrow's the monthly conference."

He got up and emptied the ashtray. He poured himself a strong whisky by way of congratulation. He lit another cigarette. He went to the phone.

He dialled part of a number and hung up. He fretted and lit another cigarette.

The cat blinked contemptuously and went to sleep.

"What the hell," he said. "Nothing venture, nothing win."

He made his phone call.

71

# 8

Georg Frankl's tough and searching eyes were brown. The skin on his face and his almost bald head was a lesser brown. The head and the face were round, but the face led with the chin. He was clean-shaven and his complexion had a healthy shine from the natural oil in his skin.

Frankl was in his large and elegantly, comfortably, furnished bedroom, looking at himself in the pier-glass. It was that kind of room, a sanctuary of tradition, glowing with the quiet strength – affirming strength, say – of eighteenth-century wood.

"You have a useful face for a disingenuous man, Old Georg," he told himself and that image of himself in the glass, but he said it silently, since the room was most certainly bugged, and the wisest thing was to divulge nothing that need not be divulged.

He was forty-seven. He had the habit of soliloquy, or self-reflected dialogue, and had called himself Old Georg for years.

He was wearing a pale brown suit and shirt and tie, which were as close as could be to the colour of the hands and neck that emerged from them, and brown socks and shoes. It was what he usually wore, unless the part called for something else. He had this gift, that he was an anonymous figure in a crowd, and he knew that these clothes helped.

Downstairs, a small crowd was gathering for the meeting, and he did not suppose he would be anonymous among them, not in any realistic sense. All the same, he carried that private feeling of anonymity within him, the hidden persona of invisibility which was the core of his given skill of moving unseen through the streets of cities.

He was nurturing that feeling now, because something was up.

He knew it in his bones: this was to be a bad meeting. "Rather a special dinner party," Colvin had said, and that was all he had said, but he said it in the manner of a physician failing to conceal from his patient the fact that he suspects the worst.

"Relax, Old Georg," he said to himself. "Do the breathing exercise."

He did not do the breathing exercise. He had been fretting away at worst-case scenarios ever since Colvin spoke to him. He had nothing much against Colvin (beyond that he was an incompetent man confused by his double role of host and warder), but he took a dark view of the dinner party. The English had a talent for dining, along with a talent for hypocrisy. For them to invite a man to dine in order to help them carry off the delivery of some appalling news would be so true to their character that by now he was certain this was what he must expect.

The phone rang. Colvin's voice said: "We're ready for you."

"Ready for me?" Frankl said, objecting to a phrase which at once geared up his apprehensions another notch. "I understood I had been invited to dinner at eight." He laid a stress on the word invited.

"Ah," Colvin said, swimming clumsily towards the words he needed, "Yes. But we're having pre-dinner drinks just now in the drawing-room."

"Thank you," Frankl said. "I don't want an aperitif, I shall see you at eight o'clock." He replaced the receiver. He went about the room turning off the lights and then went to the window and lifted the sash high, and leaned out.

A gusting wind had begun to lift into the frosty night, and the chill of it struck at his hairless head. Perhaps it would help to freeze his neuroses and to slow down his over-working brain.

He listened to the rustle of bare twigs as the wind passed through the trees. As his vision settled he saw that it was not yet full dark. The hills behind the house rose to their ridge in a grey bulk against the ethereal blue-shot blackness of the sky.

Frankl's working life had been for the greater part a city life, a life in many cities, a life of taxicabs and aircraft, streets and offices, sometimes in hotels and sometimes in houses that would see him, at most, for a tenure of six months before he moved out and away.

But Frankl had been brought up in the hills of Istria, and the child-memory within him responded to the wild country that lay beyond that ridge, and into which he had hardly penetrated. He might go there yet.

He heard movement below him in the dark. A faint light came on as a car door opened and a figure stooped into the car and came out again. He saw that the figure was a woman's. She lifted her face to the window. Frankl raised a hand, which she may or may not have been able to see. The woman pushed the car door to, and went towards the house and out of sight.

Frankl switched on a lamp. Time for this dinner: this English dinner table. His eye caught his polished shoes and a small bitter spirit woke in him. He took off the shoes and stepped into a pair of sandals. A touch of – what? – the Levant, would they think? Bad form, anyway.

He left his bedroom and went downstairs.


Meals were served in the kitchen, because in the dining room a ferocious infestation of dry rot had been found and the walls stripped of their panels to reveal the revolting fungus. After that, nothing had been done: the Secret Intelligence Service was not much in the way of dealing with the graver domestic crises.

When Colvin ushered in the visiting party, or to be more accurate, led in Sir John Arkley while the others followed, Georg Frankl was standing in front of the Rayburn cooker, making idle chat with Louise the cook.

Frankl had never met Arkley, but he had seen photographs. The photographs had been taken before the great man lost a leg, but the face was hardly changed. He came in smiling, thought Frankl, like a wolf with an unnaturally depleted conscience, even for a wolf. It was with phrase-work like this that Frankl, in situations such as these, was accustomed silently to oppose his enemies.

"Ah, Georg!" Colvin said, and advanced, according to some privately conceived protocol, on an axis three inches behind that of his overlord, but with an arm held forward in an upward tilted arc so that the hand, travelling well before and at the same height as Arkley's eyes, conveniently signalled to them the existence of

Georg Frankl. ". . . But the dog is better?" Georg was saying to Louise.

"In a fair way to being better," Louise said. "But I was up all night, you know. And it has put me off my stride. I have fears for the soufflé. I can trust you to make sure no one opens that door when I'm taking it out of the oven, can't I?"

Georg had a great liking for this woman, despite the fact that by this moment in her life she was in a highly developed maternal mode, having, as a single parent, brought up a son, now twelve. Had the child been a daughter, his liking for the mother would have been more direct. As it was, he felt the sexuality of her encumbered by an excess of maternalism towards the male.

She was a woman whose bucolic flush and fullness went with great sensual prettiness. Her hair was glorious, a black and curling mane shot with undisguised grey, that flowed to her shoulders. But to Frankl, who had taken plenty of the time available to him doing nothing in particular during his stay in this house, it had come to seem that the movements of her body, even when she was engaged in dealings with others, expressed the relationship with the son.

"Frankl!" a vexed voice said.

He gave his attention to Colvin and Arkley at last.

"How do you do?" he said.

It had even occurred to him that they had put her here because he was Jewish: that they had ideas about Jewish boys and their mothers. Certainly, since she was the only woman in the ménage, she would have been chosen for him by the casting directorate of MI6.

That kind of thing, though, meant nothing to Georg. For him, Louise Alcorn was a human being whom he valued. He held her arm, the one with which she held the saucepan while the other stirred. "You may trust me," he said. "When you are ready to take the soufflé from the oven, let me know and I shall guard the door."

He looked Arkley in the face and allowed his eyes to run over the worsted grey suit with blue flecks in it. He made the slightest lift of a hand, almost a private gesture, as he recorded the stick that helped support the artificial leg.

"How are we to seat ourselves, Sir John?" he said.

Arkley scanned Frankl in return, as if he were looking at the lie of the balls on a billiard table before bending, not very competitively, over his cue.

"It's not my party, Mr Frankl. Louise will tell us where we sit," Arkley said. "You are being made comfortable here, I hope. Come." He touched Frankl with his free hand and so drew him towards the table. "I wonder if we need introductions. I dare say you know each of us. You will be pleased to see Mr Mullen, I know."

Frankl was pleased. "Roberto," he said. "This is good."

"Hi, Georg," Mullen said. Frankl saw that Mullen was ashamed of what was to come.

"You are friends," Arkley said. "Then you must sit together. We shall defy Louise. I'll sit here, and will you sit on my right, Mr Frankl, or shall it be Georg?"

"It shall be Georg," Georg said.

He sat himself next to Arkley, who took the head of the table and then vanished behind the appearance – which Frankl punctiliously stigmatized as meretricious – of a beneficent trance. Before vanishing, Arkley said only, "How *homely* to dine in the kitchen," as one who had never boiled an egg or made a slice of toast for himself in his life; and thereafter tilted his hawk-nosed piebald-moustached head a little up and to the side, and sat there immobile, except for his bright eyes, which flitted haphazard about the room, now on Louise at the stove, now to this corner of the ceiling or that, but always back again to one or other of those at the table. He had the air of a conductor evaluating the sound of his orchestra.

Mullen sat beside Frankl. Opposite Frankl was a young woman, dark and beautiful. She had a quick intelligent look to her, which was not muted by her quiet and peaceful state.

"Mr Frankl," she said. "My name is Anna. Arkley has no manners" – he heard a contemptuous, but also affectionate, comment in this use of his host's surname – "so I'll introduce you. Mr Mullen you know. Next to him is Isobel Shepherd, and opposite Isobel is Martin Ennis."

Georg bowed across Mullen's lap to Shepherd, and down the diagonal to Ennis. Shepherd smiled warmly and said hallo. Ennis gave him the respect, or the reserve, of not smiling and said that it was deeply interesting for him to meet Mr Frankl.

He liked Isobel Shepherd's face, which was an over-narrow, elongated oval with a long straight nose and fine wide eyes and mouth that summoned up, for Georg, one of those Winterhalter women – which one he could not remember. He thought, too, that Shepherd looked very bright.

It was a pity all round, really, that she, along with Ennis, was among his enemies for the evening: privy, at any rate, to whatever Arkley was up to; part of his back-up. They made an unlikely team, but Georg, who required scenarios in times of crisis, resolved that they had once been lovers in a way that contented them with each other afterwards, so that when their affair was over they had redefined their borders at their own private Congress of Vienna, and had emerged as inveterate allies.

He wondered what Arkley *was* up to. He thought he had been wondering long enough. What was he, Georg Frankl, going to do? Was he going to sit through the meal according to that convention one kept reading about, and wait for Arkley to get down to business when the coffee came?

Like hell he was.

"Georg!" This was Louise. She gestured at the oven, and then at the kitchen door. He got up and went to make sure that none of those prowling security people, who had a *laissez-passer* to go anywhere at any time, opened the door to deflate Louise's soufflé.

He was behind Arkley. The ideal moment. As Louise put the soufflé dish, steaming like Krakatoa on the point of eruption, in front of her place at the foot of table, Georg approached the back of Arkley's head and put a hand on his shoulder and applied an intimate pressure – a thing he would have detested himself. Indeed, he felt Arkley shudder.

"Arkley," he said, and pressed down and felt Arkley's outrage again. "Sir John," Georg said. "Why do I feel as if I am a kidnapped hostage and that you are the Bandit King?"

He did not wait for Arkley not to look round, but went back to his seat beside him. "Perhaps it is that this feast takes place in the kitchen," Georg said, "as it might in Sardinia or Corsica. In such circumstances."

"Fish, a delicious fish soufflé," Arkley said, sniffing with a deranged air, but he caught control of the situation again at once, and turned upon Georg.

"Do you know," Arkley said, "I suppose you do know, since they were your own people, that when the Jews in Odessa sensed from the mood of the populace that a pogrom was on the way, they used to take down the fences between their gardens – in the ghetto, you know – so that when the killing started they would have a chance to make a run for it."

"Yes," Georg said. "I've heard of that sort of thing."

"Thank you," Arkley said, as Anna passed him his plate with Louise's fish soufflé on it. "Louise," he said, "how delicious. There is no one like you."

Arkley said to Georg: "I was sure you must have. I wondered if perhaps your remark about kidnappers and bandits meant that you were starting to tear down the fences."

"To make a clear run for it," Georg said, not as a question.

He'd thought he had served Arkley an ace, but Arkley had sent it back hard and low across the net.

"Eat it," Louise said commandingly, "while it's hot."

Her soufflé had been distributed round *her* table, and Georg was not sure if she had intervened out of her pride as a cook, or if she was giving him a helping hand by cutting short the exchange with Arkley.

A silence descended upon the diners as the wonder of the Alcorn soufflé broke upon their palates. Even those who lacked sensitivity in that area fell into a bemusement for which, perhaps, they could not account, and a gourmandizing speculation ran among the outsiders, who began interpreting the silverware in front of them to reckon how many courses were still to come.

The dinner went its way.


Refulgent, later, in the drawing room, Arkley sat himself in the centre of a couch. He surrounded himself there with an Augustan nimbus that repelled proximity, and the rest of the diners dispersed themselves according as their natures responded to this implicit ordinance.

Ennis moved at once to the armchair most adjacent to the seat of power. Thwarted by this, Colvin performed an irresolute dance in which his body moved with a virtuosity that his feet could not match, so that his torso and limbs emblemized a mime of hesitation; Isobel Shepherd and Roberto Mullen, the latter after offering the place with a gesture of the eyes to Georg Frankl and having it declined, shared the other couch at right angles to Arkley's.

Anna stood with one knee on the club fender and looked into the wood fire, an act of isolation which appeared to inhibit Colvin as much as the imperium claimed by his master, for moving towards the fireplace he swerved and settled on an upright chair which he placed at the edge of the space between the two couches, so that he had secured himself to the circle, as it were, but was perforce a little out of it.

Georg stood by the door and thought for a witty instant of saying goodnight and going upstairs to bed, but his eye caught Anna's in the mirror over the fireplace and at her smile, choosing one whim instead of the other, he made his way to the fireplace and sat on the fender.

"I thought, Georg," Arkley said, "that I—" Here he broke off and frowned, beetled the brows, pulled the moustache, as if this preamble was not meeting the respect it deserved.

"Are you comfortable like that, Georg?" he asked. Georg was in fact extremely comfortable, with his back now against the chimney piece and both sandals lying on the carpet, hugging his bent legs with his feet up on the padded leather of the club fender, his chin resting on his knees, and the fire warming his flank.

Georg knew Arkley was merely telling him he was aware that this business of sitting perched up there in his socks was a refusal to accept the style of after-dinner-cum-conference formality that Arkley thought convenient to the occasion (whatever this might be revealed to be). It was, however, characteristic of Arkley that his tone of voice had carried not only the implication that he was delivering a rebuke, but also the assumption that he owned a right to disapprove of persons who sat like gnomes on fenders after dinner. Georg could hardly be bothered to deal with this – he wanted to get to the point – but he thought it might start some useful adrenaline if he gave the riposte.

79

"No need to be effusive, Arkley," he said. "If it wasn't comfortable I shouldn't sit here. What about you? Leg giving you no trouble, I think? Let's get on, then. I keep country hours here, you know. Early to bed and up with the lark."

Arkley, a monument of impervious obsidian, waited through this farrago and then went on as if Georg, and not himself, had interrupted him.

"To business," Arkley said. "Ennis, I wonder if you would be kind enough to tell Mr Frankl what we have in mind for him."

Ennis, who was lighting a cigarette when he heard this instruction, at once stood up, gathered in the ashtray at his side, and in an act of surprising grace (so it seemed to the wary and sceptical Georg) came and sat on the other end of the fender.

"It's time to move you forward," Ennis said in such a positive and encouraging way that Georg almost believed he was going to be offered an advanced place on a career ladder.

In his real mind, however, he knew better. "Forward," he said, with no inflection in his voice.

"It would be of enormous use to us," Ennis said, "if you—"

Georg interrupted: "I have already been of enormous use to you," he said. "That's why I'm skulking here."

"Of how much use remains to be seen," Ennis said. "The fact that you have been compelled to skulk here is not a measure of the use you have been to us. It is a measure of the hostility that your betrayal of them has drawn upon you from your late masters, and of that alone. And you cannot skulk here for ever."

Georg met Mullen's eyes as they moved without expression across his own, saying as clear as day, yes, this was how it was going to be. He thought again, as he had thought on entering the room, of going up to bed. Telling them to put it down on paper, so that he could deprive them of their fun and games.

Instead he said: "Talk on."

Ennis was saying now: "If you were to go one step further with us, it would be appreciated."

"Can you please specify," Georg said, "the form this appreciation will take."

The reply took him aback.

"Fifty thousand pounds down, in advance," Ennis said. "Over

and above, we will honour all reasonable and necessary expenses. The fifty thousand will be your entire fee for what you have done for us and for what we now propose to you."

Georg's eye fell on his socks. The big toenail on his right foot needed cutting, it was putting a strain on the wool. Fifty thousand, and with a bit of haggling he'd have more than that out of them.

"Tell me what you want," he said.

He looked down the length of the room. A handsome room, with the elegant doors at the far end that led to the dryly rotting dining room and were flanked by bookcases to the height of the architrave; its range of three windows on his right, across which the plain linen-coloured curtains were drawn; a pair of good country-made tables between the windows, and a Regency bureau on the opposite side of the room; and a pleasing combination of Dutch and English paintings, landscapes that mostly ran to being also skyscapes – fishing boats at Scheveningen, cows by a Norfolk stream with pollarded willows, that sort of thing: nothing very much – his fifty thousand would buy all of them – but good work, apt for this long room with its cool white walls and woodwork.

Here, then, in this harmonious and gracefully dated domestic setting, Georg Frankl confronted Arkley, who sat enthroned in the character of Renaissance prince, with that kenspeckle hair and moustache and the high colour in that old, strong, stern, handsome, wicked face, watching his Machiavelli expound for him his disingenuous designs.

Beyond Arkley's shoulder Georg saw the beautiful girl reading, folded into her chair at the far end of the room, a hand toying with the ends of her hair. He looked at Isobel Shepherd and young, well, youngish, Roberto Mullen, and wondered where they came in. Colvin was in an expectable style, wearing a serious mien but with his eyes a little wide, astonished to be in the presence of the Prince while the great man's mind was unfolded before his eyes.

Ennis had been to the drinks table, and helped himself to a glass of cognac and one, too, for Georg. Georg allowed himself a sniff and a sip, and set it on the hearth beside him.

"Salut," Ennis said. He took his place again at the other end of the fender. "What we want you to do is make contact with Brigadier Markish."

"That's absurd!" Georg said. "Ben Markish . . . after what I've spilled to you. You ask a lot."

"Yes, that's what we want you to do," Ennis said, "make contact with your friend Markish."

Georg said: "Ben Markish is not my friend. I don't even know Ben Markish. I met him perhaps twice when he was in the army, but not since he went into arms sales – and that was years ago."

"Find out from Markish," Ennis said, "where that CBR shipment he sold is going. Find out very fast; three days, how does that sound?"

"It sounds fatuous," Georg said. "Three days? Listen," he said, "never mind your three days. Three days, three months: what's the difference? This will get me dead, you know that? Certainly you know that. Even if I get to Markish without being spotted on the way, do you think Mossad don't keep an eye on him? As soon as I get near him they'll have me."

Ennis said briskly: "You took the risk of getting yourself dead when you came to us. We didn't ask you to bring any of Mossad's secrets to us. You came entirely of your own volition."

Ennis was rattling all this off in the remorseless style of a schoolmaster who was going to keep it up until the bad lad before him broke down in tears. It was exactly the kind of thing Georg had expected of these people, but it put him into a fury.

He was seized by a huge urge to chop Ennis across the throat and throw him into the fire. It was quite a good-sized fireplace. Instead, he stood up and said: "Ennis, hold on for a moment."

He took a log from the basket and put it, rather than Ennis, on the glowing coals. The fire had gone down and there was room for another log. This one he dedicated to Arkley. He decided it was one of those rare occasions when he could have a cigarette, and although Ennis's pack of Silk Cut was sitting there beside his ashtray he padded, in his socks, over to Mullen.

"Roberto," he said, "give me a cigarette, will you?"

Mullen handed him one, and lit it for him.

"What do you know about all this, Roberto?" he said.

"Not a lot," Mullen said. "I'm learning it at about the same speed you are. Ennis makes it pretty boring, though, doesn't he?

I'd wandered rather, I'm afraid. I was thinking about six-furlong sprints at Brighton.''

Georg put his face down, about three feet from Mullen's. "Roberto," he said. "They're going to put me up there to get me shot or blown up or bombed or tortured to death, and you tell me you're thinking about race horses. Why are they doing this? Your people, Roberto, have thrown me to the wolves," and as he said it he flung his left arm out behind him towards Arkley.

It came to Georg that Mullen had the guilt he had been showing earlier well under control. His face looked clear and intelligent, as if he had made a good decision about the Mullen-Frankl question.

"Thrown you to the wolves?" Mullen said. "Yes, that seems about right."

Georg's eyes flickered sideways and caught Isobel Shepherd watching him, close and intent. "What are you thinking?" he shot at her.

"What are you?" she shot back. She watched him longer, and then nodded, as if she had learned something. He had a twinge of uneasiness, but let it go.

The beautiful girl at the end of the room smiled at him as if all was right with the world, and then resumed her book.

He went back to the fire. "All right, Ennis," he said. "Let's play it out. I didn't come to you people. I went to Mullen's people and you lot grabbed me out from under them. Now you're going to do the dirty on me, and you're not going to give me a choice, are you?"

"There now," Arkley said from behind him. "I knew that sooner or later it would be a pleasure to deal with you, Mr Frankl."

Georg smiled and turned to see Arkley in the act of standing up. He was shunting himself to the end of the deeply upholstered couch, supporting the weight of the false leg with a hand under its thigh. Even the fool Colvin had enough sense not to offer to help. Arkley leaned on the arm of the couch and got to his feet, settled himself steady with his stick, and came up to Georg.

"You know you're going to do it," he said. "You want to be away from here; you don't trust me and you don't trust my people. We don't trust you – and how wise, in this, all of us are.

As to the money, you will either have it in your hand before you set off, or we will dispose of it for you as you think best.

"As to your mission to Brigadier Markish: accomplish it and we shall pay you another fifty thousand, and if not, not. Payment by results. Truly, you will be in some danger, but then you are a capable man, Frankl, are you not?"

Arkley gazed into the fire, watching all unawares as the logs that Frankl had consigned to the flames under the names of Arkley and Ennis hissed and snapped their way to their fiery end.

"That shipment is moving," Arkley said, "to Africa, as you tell us. It is on its way to somewhere, and it is British."

He went to where Georg had sat before on the club fender and dropped onto it with comparative ease because of the difference in solidity and height between it and the couch from which he had just risen with such difficulty.

He sat looking up at Georg. He did nothing to make it happen, but power came out from him like perfume from a rose, and Georg felt himself yield a little to its scent.

When you thought about it, Arkley was old, but sitting there with his straight back, his brutally strong and handsome head with its mad flourish of black and white hair springing from it, with that cruel and sensual face and those cold, fierce eyes; the whole man as relaxed, now, as if he were dealing with nothing more critical than whether to choose the Aloxe-Corton yet again or give the Calon-Ségur a chance: to Georg, standing there, over against the mighty Sir John Arkley, head of Britain's Intelligence Service, the man's age was nothing like a weakness but rather an element and a sign of his power. The pack might be waiting to bring him down, but none that lived still had dared it yet.

"You will have known before we met tonight," Arkley said, "and by now you will have confirmed it for yourself, that there is nothing sentimental about me. I am not," and an enigmatic smile glimmered under the moustache, "an Edith Cavell or an Axel Munthe in wolf's clothing. I mean by this to say that patriotism and plague are nothing to me.

"So. In those green packing-cases, divided half and half, as we understand it, between chemical and bacteriological weapons, the death of probably millions is going into Africa. This raises no humanitarian feelings in me. You say it raises humanitarian feelings in you, and that is why you brought your knowledge of it, such as it is, to Mr Mullen, with whom you had dealings once in Tel Aviv."

He broke off and his eyes washed over Georg's face like a north-easterly airstream. "Yes," he said again. "Your knowledge, such as it is." He tapped his stick on the toe of his shoe. "You brought to Mr Mullen. So it went upwards and came to Downing Street, and no one in Britain knows about it save at the highest levels of the Home Office, the Foreign Office, the Ministry of Defence, and the Prime Minister's office; and even at those levels, only those with need to know are aware."

There was nothing ironical in the smile that gleamed now. "So you are right, Frankl," and he reached out and touched Georg lightly on the side of the calf with the stick, "to be scared shitless about the idea of undertaking this mission. Secrecy has undoubtedly been compromised. Not everyone is so security conscious as you and I. If I confided a secret to my dog, I would kill it after."

His face moved with discomfort. He put the stick under the artificial leg and used it as a lever to shift the leg so that he could ease himself forward.

Georg stood unmoving, acquiring the man before him.

"These noxious substances are British," Arkley said. "That is my only interest. I am not even interested to know how they reached the market in which Brigadier Markish operates. My interest is that they are British and must not be used. We have fed the little we know from you and the little we know about Africa," – another of those dark, unspeaking smiles – "into the computers and let them run scenarios for us, through the Saharan and sub-Saharan African states. Do you know that the likeliest case is the worst case? That they will be used against Islamic fundamentalists? Britain cannot afford to have this happen. If they are so used, and it becomes known that they are British in origin – no matter how they got there – it will corrupt our relations with half the world."

Frankl said: "If your security is blown, Ben Markish will know I've exposed him to you and he'll want to kill me. If there's Moslem faction-fighting in this I'll get caught in their crossfire and some of *them* will be trying to kill me. If I get anywhere near Ben Markish, Mossad will kill me. Half the bloody world will be trying to kill me, and not worrying one tiny bit about corrupting its relations with me."

Arkley planted the stick and stood, and came right up to Frankl. A triumphant expression shone on the florid face. "If these CBR weapons are used against Moslems, fundamentalist or otherwise, what such an event would do to Israel's relations with half the world – when you consider that the middleman is *your* Brigadier Markish, once a shining light in *your* military elite – does not bear thinking of. But I expect . . ."

Here he thumped his stick on the floor for emphasis, but it encountered one of Georg's discarded sandals and the thump was muffled. Arkley reversed his stick and hooked the sandal up into his hand, where he let it dangle from a finger while he completed his peroration.

"I expect you, and even Mossad, have contemplated that awful possibility," he said. "Who knows over whom you may not trip before your mission is over. You see, I know you will do this for us. You will, won't you, Frankl?"

"Seventy-five thousand up front and I'll do it," Georg said.

"And," Arkley said, "the other reason you'll do it is that if I confided a secret to my dog, I'd kill it after."

"Oh, that," Georg said, "goes without saying. I knew that of you."

"Of course you did," Arkley said. "Ennis will arrange it all, and your friend Mullen will put you on your road. Ennis, one hundred thousand for Mr Frankl: seventy-five down, twenty-five on completion. Mr Frankl will trust us, I am sure, for the balance. I will say goodnight to you all now."

He looked at the sandal hanging from his finger. He looked at Georg. He turned and tossed the sandal into the fire.

"With seventy-five thousand pounds," he said, "you'll be able to get yourself a decent pair of shoes."

He looked at Georg's feet. "Take my tip," he said. "If you live to collect the other twenty-five, get yourself a last at Tricker's."

# 9

Seddall was up at seven, raring to go. He sang *"Il mio tesoro"* in the shower, after the true lyric style of Anton Dermota in the Salzburg recording, and while he steered the electric shaver about his face he made an ambitious attempt at *"Der Lindenbaum"*, but lost the words somewhere about his Adam's apple.

He had a particular middling dark-blue suit which had the best cut pair of trousers he had ever seen – since most of his respectable clothes were cut by the same pair of scissors, this was unaccount-able: art, he supposed – and wearing these, he put the bacon under the grill and the butter for the eggs on to heat.

He hummed his way into his shirt, socks and shoes, giving the latter a light rub with yesterday's handkerchief borrowed from the laundry basket, and went to turn the bacon, put the eggs in the hot butter, and drop two slices of bread into the toaster.

"Sacha, my sweet," he said as he passed again the black cat, who sat in the hall waiting for the mail, "how very matutinal one feels today. There's nothing like being up with the lark."

Sacha, whose only reason for being up with the lark would be to catch the wretched bird before it soared off to the heights to warble insults at the baffled predator, found this cause enough to make her morning snatch at Seddall's stroking hand.

He was on the watch, however.

"Missed, you fiend," he said, fond but triumphant, and ran back upstairs to his camp in the future study. Whisking the tie round his neck, he caught his eyes in the glass and stopped in the act of making the knot. He had seen that the eyes were wicked, with the glee which he knew to be that of the conspirator.

"We must moderate the mood," he said. "We have still to hear from the Herr General."

Waistcoated and with the jacket slung over a chair, he sat down at the kitchen table to excellent bacon and perfect eggs. He had become quite soigné about this cooking.

Sacha, who had forgiven them both for the bloodless spat in the hall, came in for some egg-yolk. It was a curious fact that since she and Seddall had been living alone here together – with Olivia away in France and Bayard the dog down in Somerset with Mrs Lyon – Sacha had begun to accept morsels of cooked food. Up until now she had been inflexible in eating nothing but her own kill, and while it was true that the move to this house had taken her away from the park that had been her hunting ground, she was feeding pretty well off the wildlife round about. Seddall was inclined to value the change in her as a compliment to his cooking and a deepening of their relationship.

He lit the first cigarette and looked at the time. "Seven fifty-five," he said. "Too early for the Herr General."

The phone rang out.

"Good God," Seddall said, and grabbed for it.

"Seddall," he said.

"Morning, Harry," the general said. "I'll do it," he said. "I've fixed the meeting and I'll keep out of your way. These meetings are at eleven. You'll find a bit of paper on your desk saying where – the site varies. What I have to do now is nobble the politico, and you can never count on that."

"By God, sir, well done, sir" Harry said.

"You sound like Uxbridge at Waterloo," the general said. "Which reminds me: he lost a leg in that one, same as our friend Arkley; and you could get your head in your hands for this one. You're a conniving bastard, Harry, but so is Arkley. Watch your step."

"You will be amazed at how circumspect I shall be," Harry said.

"That'll be the day," the general said, "but I wish you luck. And Harry, I do mean this: if it all goes badly for you and you end up on the street without a penny, you can always take pot luck with us till you find your feet. You can sleep with the dogs; they trust you, the poor innocent brutes."

"I could buttle for you," Harry said.

"That sort of thing," the general said. "I'm off the scene on a vital mission, that is understood."

"What did you come up with?" Harry asked.

"I did not specify," the general said, "but I sounded powerful solemn, I can tell you. I almost believed myself. In fact, I've an aunt in Norfolk I ought to see. I'll take her to lunch at the Feathers in Holt and be home for dinner. Good hunting."

As Harry put on his hat, he heard the clang of Sacha's sally port at the back door. Olivia wasn't the only one who went in for independence in the relationship.

He hailed a taxi in Thurloe Place and went down to Whitehall to do battle.


The room was not small, but in its proportion to the high ceiling it was well composed, and since it was gravely and not superfluously furnished this gave it, for Seddall, the intimacy that belonged to the council chamber of a secret society. Indeed, as there were to be only four of them at the octagonal table, so that each man would be flanked by an empty chair, the suggestion that they were in an inner council was irresistible.

However romantic this conceit, its melodramatic buzz of being at the heart of secret government – since he himself had achieved his place here by chicanery – served to heighten in him a sense of the stakes he was playing for and to flush even more adrenaline into his system.

Opposite sat Arkley, transfixed, glaring at him. Fury had stretched the skin of his face over the bone. He was poised like an enraged duellist ready to fall upon his enemy. This must be a good fight.

On Seddall's left was Colin Duncanson, one of those career-driven Border Celts whom Johnson would have called a Scotch-man on the make. He had dank black hair, combed flat and unprepossessing across his scalp. His face was strange: patched white and red with a lifeless, untouchable look to it, like marbled meat in a butcher's shop. The mouth was long and ugly, its lips scarlet as if too full of blood, and was set in a rictus, so that in all moods he seemed to smile.

Duncanson, in contrast to Arkley's statue-like stillness, looked now at the table, now at Seddall, now at Arkley, now at the chairman's vacant chair, most often at this corner of the ceiling or that. Neither of them had yet asked Seddall how he came to be there.

Seddall was in a mixture of two states. He was in the enjoyment of that internal balance which is also cogent and active, and would have let him sit silent throughout a dinner party with unquestioning certainty of self, if that was what he felt like doing. The second state was that of a man in a poker game which is too rich for his blood, but who knows he is riding on that beam where nerve and concentration are at the pitch where risk is essential to fulfil them.

The chairman came into the room and had walked three paces onto the carpet when, as if he had walked into an invisible barrier, his head turned aside and he stopped.

"Well, well," he said, and came briskly on. A secretary or assistant walked at his heel.

The chairman sat down. "There's no water," he said to the assistant, who went out.

"Arkley," the chairman said to his right, "Duncanson," he said across the table. "You're Harry Seddall," he said to his left. "Oliver Quick. How do you do."

"How d'you do," Harry said.

Arkley, while continuing to stare at Harry like a basilisk, said: "This meeting cannot possibly continue. Seddall is not the head of his service."

"Duncanson, what's your view?" Quick said.

Duncanson looked calmly at Arkley, at Seddall, and at Quick. "Unformed, as yet," he said. He smiled, which is to say the permanent smile became real. "Giving help to none," he said.

Quick was interested. "Giving help to none: is that a quotation?"

"No," Duncanson said. "It was my comment."

"Sir Oliver," Arkley said, abandoning the surname format. "Seddall is not a head of service. He should not be here."

"General Kenyon can't be here," Quick said. "This meeting will have a limited agenda to which Seddall is relevant."

"Downing Street *fiat*," Duncanson said, noting this fact without much interest: indeed, as one who recognizes one of those familiar and reassuring events that removes uncertainty.

"Downing Street covers a multitude of sins," Arkley said, inflexibly irate. "It could mean the Chancellor of the Exchequer, the Prime Minister, or merely the Cabinet Office."

"By which last you mean myself." Quick said this in a brisk and pleasant enough tone, but you could tell no more from that than from the appearance of a large dog that was neither wagging its tail nor growling. Quick was certainly large. He had the over-fleshed bulk of a self-indulgent livestock auctioneer who took an extra commission in beef. The face was pudgy and high-coloured and ugly, with a large wide nose and a short, clamping jaw that pushed the lower lip up against a straggly Mexican moustache that was incongruous both on that face and to his professional standing.

He used no style to assert himself, to let you know how tough he was. What it was, Seddall thought, was that the man was enormously at ease.

"Arkley," Duncanson said, "what's the point of this? Let's get on, huh? This isn't a formal meeting. You can't register your discontent in the minutes or any of that crap."

"If I could, I would," Arkley said. "As it is, I'll register it elsewhere."

"Always good to discard your low cards early in the game," Duncanson said insultingly. "I take it that means we can actually get on now."

"Georg Frankl," said Oliver Quick, "came first to you, Duncanson, saying UK-derived CBRs were moving from the Gulf to Africa. Seddall also interviewed Frankl, and was asked to act. Frankl was then passed to you, Arkley, and you housed him. You were given Cabinet background and asked to act. You go first, Seddall."

Seddall slid the Churchyard diary into the centre of the table, and gave a précis of it. He would have liked, without quite knowing why, to hold back on Taif Awdi's part in bringing the diary to him, but he could not believe that neither Arkley nor Duncanson had received a record of Taif's call.

"Churchyard wasn't that reliable, was he, Seddall?" Arkley

said. There was nothing hostile in his voice. He had apparently started to cool off from the anger that had overtaken him when he saw that General Kenyon had sent Seddall to stand in for him at this meeting.

"No," Seddall said. "Churchyard was flawed. We have to take that into account. On the other hand, he got a long way. He was a good man in the field."

"That why you kept him?" Arkley said. He smiled like a wolf. "I didn't know you had it in you."

Seddall sent a lazy smile across the table. "Arkley," he said, "if I'd dropped him, you'd have taken him."

Arkley bowed, briefly, his head, and pretended to appear enigmatic.

"What was Churchyard's flaw?" asked Sir Oliver. "Does it impeach his report?"

"He tortured a man to death on an operation I was running," Seddall said. "He was out to redeem himself. What Sir John means is that he may have decorated his story to that end, and of course that is a possibility."

Duncanson bent his rictus upon the table and revolved the diary with a forefinger. "That's really quite vexatious," he said, "because this Bedayatt merchant of yours can corroborate, if we take him at face value at least in this respect, what happened in the desert. But he can't affirm what Churchyard says he picked up in the Gulf, that this little cargo of CBR was reputed to be on its way to a woman. It's the crucial part of his story. It offers something to act on, and yet it may or may not be decoration."

Sir Oliver said: "I can't for the life of me come up with a woman of political dominance in West Africa. In fact, in West Africa it's an unlikely postulate."

"That's what gives it its charm," Arkley said. "That's what fetches us. It's too unlikely to be an intelligent invention."

"Which doesn't mean it's not an invention," Seddall said.

"Quite so," Arkley said. "Now then: I have discharged Frankl from his sanctuary with us, paid him a fair fee, and sent him to discover from the Israeli arms dealer, Ben Markish, what he can of the expected use to which this CBR may be put, and by whom."

"I could have borne to be consulted about that," Duncanson said.

"What does that mean?" Sir Oliver asked.

Arkley said: "Duncanson made a deal with Frankl. I have broken it."

"We don't have time here for these accountings," Sir Oliver said. "This arms dealer . . ."

"Brigadier Ben Markish," Arkley said. "He had a role in this, according to Frankl."

"Brigadier?"

"Ah, yes," Arkley said. "Retired, of course; expatriate Israeli living in Paris. A respectable arms merchant."

"There is something unclear to me," Quick said. "What do we make of Frankl?"

Arkley looked at Seddall. "I'm not at all sure," Seddall said. "Either he's ordinary, or he has such a gift for dissimulation that he can put himself across as ordinary. Of course, to be able to do that is the hallmark of a good agent. Equally, in my trade I'm supposed to be able to detect it. I have no trace of him in Mossad. I've tried Defence Intelligence in Washington and so far they've struck out."

Arkley looked at Duncanson. "Same as Seddall," Duncanson said talkatively.

"Yes," Arkley said. "It's my pigeon, and we're looking in Tel Aviv, but so far all we have is what he tells us himself. He's a deputy head of section at the Institute, no more than that; which means that he's a field agent and when he's at home he's useful on the desk. It may well be true."

"The Institute?" Sir Oliver said.

"It's an affectation of Arkley's," Seddall said.

"Mossad means 'the Institute'," Arkley said, "in Yiddish."

"Not Yiddish," Duncanson said. "Hebrew."

Sir Oliver rode over this. "I gather Frankl claims to be unclear about what connection there might be between Mossad and this retired-brigadier arms merchant. It was known in Mossad, but Frankl found it too appalling to think Mossad might be itself involved. So do I, come to that. He could not resolve the question for himself one way or the other. Obviously there was no way

93

Israel was going to mount a major operation into Africa which was not in its own direct interest and thereby raise fresh Muslim resentment against itself. Equally, Mossad (as opposed to Israel as such) might conjecture an advantage from a disaster in Africa for which Britain might be blamed" – at this Seddall saw the fixed rictus on Duncanson's face glimmer into life – "and they were still no more than talking about it at the Institute," and Quick leaned his eyes on Arkley, "so Frankl thought he must do something or hell, in the exact sense, might be let loose in Africa."

Arkley was stroking the black side of his piebald moustache. "Yes," he said, "We could not get him to go past that."

Sir Oliver said: "How far do you believe him?"

"It is not going to matter," Arkley said.

Seddall, on the alert at once, slouched low in his chair as if the meeting had begun to drag.

Arkley said: "It is Frankl who created that question by coming to us: how far are we to believe him? If Frankl has something else in mind, I have pre-empted him. For the rest, I have moved against the perceived threat and I can tell you, Sir Oliver, that the Cabinet Office will not want to know what I have done."

That plump auctioneer's face looked at him as if he were a Texel-cross, with no great show record. "What does that mean? You only heard about this proposition that the CBR is destined for some woman in West Africa three minutes ago. You have still to learn what Frankl finds out from Brigadier Markish."

"What about Frankl?" Duncanson said. "You're covering him in Paris?"

Seddall rubbed the palm of his hand on the back of his neck and then brought the hand to his face as if to smother a yawn.

"I'm doing all that is appropriate," Arkley said. "I remind you that I am restrained by my instructions from sharing my intimate knowledge of a British end to this business with my staff. That I have," he sent a dark and flaring look round the table and let it rest on the chairman, "*carte blanche.*"

Quick kept his eyes on Arkley. "And you, Seddall? What do you intend to do?"

"What I'm going to do next," Seddall said, but not, it seemed, to anyone in particular, "is think, over a lamb cutlet."

For the third or fourth time at this meeting, Duncanson came in out of synch. "Arkley," he said. "I gave you Frankl. I want more than this. When did you send Frankl to Paris?"

Arkley discussed it internally for no more than a moment before agreeing with himself that he would answer. But he did discuss it, and Seddall had seen him do it. "I had him flown over last night," Arkley said.

A curious silence followed, in which Arkley's head turned a little to the side, as if he were listening for something. It was as if he were adrift in some cosmos of his own. During this silence the light in the room seemed to darken, but when Seddall looked to the windows the sun was as bright as ever, and when he looked up at the small chandelier over the table none of the bulbs had gone out.

"Duncanson," Arkley said. "That young officer of yours who was with me last night – surely he has reported to you? He drove Frankl to the airfield."

"Not yet," Duncanson said. "I am straight from a working breakfast. I've not been to the Office this morning."

"Nor I," Arkley said. "I had sleep to catch up. I must make a phone call." His face, the grizzled phiz of a chief of the Camorra, was harsh and closed. Behind his descended eyelids, Arkley was listening to the admonishing voice in his head. "You would know how Frankl's flight went," Arkley said to himself, "if it were not for that girl. She comes to you at night like the young Shulamite to King David in his age. No matter. The Frenchman does not fail."

Round Seddall more light went from the air.

Arkley spoke aloud. "No," he said, "no matter."

Seddall watched Duncanson's eyes, fierce and black like a gypsy's, hunting into the man behind Arkley's face. Seddall felt ill and filled with lethargy, as if he would never be able to leave this room.

He went on watching Duncanson, but out of the edge of his eye he saw the bulk of Oliver Quick lift in his chair as the intuitive knowledge that was turning in the air above the table began to reach him.

Duncanson himself now sat back and stared out of the window

behind the chairman's head. On his marred face it was as if the shadow of an ancient wrong had fallen.

"You have . . ." he said. "What was the need, Arkley?"

When Arkley unhooded his own eyes and brought them up to meet Duncanson's, Seddall saw it: the glint of morbid cynicism arrogantly held. He had never had such a sense in any man of Lucifer poised above the pit.

"The imperatives are mine," Arkley said. "They must remain mine." All of a sudden he was completely with them. He was, for the first time that morning, one of them. "You know damn well, Duncanson," he said, the voice incisive, himself dominant and ebullient, full of that quality the ancient Romans prized, of *auctoritas*. At the same time his whole being was alert, the face ruddy and animated and the blue eyes bright and alive, as if life were a dance. "You know damn well that these things have to be done. The stakes in this are too high to take the risks of omission."

Sir Oliver Quick came in, and Seddall knew from his tone that he would be out of there in minutes. "What are you saying, Arkley?"

Arkley leaned forward over the table, adjusting his prosthetic leg to the movement with the ease of one who had worn it all his life: "I am saying, Sir Oliver, that I have arranged for the ambiguity, the doubt, the uncertainty posed by the questions we cannot answer about Georg Frankl within the time that we would need to answer them, to become irrelevant."

"Sweet Christ, Arkley," Seddall found himself saying, "such as they are, they were irrelevant when he was holed up in your fucking safe house. It was you who kicked him out."

"You're being absurd, Seddall," Arkley said. "For all you know Frankl is an accomplished killer for the Institute. You know nothing about him. I do. I know that he is not ordinary, I know that he's good: that was your own antithesis, that he was one or the other. By good, you meant very good. Frankl's very good. I can smell that a mile off. What we have to deal with here is unspeakable in the terms of what it might mean to the Government, never mind the possible thousands – thousands? say a million, two million – in Africa. I would cut Frankl's throat here in this room if I had to. He is a man in play and not on our side of the board, and he is an incalculable risk. Time is not on our side. I take him off the board."

He suited the action to the word, cutting a hand through the air in front of him.

"Furthermore, doing so is an integral part of the overall operation I have mounted in response to the Cabinet instruction notified to me by the . . . appropriate Minister."

Sir Oliver Quick consulted his wristwatch and dropped into the vulgar tongue. "Adjourned," he said, "and that little fucker never brought me any water. Otherwise, a satisfactory clearing of the air, I think we're able to say."

Duncanson, too, embraced the idea of conciliating that abstract concept, the ethos of the meeting. "Endorsed," he said.

Arkley said nothing, and it was to Seddall that he said it.

Seddall gave it back to him, nodding his head at Arkley once or twice with a sour smile to congratulate him on his performance.

After that Seddall did not hang about, nor wait on whatever protocol there might be. He gathered in Churchyard's notebook, pushed back his chair and stood up.

"Must rush," he said, "early lunch date," and left the room and the building.

As he emerged, a taxi stopped for his upraised arm. "Cavalry Club," he said through the window.

"Cavalry Club?" the driver said. "I wouldn't 'ave time to get out of first gear. You must be bloody jokin'."

"Five quid," Harry said, and opened the door and thrust the note at him.

"Hop in, mate," the driver said, and went there.

At the club, Harry made straight for the secretary's room.

"Borrow your phone?" he said.

# 10

Toko was singing again, no longer in the desert but this time into the sex and smoke and sweat, the liquor fumes and smells of food, of the Pigalle boîte where she earned her keep.

> *Parlez-moi d'amour*

she sang,

> *Redites-moi des choses tendres,*
> *Votre beau discours*
> *Mon coeur n'est pas las de l'entendre,*
> *Pourvu que toujours*
> *Vous répétiez ces mots suprêmes,*
> *Je vous aime.*

She was singing well tonight, she was in voice. In her sweet, rich, cream-like voice she shaped the song into one true *bel canto* flawless piece of art entire.

With the help of Pierre-André at the piano (who was in that ideal state when the heroin had been good, just enough, and taken not too long ago) she used the mellifluous voice in exact obedience to the score.

There was no deviation from the metronome, no falling into false sentiment with indulgent lingering on the end of the line. She gave them no pseudo-romantic slurs; she moved cleanly from note to note. She sang with a stern passion that refused to sully the purity of the song, and of her voice, with such melodramatic tricks as vibrato or letting the husk come to her throat.

She stood naked and covered with oil, at one with her own spirit and the song and the man at the keyboard; and with them alone. She sang into the smoke with a serene scorn, as if by singing from all the candour of her bare body and at the same time pandering to the rat-assed, lecherous, voyeuristic, crowd sitting at their tables all around her, she brought to their most ecstatic pitch the emotion of the song, the exquisite beauty of the song, the exaltation of her singing.

At the far end of the room, a man came in the door and took a stool at the battered zinc-topped bar and put a leather bag on the floor beside him. The barman took down a bottle and poured into two glasses and slid one across. They lifted the glasses and nodded to each other and emptied them. The barman filled the newcomer's glass again and left him to himself. No word had been exchanged.

The newcomer sat with his back to the nude singer and her audience. He was a tall man, built like a rock, and he had a bullet head with sandy hair shorn to the scalp. He had a three-day stubble and wore a loose cotton tropical jacket over shirt and trousers that looked as if they'd been slept in.

He sat and drank calvados with a grim mouth, but every now and then a smile twitched onto it and away again. He was completely self-contained, content with his own company and the drink before him and the cigarette he smoked that stank of cattle dung.

Toko sang with the lights in her eyes from a rig hanging low over the tables. She saw little of the audience and far less of what was going on down at the bar. Her only human contact was with Pierre-André at the piano, and now in the middle of the song – the two of them on a roll with the music tonight, in such a rapport – she gave him the side of her eye and saw him smile and shake his head.

The next moment she felt it, all over her body and inside her. "Oh, dear God, my pussy juice is running," she said to herself even as she sang. "Dujardin's here."

She sang the last verse like an angel and took the applause and the raucous shouts as she always did, waiting without sign of acknowledgement until the noise tailed off. Then she stepped down from the rostrum, laid a light hand on Pierre-André's head, and went through the audience towards the bar.

When she was still in among the crowded tables she saw

Dujardin, sitting sideways there at the bar, leaning an elbow on it, leaning his head on his hand, watching her come to him.

An arm grabbed her round the waist and threw her on her back on top of a table, among the plates and glasses and bottles. First there was the shock of being swept off her feet; then, together, there came the anger, and the pain of broken glass and other things cutting at her and bruising her.

Then fury burst through her as she was pulled off the table by arms and hands which clutched her damn body, her breasts, her belly, her thighs, and dragged her down till she was across the laps of two men: and one of them was hard, for fuck's sake, right up there he was, and one of them, of course, got his fingers on her cunt and groped in there where she was already wet, but wet for Dujardin.

Toko went berserk. The men who had their hands on her were easy meat, they were drunk, laughing, at play. She whacked her right elbow twice into the balls of one man, and scored. She heard him squawk and go loose on her at the same moment that she slashed the other across the throat with the edge of her hand. That one fell off his chair and she went to the floor after him, saw that he was helpless (or thought he was, the poor specimen of manhood, just because he was hurt) and stood up and stamped her heel into his balls, too.

"Hey, don't kill him, Toko," a voice said. "If you kill him, we might get closed down." The voice belonged to the owner, a Pole called Tadeus Krubski. "I'll sling them out. All you have to do is yell, and me and the boys will handle these bastards."

"Oh yes, sure you will," Toko said. "Tad, his fucking hand was inside me. No one but me could have been there fast enough. And he was *mine*, Tad, when he did that."

The Pole looked down at the sick man on the floor, who stared up at him out of a pallid face. Tad kicked him with all his force in the kidneys. The victim's body shuddered at the blow, and he let out a sound between a gasp and a shriek.

Tad turned to the other man, who was on his feet now, supporting himself with both hands on the table. "Bastards," the man said to the two still sitting across the table from him. "I won't go drinking with you again in a hurry."

"You brought it on yourself," one of them said, and then said to Krubski, "But you've done enough to him now," and he jerked his head at the one on the floor.

"Ah," Tad said. "I've done enough when I say so."

The two on the other side of the table stood up. "No," the spokesman said. "You've done enough."

Here and there at tables round about other men began to stand up.

Toko was still naked and still on her way to Dujardin. "Big men," she sneered at them. The two men were big, but that was incidental: she was talking to them all, to Tad and the others who had begun to scent a full-scale rough house. "The party's over. You guys," she said to the two, "take out your friends, and when you've done it, come back if you like. You've done nothing bad, not yet. Pierre-André," she called to the pianist, "play some music."

Pierre-André began to play a *mouvement perpetuel* by Poulenc. She knew it was his way of taking the piss out of all these idiots.

One of the big guys took the shrimp off the floor and humped him onto his shoulder. The other one took the arm of the man leaning on the table and said: "Come on, you're out."

Tad said: "And he doesn't come back. He's black-balled."

"Oh, hey! His balls are black all right," Toko said. And she went down to the bar laughing.

"Shit, Dujardin," she said, "you sure came running to defend my honour."

"Come here," he said, and got off the stool and took her into the span of his arms and held her loosely. "It'll be a cold day in hell before you need me to defend your honour," he said. "But when you want it, I'll do it."

She felt him up and down and around; her hands ran all over him. His hands moved over her, more slowly than hers moved on him.

"You've got blood on you," he said, "and what's this? Turn round. Yes, you've got some splinters of glass. Give me a bottle of cognac, Tad," for Tad had come up now and was behind the bar, "and have you any tissues? Here, my Toko, sit on this stool in front of me and I'll do a little doctoring on you."

"I don't know that I like you sitting bare-assed at the bar, Toko," Tad said, as she got up on the bar stool. "It's not that kind of place."

Dujardin dropped his chin onto his chest and brought it up again. There was no change on his face and he did not look at Tad, but the Pole said: "Sure, here's the cognac and yes, a box of tissues. Let me get her a robe, though, for when you're through."

"Wowee!" Toko said as the brandy bit into the cuts on her back. "Is that your drink?" and she swallowed a big mouthful of calvados. "Where have you been, Dujardin? The last few weeks I seem to be doing nothing but fighting off men."

"First I was in Peru," he said. "Then I was in jail in Peru, and then I got mixed up in a little fight with the Shining Path, and then I came here."

It was a wonderful feeling, to have his hands on her back: for though he was doctoring her, they were the fingers of her lover that did the doctoring. They were at once strong, clever, ruthless and tender, and where they touched, and deeper, they woke fire.

It was too much.

"I want to go home, Dujardin. Have you got a car?"

She slid round on the stool, inside his arms.

"Yes," he said. "I have a car."

He bent forward and they kissed with the outsides of their lips. She let her head fall forward. "Oh, God, Dujardin," she said.

"Yes," he said. "Let's go."

He picked up his bag from the floor and slung it on his shoulder, and all in that movement she put her arms round his neck and he gathered her up in his arms.

Tad came up with a dressing-gown. "You people!" he said. "At least have this over her."

And since Dujardin was moving now to the door, Tad went with them, putting the robe over Toko and tucking it in round her as best he could.

He held the door open for them and Dujardin went through. The robe caught on something as they passed to the street and fell to the pavement.

It was a dirty night, cold and with sleet falling in a blustery wind.

Tad, with the robe in his hand, watched Dujardin carry Toko across the street and set her down while he fished in his pocket for the car keys. Toko stood naked on the road and reached out to touch Dujardin's neck while he bent to the car door.

He opened it, and still she kept her hand to his neck and he stayed there holding the door for her, and leaned his neck and head into her caress: while the wind blew, and the sleet fell on them, and people and traffic passed, the lights of the cars moving and shining on her dark skin, and on the passion of her hand on his neck and on the passion of his head moving to her hand.

Tadeus Krubski thought it was the most beautiful picture he'd ever seen. "You people," he said to himself.

At last Toko brought her hand forward, round the side of Dujardin's face, and let it fall, and got into the car. Dujardin went round the other side and got in and drove away.

Tad stood in the entrance, out of the wind and weather. He lit a cigarette and smoked for a while, and then went back inside.


In the afternoon, they left the apartment and walked to Chez Bernard for breakfast. It was still cold, but it was a bright day, hardly a cloud up there. Toko wore a woolly sweater of Dujardin's and black leather trousers. Dujardin wore jeans and an ancient and capacious leather jacket that came down to his thighs, and a gun, the new Beretta 9mm, in a holster under his armpit.

He ordered steak and eggs and chips, and Toko had a croque-monsieur. After he had eaten, Dujardin got himself a cognac and Toko had another croque-monsieur.

Dujardin said: "We've got a job."

"You and me?" Toko said.

"You and me."

"Great," Toko said. "Who we going to do it to?"

"We do it in West Africa," Dujardin said, "and we do it to a woman, but we won't know who it is till we get there."

"We're in business already, aren't we?" Toko said. "You sitting with your back to the wall and carrying."

"I'm always in business now," Dujardin said. "Since I fouled

103

up in Peru and let those sons of bitches put me in that filthy prison, I always will be in business."

It was one of the best things about Dujardin, that he took his own share of responsibility when things went wrong.

All the same, as part of the creative war between them she held an inflexible line that she didn't let him cross without a fight. "Sons of bitches?" she said.

"What?" Dujardin said.

"Bitches," Toko said. "You called them sons of bitches."

Dujardin clasped a hand round her arm with that suggestion of force in his grip that told her, which she knew perfectly well, that he could crush it with one hand – if she let him. "Dogs, then. Sons of dogs," he said, "and daughters of bitches, because there were women with them as well. Will that do?"

"That will do fine," Toko said. "What are you going to do to my arm, Dujardin? You didn't do enough to me last night?"

"No," he said, and took his hand away, "I didn't, and neither did you, to me, but I guess you don't have a date with anyone else tonight, do you?" And, looking at her, he smiled.

He was not a smiling man, Dujardin; even to her, his smiles were rare. They were always better for that, and for the grim mouth they came from, but most of all for the fact that when it was to her he smiled, those hard grey eyes of his came to life.

They did not soften, she would not have wanted that – well, perhaps she would have, now and then; but again, perhaps not, because though it was a tough thing to be always in this contest they waged, not so much with each other as with life and death, to keep themselves free and equal, she valued the toughness of it.

So, Dujardin's eyes did not soften when he smiled at her, but the life that came into them had sometimes so primitive a force in it, even a ferocity, that it took her back to the time she found herself looking into the eyes of a panther: not out in the bush, but in a zoo. In the bush she'd have had to kill it, for her life. In the zoo, she had wanted to free it. She freed it, instead, in Dujardin, and nothing in her life would ever beat that.

He looked around and then got up and went to the washroom. She watched him go and let herself feel good about him, then turned to taking in the café.

104

It was that time in late afternoon when the place started to fill as offices in the neighbourhood began to empty. At first sight she saw no one who gave her that sense of difference which meant something was wrong, but it was not usually first sight that told you; unless you were dealing with amateurs. She went on taking in those who were in already, those who came in, and those who went out.

Often you did not know who you were dealing with until you were right into it with them already. Everybody hired out to everybody else these days, or did favours in return for favours. You could be dealing with Abu Nidal, or the Basques, or the IRA, or the SDECE, or Shin Bet doing one for US Military Intelligence, or Mossad doing one for Shin Bet, or MI5 doing one for MI6, which was actually for the FBI, or the Camorra moving in on the Mafia, or the CIA doing one for the Australians (whatever they called themselves) but actually farming it out to the Mafia, who were doing it, as was everyone else, for money.

Who was that Sicilian who said it? She couldn't remember; only that he said: "So long as nobody's talking money, nobody's saying anything." Right on, Siciliano.

It was as if hardly anyone took in their own washing any more, and now here was someone farming one out to her and Dujardin.

"When and how do we get paid?" Toko said, when Dujardin rejoined her. "And I mean when and how do *I* get paid? And where in West Africa? And who're we working for?"

Dujardin said: "We get seventy-five thousand pounds in English notes between us. Half to you and half to me. All we have to do is lift it off this man who thinks he's been paid it to do something else.

He's expected in Paris tomorrow. And we receive our air tickets tomorrow – and that is when we know where we're going, at least in the first instance – and passports and all appropriate visas, and cholera and sleeping sickness certificates, or whatever it is you people have to get you sick in Africa. We fly out tomorrow night. The man who hired us is English. I think he sprung me from prison in Peru, but he didn't say, so I didn't ask. Why waste time with questions that won't be answered? How do you like it so far?"

Toko looked at him. "It sounds too good," she said. "It's simple where it should be simple and it's dirty where it needs to be dirty. Who's doing this?"

"Aha," Dujardin said. "That is quite a question. His French was excellent, but he was plainly English and not trying to hide it. I know who he is. Perhaps I'll tell you, perhaps not." He hunched himself forward over the table and put his face close to hers. Dujardin was not a man whose skin tanned well, but she was used to seeing that seasoned face of his ruddy with health. Now, after the months he'd spent in prison, it had a seedy, clay-like look to it, with a yellow tinge.

"Dujardin?" she said.

"What is it?" he said, irritated at being interrupted.

"You fit enough for this job?"

"Why not?" he said. "We're not going to hike two or three hundred kilometres over the mountains or through the jungle. We're flying in to do a fast hit and get out again."

"Sure," she said, "a cakewalk."

"To hell with you," he said. "If you think I'm going to let you down, I'll do the job by myself."

Despite the jail pallor, his expression was as hard as nails. She thought that he might be laughing in there, but with Dujardin you could not be sure. He leaned back and gave his shoulders a shake.

"All right, then," he said. "It's the English hiring us. And this was all on the phone, you understand. I mean this was all quite sensible; not clever, but sensible. It means I was tracked when I flew out of La Paz. I went to the embassy for papers; I imagine they were watching, just in case. La Paz was so close over the border, where else would I go? That's sensible. I think the whole operation is simple and sensible. It inspires confidence."

Toko had maintained her running watch on the café. "I don't see any bad sign in here," she said. "What's next? Let's do what's next."

Dujardin said: "Next? We will be in the apartment tomorrow morning and we get a phone call before noon. He told me your phone number. I didn't tell him. Whoever he is, he knows a lot about both of us. We may have to do something about that, after."

"We'll play it as the cards fall," Toko said.

"Are you singing tonight?" Dujardin said.

"Are you crazy?" she said. "No, I'm not singing tonight. If we're going to be up tomorrow morning, then I think we should go home about now."

Dujardin put money down, and they went home.


At a quarter to twelve, when Dujardin was making coffee in the kitchen and Toko was in the bath, and the bright autumn sun was shining in at the windows, the phone rang.

"He's on the way," the voice said, "but he has not settled yet. You will wait there?"

"No problem," Dujardin said.

"It may mean, perhaps, a twenty-four-hour delay in your holiday plans. You apprehend me?"

"Yes," Dujardin said. "We'll play it as the cards fall."

"As you are accustomed to do," the voice said.

"You leave me with nothing to say," Dujardin said. "I await your call."

Four hours later the phone rang again.

"Your man is at the Hotel Talbot, rue de la Force, in the sixteenth," the voice said. "You should go there now. He may go out tonight to meet someone. The someone lives in Neuilly, 27 rue Mazenc. Sometime tonight your tickets and travel documents will be put through your letter box. Do you want to repeat those addresses to me?"

Dujardin repeated the addresses.

"Good," the voice said, and hung up.

"Target in place," he said to Toko. "Time to collect our fee."

Clad in dark clothes, and Dujardin carrying his shoulder bag, the two assassins padded downstairs on rubber-soled feet to the car and set off. Before them, the declining sun hung like a scarlet shield in the autumn sky.

# 11

Georg Frankl sat with his eyes closed in the dark and comfort of the cinema in the Champs-Elysées. He felt like a diver in a decompression chamber. If ever a man needed time to get his act together, he thought, that man was he.

The last twenty-four hours, spent in the unwanted and extraordinary company of Roberto Mullen, unreeled in random flashbacks before his mind's eye to the soothing racket of French gangsters digging their way into a bank vault with a pneumatic drill.

"I'm going to do it," Roberto had said. "I owe it to you, and I'm going to do it."

Some hours and many miles before this declaration, Mullen had ushered Frankl (and an attaché case holding £75,000 in fifties, twenties and tens) from the rustic safe house into the Volvo, and had driven him, in almost total silence, to a Royal Air Force base in Wiltshire. The silence had suited Georg well, since he had a few questions to sort out in his head.

The difficulty of dealing with Arkley was not that the man was incomparably devious, but that he let you know that he knew you knew this. Georg was going to need plenty of psychic space around him to allow his mind to find a perspective on the late meeting with Arkley.

Psychic space was not available to him on the ride in the Volvo. Mullen's silence was a busy one. Georg knew that Mullen was riding a lot of guilt. He had got promises for Georg, before Georg opened himself to Duncanson at MI5, which had been thrown to the wind tonight by Arkley. The promises had not been that terrific, since no one could guarantee Georg perpetual anonymity. They had not been up to the Americans' Federal

Witness Protection Programme; but they had offered him a measure of security that he could have used as a breathing space to hide himself in the world.

Sitting in the Volvo, beside Roberto Mullen, watching the head-lights carve their way into the night, Georg had therefore received those emanations which one human being in a state of tension and unease can discharge at another; so that the unfortunate Georg had experienced, as if it were an infectious itch, the disquiet of which he was himself the object that was troubling Roberto.

Frankl opened his eyes and saw that the criminals on the screen had arrived, inevitably, in a convoy of three cars at some isolated farm. They seemed to have come away with at least ten times as much money as Georg had got from Arkley.

He closed his eyes again and remembered that during the journey in the Volvo Mullen had spoken twice.

"What are you going to do?" Mullen had asked.

"Do?" Georg replied irritably. "What do you mean, what am I going to do?"

"I mean, are you going to do what Arkley wants?"

"Perhaps, perhaps not. I'm going to think about it," Georg said.

The car swept on, miles and miles, about an hour by the clock on the dashboard, and Georg had almost got himself to sleep when Mullen spoke again. Apparently he had been brooding over that last exchange for the length of half a county.

"You don't trust me now, do you?" Mullen said.

Georg refused to meet this. "I trust myself," he said. "I always have."

There was a kind of pause in the night, and then the car's speed leapt up.

The next thing Frankl knew, the car was stopped at a security barrier and flanked by armed air force police.

Mullen showed his credentials, left the car, and was taken into the guardroom. He came back with an RAF squadron leader who got in the back of the car. Mullen set off, under his direction, through the winding maze of buildings and onto the airfield.

The great hulls of Hercules aircraft parked in echelon loomed out of the dark as the car ran down the perimeter. It stopped beside a much smaller aircraft parked on its own. Out of the car, with the sky black and starry overhead but that first light before the dawn diminishing the dark in the east, Georg smelled the aviation fuel.

"I love the smell of avgas in the morning," he thought irreverently, but with real feeling: it meant he was about to escape from Roberto Mullen and the Mullen burden of moral doubts.

At this point Mullen emerged from his dark reticence into an effusion of unpersuasive joviality. He might have been seeing Frankl off on holiday to some sun-smitten beach; but his chatter was that of an embarrassed tour guide who knows that the hotel is not as advertised.

Mullen's babble – "Well, here we are. It's a good, clear morning. Going to be perfect weather for flying" – was drowned by the take-off of one of the giant transport aircraft.

As the plane hoisted itself into the air, his voice emerged saying strangely: "At least we've got you plenty to wear." Georg watched him as he went to the back of the car, from which he extracted, as well as Georg's well-used bag, two leather suitcases.

"Plenty to wear?" Georg said. "What does that mean?"

"Couldn't see you go off to the ends of the earth at a moment's notice without a wardrobe," Roberto said. "Jan and I did some shopping for you."

The RAF officer, who had boarded the Defender, came out again and was followed by a crew member. "This is your cabin steward," he said to Georg.

"Will Speary," the steward said.

"Georg Frankl," Georg said.

"Yes," the steward said, "I know who you are." He was lanky, sharp-faced and dark-haired. He looked alert and intelligent, but he was young and he had said more with these words than he had meant to, thereby indicating that he was not merely a cabin steward.

"Of course you know. But so long as you can open a bottle of booze, that's all that matters," Georg said, and patted his arm. He must have been more wrought up than he'd realized. It was no habit of his to patronize the young.

It began to seem that his departure was to be prolonged by

reluctant connections with other people's personalities. First Mullen and now this young man of Arkley's. Well, in a moment he would say goodbye to Mullen and he could sleep, or pretend to sleep, on the plane.

"I take it these are going on board," Speary said. "Two suitcases and one bag."

"Yes," Roberto said, "that's the lot."

Speary took the luggage onto the plane.

"Roberto," Georg said. "These suitcases. I packed my clothes. I buy my own clothes."

"Of course you do," Roberto said. "The fact is, I had no idea what the actual plan was. Where you would be going or what nick they'd send you off in. So Jan and I went shopping. I mean, don't worry about it, it's all on the Department."

"Who's Jan?"

"Jan? Joanna? She's a colleague of mine," Roberto said. He said it with a kind of irrelevant earnestness, as if his mind was on something else. "Best get on board, I should think," he said.

"If you would," the squadron leader said. "We have another Hercules going off to Germany soon."

"Right," Roberto said. "About the car . . ." he said. "Thanks."

"Perfectly pleased to do that," the officer said. Whatever that might mean. He shook Georg's hand, rather as a way of getting the show on the road was how it felt, but if that was so, Georg was with him.

He turned to the door to see Mullen climbing in. There was to be an assiduous farewell then. Georg sighed and followed after.

In the cabin of the plane, which would have taken twenty passengers, Mullen sat alone. Georg, surprised to see him sitting, supposed him overcome by stress or fatigue. Georg went to where he sat and, buoyed by the imminence of departure, put on a good face to say goodbye.

"I'm coming with you," Mullen said.

"No, no!" Georg said, rejecting this utterly.

"I owe it to you. I'm going to see you safe into Paris and make sure there's no one on your back."

"This is rubbish," Georg said. "I won't have it." This half-man, half-boy was going to wreck everything.

The door thunked to. Speary, the *soi-disant* air steward, came towards them.

"Get yourself a seat and belt up," Mullen said ambiguously. "We'll talk later."

Georg went as far from Mullen as he could get and sat down and belted up.

Mullen had just about decided it would have to be Almayer's Folly at Brighton. The horse was entered for a six-furlong handicap sprint and was a confirmed front-runner and fast breaker. So far, so good. He was owned by a man called Bell, who had a flourishing little pub in the Borders near Kelso and for the past ten years or so had never been without a horse, sometimes two. Roberto had studied Bell's form, how he and his trainer managed his horses. He thought they were exceedingly clever, and with some Scotch cunning in there from Bell.

The twin Lycoming engines made their big sound, getting up their head of steam and the plane began its take-off run.

The horse had only run five times this year. He hadn't been entered for a race till the ground was rock hard, and then they'd been careful with him, used him sparingly. And the season ended next week.

Roberto's head felt clearer. He'd been thinking about this bet all the way down in the car, but he'd been distracted by the grim sense of hostility he'd felt from Frankl. He had always thought that being cooped up in a car was the worst possible situation for having a row, especially for the one driving. A silent row was just about as bad.

He had known Frankl would feel betrayed. How else could the man feel? At great risk to himself, he had done the British Government a service, burning the boats of his past life behind him (so to speak) and, instead of getting helped forward into a new life on the far side of his personal Rubicon, he had been tossed ruthlessly into the river to sink or swim on his own.

Roberto was pleased with the aptness of this metaphor. It said to him that his mind was working clearly again, now he had decided that Almayer's Folly was going to bring home the bacon at Brighton.

All the same, the weight of Frankl's hostility sat heavy on him.

He wished he could tell him how he planned to make amends, but he could not talk to him with Arkley's man Speary on the watch. He could not talk to him until they were alone in a secure place.

These thoughts flew through Roberto's mind as he stood outside the café about to cross the road and go round the corner to Markish's office.

When he told Frankl he was going to take his place – that he, Roberto, was going to perform the task that Arkley had laid on Frankl – he would have wished that the other man had not responded by falling into a fit of merriment. It rather took the shine off.

"By God, sir," he had said, when he was able to control his laughter, "you're a credit to the regiment."

Then he calmed down, more or less, and sat up straight. They were parked in a side street, in the hire car that Mullen had driven from the airfield into Paris. "All right," Georg said, "do it. So now, what are the logistics of this?"

"I'll take the false passport Ennis gave you," Roberto said, "and one of those suitcases you were so snotty about, because I've been wearing these clothes for a day and a night now. Then I'll check into a hotel. And then I'll see about Markish."

"And what shall I do?" Frankl asked.

"You will do what you like," Roberto said. He smiled valiantly in the dawn light at this man who had found so much amusement in his proposal to make the *amende honorable*. "You take the money and run. Find somewhere safe for yourself. Just tell me where you want me to let you off."

Frankl had recovered himself. "This is a fine thing you are doing, Roberto," he said.

"Piss off," Mullen said, but he was quite pleased.

"Drive then," Frankl said. "I'll tell you when to let me off, and I'll fill you in on Ben Markish as we go."

Roberto drove. He let Frankl off at a street corner near the Champs-Elysées, with the rush-hour traffic in full swing, where Frankl said he'd get himself a taxi. They made an insufficient farewell, when you considered that the scenario was that they would be unlikely to meet again.

Mullen sat in the good suit that he had been wearing now for almost twenty-four hours and looked up out of the car window at Georg Frankl standing on the pavement between his old suit-case and his new one, in that awful brown suit, holding the attaché case with all those thousands of pounds in it – minus a thousand that he'd insisted on giving to Roberto to help him in his mission, which was to have been Frankl's mission. A man couldn't fight a war without funds, he'd said, don't make such a fuss.

It was just as well, because Mullen was travelling skint and, being rather more than technically AWOL from the Department as a result of his sudden resolution, he could expect no help from that quarter.

"Good luck," Frankl said, standing there in all these circum-stances of luggage and unknown destinations and the mysterious future; a Flying Dutchman, well, no, a Wandering Jew, in the making. Mullen took in all at once, like a revelation, what a strong character this guy was. He felt the search of those brown eyes, the force of that very ordinary round face and head leaning down at him, and had a sudden knowledge that this man was the master of himself and his own life in a way he had not known could happen with a human being.

These realizations had disconcerting effects in various places within Mullen. In his professional mind, he wondered if Arkley knew who he had been dealing with in Georg Frankl. In his own self, a sense of unease stirred, which in its first awakening had brought with it a moment – swiftly passed – that seemed like panic: and behind the unease came the idea that – by comparison with the recently illuminated Frankl – he was not held well together. He wished he had just met the man and was about to get to know him, and instead of this the man had just wished him farewell. He put his hand through the window, the gesture feeling clumsy even as he made it, and Frankl shook it formally; Frankl standing there stooped, a traveller stranded on the edge of the pavement, a man who looked unimportant, uninteresting, unmemorable.

"Good luck to you," Mullen said. "Take lots of care."

"You do the same," Frankl said. He smiled. "We are parting

like lovers," he said, "or like a couple who have found they will not be lovers."

"I don't know," Mullen said. "That happens all the time."

"Ah," Frankl said. "You mean it happens to you all the time. Then I wish you good luck with that as well."

"All right," Mullen said, not saying thank you; thinking this was all too close for comfort.

Frankl stepped back. "Never mind," he said.

He nodded, and Roberto nodded back and put the car in gear and drove off.

It occurred to him that Frankl was not held together but simply was together, out of some quality of his own nature. He drove on idly, looking for an escape from the traffic so that he could find a café where he could sit and think.

When he had nudged the car into a space at the kerb, he got out a cigarette and lit it and had his think.

Roberto knew that he himself was viewed in the Department as pretty raffish. And since he was so, he had been pleased up to now to acquit himself of being infected by those traits of archaic snobbishness which survived, so eccentrically, in the upper reaches of the British Intelligence world.

Now he had a bad feeling that maybe he was as much a sucker for English social prejudice as anyone else: it had hidden Georg Frankl from him.

He'd met Frankl a year ago in Israel, and again when he came to London to spill the beans about this malarkey that had brought them both to Paris, but it was only in the last hour he'd begun to learn how much of a human being lived inside that exterior: and how much authority.

He knew why, too. It was that Frankl was ordinary to look at. He had no style, no attitude, no *empressement*, no *figura*. He was never on, he just was.

You knew there was something about Frankl. You knew he was deep, that the mind was quick, that he had uncanny perceptions, and that there was something behind those brown eyes that called to women; you even knew that there was something extra about Frankl.

Qualities like these, however, were likely to remain invisible to the people Mullen worked for, unless the man they belonged to reflected in some way – and even a foreigner could do this – their idea of how a man should present himself if he were to be recognizable as one of the élite. They had remained invisible to Mullen. He thought that when he was back in London he would try to find out a bit more about Frankl. It had begun to seem impossible that Frankl was what he had said he was: just a small man in Mossad.

He threw the cigarette out of the window and put the car back in the traffic.

# 12

Ben Markish was working late to the music of J. S. Bach played by Andras Schiff, who had just moved from the Prelude to the Fugue of the Seventeenth in the second book.

Markish was working with a student – well, they were all students – who had asked him for a light at the Place St Michel. The girl was not sure if he was making love to her with his body or his mind.

"Do you never come?" she said. Then she said, "Oogh!" and lost control of her head at some cumulation of one of those slow, poised, mysteriously timed movements he made inside her.

"Hush," he said. "*Je suis content. Et toi?*"

"*Ah, oui,*" she said, and smiled that ravishing innocent salacious floppy smile.

Above her, his face was beautiful and brutal, but not cruel. Except that this was cruel, this exquisite progress of agonies that rose and fell, and then rose higher it seemed. But it was not measurable, since it was the continuousness of it that grew within her, that intolerable succession of wantings and torments that she half wanted to explode and half wanted to go on and on until she went crazy.

Which was what was happening anyway, because every time she tried for release he tricked her away from it with that clever, sadistic, self-aware and intuitive cock of his. Oh, Christ, that sweet thing! Now she was going! Yes! Oh, no, no, no, unbearable.

That sound was forced from her again, and again. She came down, that little way, and her eyes focused up on him once more. His eyes intent on her *were* cruel, but he was losing it himself now, and as he lost it his face went and his eyes were feral . . . and . . . Bach and Schiff went from A flat major to G sharp minor but the man and the girl weltering on the floor were lost to all amazements but their own.

After a while, the noises of their love-making and the sound of the music had all stopped, and the room was quiet except for their breathing. The girl lay on the carpet with one arm flung out and one knee bent, and looked at the white ceiling. Her flat stomach quivered, every now and then she took a deep breath and sighed. Markish too lay on his back, some of him still on the rucked-up bath towel he had thrown down for them to make love on.

When his breathing had steadied he rose to his knees, got his cigarettes and lighter from the desk, and lay down again. They reclined there, smoking. The girl got up to find an ashtray and then knelt, looking down at him. "You're beautiful," she said.

He didn't tell her she was beautiful, which would have been true. She had the straight back and slim body of a Diana, long thighs and breasts of a perfect size, with nipples the pure pink of coral, and such a good, simply drawn face, curtained, as she looked down at him, by silky chestnut hair cut to show the nape of her lovely neck.

He was not, in fact, beautiful, though he knew what she meant. The skin of his dark face was rough and he had a pug face, he knew that, with end-of-day stubble on it; and his body was stocky and quite fit and strong, but nothing in particular.

She said: "When you get there, you really like to dish it out, don't you? I thought you were going to screw me into the floor."

"Yes," he said. "That's what I like."

"Do you always do it on the floor?" she said.

"In the office, yes," he said. "There isn't anywhere else here to do it."

The girl laughed. "We could do something with that desk."

"We could not," he said. "The desk is for business."

At this moment the electric chime sounded in the outer office.

Markish sat up and tapped his cigarette so that ash fell on the girl's stomach.

"Idiot," she said, as a flake of residual heat stung her. "Who's that?"

"No idea," he said. "A surprise."

He came to his feet and pulled on his jeans and shirt. From a drawer of his desk he took a small pistol, looked at the safety catch, and tucked the weapon into his belt at the small of his back. He pulled a loose sweater over his head which came down to hide the pistol.

The girl was sitting up with her arms wrapped round her knees. "Why the gun?" she said. What was in her voice was not as much as alarm, but enough to say that she felt unsafe.

"Bah," he said. "It's nothing. I have a licence for it, to protect my premises. At this time of night, who knows?"

"You seem used to it," she said.

"I should hope so," he said. "I was a professional soldier for twenty years."

He went into the outer office and closed the door on her. He took out the pistol again to check the action. He went behind the secretary's desk and consulted the video screen.

He saw a man of about his own height and perhaps ten years younger, no one he recognized, standing back from the main door of the office with his hands held away from his sides. He was wearing an oversized overcoat and a black beret.

Markish smiled a short smile and cruised the camera about the hallway. No one else showing.

He went to the door and opened it, then moved away to the side. "Come in," he said.

Mullen came in. "My French isn't good," he said. "Do you speak English?"

"Yes," Markish said. "Who are you?"

"Roberto Mullen. I can show you ID."

"Please," Markish said.

Mullen opened his overcoat and pulled out his wallet, and took a plastic holder from it.

Markish took it and stepped further away. "Take your overcoat off," he said, "and the beret. It's warm in here."

While Mullen was taking the coat off, Markish glanced at the card. He laughed. "Mr Mullen," he said. "British Security Service: MI5. The disarming-candour approach."

"No, no," Mullen said. "It's not assumed. Part of the character, I promise you."

"I believe you," Markish said. "I shall act in character too." He took the overcoat and beret from Mullen and dropped them on the desk, and went round behind him and ran his hands over his clothes, and then did the same from the front. "No knife down the back of the neck, no ankle gun. Nothing covert about you at all, is there, Mr Mullen? What do you want?"

"I want to take you to dinner and talk," Roberto Mullen said.

"What about?"

"Chiefly about some chemical materiel presently on a journey across Africa."

The change in Ben Markish, who had been showing himself as wary but half-amused, was immediate and alarming, but Mullen saw it happen in distinct stages. Fear came first and then anger, and then these fused into a degree of menace that was extraordinary to behold. At first sight, Mullen had thought Markish was about the same build as himself, but now, at the onset of the danger which Mullen had brought with him, the man's body seemed to grow before his eyes.

That leg-breaker in London, who called himself Starker, had carried a fair amount of threat in him, but it was as nothing to what came off Ben Markish. Mullen measured the space about him and prepared to fight for England, home, and the bookies who would go unpaid if Markish got carried away and threw him out of the sixth-floor window.

"I do think," he said, "that you know what I'm talking about."

Markish looked about one and a half times tougher than Mullen. He was stronger in the shoulders, longer in the arms, and the right fist was not only big, it was clenching and opening as if it was thinking independently. Did that mean he led with his right? No, it didn't. For all Mullen knew, the first thing he would see of Markish in action was a foot coming at his groin.

Well, he would know what to do with that; the question about Markish as a fighter was, would he know what to do in response to what Mullen would do. Mullen found that he himself was beginning to want the fight, that he was ready for a fight and that it had nothing to do with Markish at all. He was in the fight already. Come on, Markish, he was saying. Come on then, do it, let's see you, Markish. So that when Markish spoke, he almost mistook the voice for the start of the fight and had to make a curious contortion of the body that turned what started as a move on Markish into a move away from him.

"Very well," Markish said, and saw Mullen execute that manoeuvre and showed a mouthful of strong white teeth. "We'll talk over dinner." He jerked his head. "Come into the office for a moment."

The girl was dressed and the office looked like an office, not like a room in a *maison de passe*.

"Héloïse," Markish said, "this is Mr Mullen. I wonder if you will forgive me. He and I must discuss business this evening. Let me give you taxi fare, and we shall see you safely into a taxi before we leave you."

He pressed, rather than put, the note in her hand, and squeezed her fingers onto it so that she felt the business card inside.

She had been pleased by his news, but now she smiled suddenly and kissed him.

"After all," she said, "it means that this evening I will do some work and feel virtuous. That is important, too. I forgive you," she said to Mullen.

They went down in the lift and out into the street. When he had sent the girl away in her taxi, Markish said: "We will take my car. You have a car?"

"Yes, I do," Mullen said, but made no protest about leaving it here. He knew Markish wanted some control, and would insist on it.

"Get in," Markish said, opening the door of a Renault 25. "We'll eat at Neuilly, and after that we shall talk in my apartment."

"Oh, shit," Mullen said.

"It's not that bad," Markish said. "It is true it makes the evening longer, but I do not discuss my business in public places. What we shall talk about, God knows, but we shall not talk business. Afterwards we shall call a taxi for you, and tomorrow you can sleep late. You look tired, if I may say so."

"You may certainly say so," Mullen said. "I am tired."

"Then you should be glad," Markish said with a glance at his passenger, "that we did not fight. I am not tired and I am extremely fit."

Mullen said: "I knew it would be interesting."

"You wanted it," Markish said. "You would have lost, because you wanted it for the wrong reasons. I think you're mixed up inside. Be careful about that. In your line it's a dangerous way for you to be."

"Jesus Christ," Mullen said. "What is it with you people, you think you know so much."

This made Markish quiet for a spell. He was a relaxed driver, deft with the car and quick to see what was happening on the road, enjoying the driving for itself.

After his silence, Markish said: "What do you mean, 'you people'? Do you mean Israelis? Jews? I don't suppose you keep running into arms dealers. And this about knowing so much about other people – what's that about? Who have you been talking to, Mullen? Another introspective Israeli? In connection with this chemical materiel, perhaps. Now, who could that have been?"

Mullen was startled. The next thing he knew the bloody man would name Georg Frankl. Markish was turning out to be a bit over the top. First of all, whoever would have won the fight they might have had, the smart money would certainly have been on Markish; and now he was doing two things at once: making a reading of Roberto Mullen the human being and at the same time homing in like a spy satellite to find out where Mullen, MI5 officer, was coming from.

He wished he wasn't so damn tired. What he would like to do was go home, spend two weeks training and sparring at this and that, eat lots of fish to revitalize the brain cells, and come back to tackle Markish again.

"Why you?" Markish was off on a new tack. "MI5 is about security, not foreign intelligence. You people don't work abroad that much."

"If you believe that," Mullen said, "you'll believe anything."

"But I do believe anything," Markish said, "in the sense of being sceptical, not credulous."

"Way to be," Mullen said, cagey as hell now. What kind of folly is this, he asked himself, coming on this self-inspired operation completely unbriefed on the target.

There was still dinner to get through. An hour and more of

small talk. What a way to spend your time in Paris. He thought of Joanna, and that was good, so he thought about her some more. He began to wonder what Frankl was doing, and then tried to make his mind blank, to give it a kind of rest.

The car ran on, and on into the outskirts of Paris.


It was a restaurant of twelve tables, tailored with surpassing elegance for the wealthy bourgeoisie and high-flying commuters of Neuilly. Roberto felt absurd in the too-big overcoat and the black beret. They were part of the wardrobe he and Joanna had bought for Frankl but which had been bequeathed to him by that humorous valedictorian, since he, as he said, bought his own clothes, and here was the impulsive Mullen arrived in Paris with nothing but what he stood up in.

As to Markish, the jeans were designer and the sweater cashmere. In any case, he was known here. He got The Welcome as soon as he was in the door.

The welcome was from a solemn woman who gave hardly a smile, and the effect of this – of being welcomed by a professional and not with the lubricating bonhomie of the restaurant business – was astringent and refreshing.

She was of the fullest height possible for a ballet dancer, and moved and held herself like one.

"Monsieur," she said to Markish.

"Madame," he said to her, with a gravity Mullen had not seen in him till now.

At Mullen she inclined her head the least bit, and he was too busy drinking up her quiet tired beauty to respond. This elicited the hint of a responsive look, so it seemed that, at least, she did not mind. He doffed the beret and a girl helped him dispossess himself of the overcoat.

He began to feel better about this dinner. Madame seated them at a table against a wall, and Markish sat with his back to the wall and looked out upon his fellow-diners. Then he said to Madame a strange thing: "Do we know everyone?"

Seven tables were occupied, besides their own. Madame surveyed them swiftly. "Yes," she said, "we do. No strangers."

123

"Thank you, Madame," he said.

"To start, I shall order you a grilled lobster, half for each of you, then roast partridge," she said. "Shall I do that? And a white and a red burgundy, or is it an evening for Perrier?"

"The wine, and the Perrier also," Markish said.

She left them.

He said to Mullen: "She tells me what I shall enjoy and I don't have to think about it. She makes me at home, here."

"I think you are at home," Mullen said.

Markish frowned. "What does that mean?" he said.

"I think you own this place."

Markish relaxed. "A share, maybe," he said, and looked complacently across the room with its Art-Deco style carried out in the furniture and engraved mirrors, the white linen and heavy silver, the staff, alert and rapid without bustle, waiting on the tables of the well-heeled and, give or take an aberration here and there, well-dressed clientele.

They ate the food and drank not much of the wine: with the partridge they had that Gevrey-Chambertin of the year when the Japanese bought most of it as a long-term investment, to hoard in vaults until it was at its apogee, when it would be up there at Impressionist prices.

"Or better," Markish said, "now that the recession has knocked the bottom out of the art market. It's very difficult, this recession," he said. "The trouble with being in business during a world recession is that the big people don't pay the little people, and men like me get squeezed for cashflow."

"What you're saying is that the wine is yours," Mullen said, "not the restaurant's. That you had it from the Japanese?"

"That's right," Markish said.

"Why are you wasting it on me?" Mullen said.

Markish smiled. "I'm not wasting it on you," he said. "I'm wasting it on me."

He looked into the wine in his glass with a kind of friendship, as if it smiled back at him, and then put it to his mouth and swallowed half of it.

"What do you want of me, Roberto Mullen?" he said.

"I thought we mustn't talk business here," Mullen said.

"A man needs time to think," Markish said. "I took time to think. Simone tells me there are no strangers here. We can talk, if we're discreet about it."

Mullen looked at him. "There's more to it than that," he said. "Isn't there?"

"Drink your wine," Markish said. "And yes, there is more to it. This place is swept every day. I can be sure no bug has been installed here. What I have to guard against is a visitor bringing a bug in with him; or her. Or sending in a trained mouse to sit under my table."

Mullen, not a connoisseur, was playing with his wine in case he might learn from it. He enquired into its warm glow. He swung it lightly in the glass and sniffed the bouquet into his nose. He took the partridge legs in his fingers and scraped the flesh off them with his teeth. He had a bite of bread and went to the wine again.

"What would you say to job-sharing?" he said. "I can do this half of the work for starters."

"What do you want of me?" Markish said, and suddenly and surprisingly he snapped his fingers up there on the other side of the wine glass before Mullen's face.

Mullen jerked back and spilled wine on the good white cloth and his shirt. "Damn it," he said. "What was that about?" He began mopping up with his napkin. "Damn it," he said again.

"What that was about," Markish said, "is that I don't believe you know what you want from me. It's true I can't make sense of that idea, but it's what it feels like to me."

"As a matter of fact," Mullen said, with some relief, "you're dead right."

The heavy, rough-cut Markish face hung between irritation and amusement. "You're a piece of work, aren't you, Mullen?" he said. "You're a piece of work, all right. You're MI5, and we both took it as too obvious even to mention that you have no authority here in France. And now . . . now you're telling me you don't know why you wanted to meet me."

"I have even less authority than you think," Mullen said. "The Department doesn't know I'm here – or rather, they didn't. They'll certainly know by now." He thought gloomily about this. Ah, well, after the tumult and the shouting had died down Duncanson would give him some pissy weeks of rotten jobs, that was all.

Then, too, there was this tiny matter of his racing debts. Having set off on this melancholy internal train, Mullen went on with it. He was having what it seemed might be a cunning notion, that to let Markish see him in this mode might help accentuate the idea that Mullen was not star material.

It was not going to be an awfully jolly return home: Duncanson in a paddy; strong men chasing him to break his legs. And Joanna would be pissed off too. He had not got a call through to her. Her office phone would be eavesdropped, and she'd not been home when he phoned her last thing before coming out to meet Markish.

He emerged from his brooding and gave Markish a shrug, which he hoped looked OK. "Where was I? Yes. I came to see you on my own kick, Ben," – get down to these first names – "I came on impulse; rather a complex impulse, if there can be such a thing." He thought about that too. Where was all this introspection coming from? Yes, of course a man could have a complex impulse.

"But," Roberto said, "I know why I wanted to meet you. Now we're meeting, I can't decide what's best to do about it."

Markish was at once wary. "I think you're being *faux naïf*, Mr Mullen." He lifted a finger and a waiter moved in and poured. Markish held his replenished glass by the stem and tilted it towards him and rocked it gently, and spoke, it seemed, to the wine in it.

"Why," Markish said to the wine, "am I sitting here with this man, this Englishman? Am I being set up? Is he a stooge, the visible player in a game where the other players are waiting outside, or at my house? I would choose him for that, he looks right for it."

He took another of those large swallows of the great burgundy. "The party's over," he said. "I don't know what you fancy you have on me, but I'll ride that. I shall want to think about you, and work out if this little game of yours means anything to me. And you will want to be getting back into town."

"Like fuck I will," Mullen said cordially. "I'll tell you what it is. I'm here instead of a man called Georg Frankl."

"Old Georg," Markish said, and a warm remembrance bloomed in the eyes and where he had been holding himself upright and back – the confrontational antagonist – he now leaned forward. "You're so devious, you English. Why not just tell me, straight out? What is it about Georg? And how is Georg?"

This jolliness about Frankl took Mullen by surprise. "Well, Georg is fine, Ben," he said. "He's just fine. It sounds as if you know him well."

Markish said simply: "I did once. He trained me."

"But you were a soldier," Mullen said. "I mean, I know you're still on the reserve, but you were a professional soldier. You reached brigadier."

"You have a problem with that?" Markish said.

Mullen was thinking fast, shuttling his mind round all the aspects of the Frankl Affair, as it suddenly became to him. "I didn't know he was a soldier," he said. "I knew he had fought, of course, but everyone in Israel has been to war. If he trained you, and you were a brigadier, what does that make him?"

Markish regarded him, running his tongue around inside his mouth as if this helped his brain to work. "How do you know Georg Frankl?" he said.

"We have him as Mossad," Mullen said, "but we don't place him very high up there."

Markish gave him a cheerful and satirical smile. "I like the 'we'," he said. "The Departmental plural, I take it. We have something we can't understand, do we? What's Georg been doing to you?"

Mullen wished he was less tired and more alert. If he wasn't careful now he'd drop Georg Frankl in the shit, which was rather the opposite of what he'd been trying to do. Invent furiously, Mullen. Give it a whirl. Put it on the train to Hartford and see where it gets off.

"Georg has been snowing us," Mullen said. He gave the rueful grin of the innocent dupe and felt, somewhere in him, that it was sufficiently in character to carry conviction.

Markish studied this notion and the histrionic mask from which it came. "Snowing us, or snowing you?" he said.

Mullen wished he could blush to order. "Well, yes," he said, "snowing me, as it happens. It makes me look bad in the Department."

"That's what this is about," Markish said. "You've come to me for help." The tone was neutral, telling Mullen nothing about whether Markish was going for this story or not; or whether, if he was going for it, he would or would not be inclined to help the story-teller.

All the beating about the bush was over, anyway. Mullen went straight in. "There's a lot of money, dealing in arms," he said. "You make a lot of money at it."

Markish made a grimace, his head moving sideways and back again, meaning that Mullen was stating the obvious.

"But now there's a recession," Mullen said. "So the money is not moving like it used to."

"I'm not poor," Markish said. "Don't overstate to yourself what I said about the recession. And what does this have to do with Georg Frankl?"

"I'm getting there," Mullen said. "Agenting a deal in chemical and biological weaponry would be worth an awful lot of money."

He watched and waited. He knew Markish was expecting this, but there was going to be some reaction.

"We're back at that," Markish said. "Of course we are. You led up to it carefully enough, so that I wouldn't blow my top this time, I suppose. I'd like a digestif, I think." He caught an eye. "You have an *idée fixe* about me and these CBRs," he said. "You think I'd stoop so low? You believe that this man you have been with for almost three hours now, is one who would sell that kind of indiscriminate slaughter of innocents just to enrich his old age?"

"I don't find it easy," Mullen said, "but I'm believing it as vigorously as I can."

"What can you do to me if I decide not to help you out with this?" Markish said.

"I don't know," Mullen said. "But I can arrange something damned irritating, that's for sure."

"Nuisance value," Markish said. "No more? That fits my image of you."

"Thanks," Mullen said.

Two glasses were put on the table. It was Madame who had

128

brought them. "You have enjoyed your supper?" she said to Mullen.

"Have I not!" he said. "I do thank you for it."

"It was superb, Simone," Markish said. "Simple and perfect. You know how well I like that."

"At the table, yes," she said, perhaps enigmatically, but probably not, for Mullen felt the fibrillation of energy that awoke in the air between them and saw her eyes start to cloud until she gave her head a shake to bring herself back to business, and saw the blood come more fully to the face of Ben Markish. "Ah," Markish said, as if grateful to be extricated from this particular moment. "You have customers."

She went to meet them, and Mullen watched her passage through the room with that graceful walk of a dancer, pictured for him in the mirrored wall behind Markish's head, so that she went from him whilst leaving behind her a screen of decorously erotic images in the naked nymphs swimming in the engraved glass. He watched her approach two slight men in suits.

He remembered that he and Markish had been getting down to brass tacks. He took a sip of the Grand Marnier, and then another.

"So," he said, watching his fingers play with the glass, twirling it slowly on the white tablecloth. "Whatever you make of me, I'm in shtook with the boss and I want not to be. As far as he's concerned, a rose has fallen from my chaplet, if you pick up the allusion."

He looked up and saw that Markish was not picking up allusions right then.

Markish said: "No!" and shifted position in a quick contorting movement, and pointed a pistol past Mullen's left shoulder.

Mullen's eyes went automatically to the mirror to be sure that going to the floor would be the best thing, and he saw the two newcomers standing at the table where Simone had seated them, she beyond and between them in his vision, and each of them with a pistol that looked huge in the hand that held it – for they were lightly-made men – and the pistols were pointing this way.

"Drop, Simone, drop!" Markish called to her in a mixture of anguish and rage across the two unoccupied tables between him and the gunmen.

Then Mullen was thrown across the table at Markish as something hit him in the back. A red flower bloomed on Markish where his heart was and he went away from Mullen, and at the same time there was a great banging noise, soon over, and the mirror was gone.

Mullen grabbed Markish's revolver from the table and went low and round and away, crouching on the floor, and caught a glimpse of a fast-departing man at the door. He came up from his crouch and ran down the lane between the tables, conscious of all those faces turned towards that corner where Markish had fallen, so that it was as if he ran through a moment in which everyone but he was frozen in time.

Some of the faces began to shout and scream as he reached the door and pushed through. In the street, traffic moved, people went past, a stall near by was still selling fruit and flowers and vegetables. He saw no one running, no car squealing its tyres in its hurry to get away, saw no one and nothing to shoot at.

He let the gun point to the ground and went back inside the restaurant.

Half the clientele were on their feet – in their outdoor clothes, getting into their outdoor clothes, or demanding them from the cloakroom girl. Others sat at their tables, looking, or not looking, at one another; wearing those expressions compounded of shame, love, doubt, fear, even grief, that Mullen had seen before when violent death fell like this upon an unknown soul.

He walked back through the restaurant, pushing past the ones who were poised, clumsy from shock, on the point of leaving.

Simone was kneeling beside Markish. His head was pillowed on a folded coat. His hand held hers and his eyes were on hers.

A man who was probably a doctor sat in Mullen's chair with his head down and his hands clasped loosely between his thighs, as if there was no more for him to do but be there till Markish died. He had tried to do something, for bits of cashmere sweater and pale blue shirt that looked as if they'd been cut away from the wounded man, the dying man, were thrown into the corner among the broken glass. A tartan rug had been laid on Markish, a bright tartan of reds and yellows. It came to his throat, and against it the skin of his face had paled to the colour of parchment with shock and the loss of his life's blood.

The dying man's eyes moved to Mullen, and then back to Simone. "The Englishman," he said. "This is not his fault. They would have come for me anyway. I got in over my head."

A change came to his face. "Ah!" he said, and his eyes leapt not with fear but with a sure and wary knowledge, towards a picture visible only to him.

When that was past, he said to Mullen: "Those CBRs of yours, they're real money."

At face value that was true; it was what Mullen had told Markish just before the assassins came for him. Yet to Mullen's ear there was another sound in it. He leaned forward, but Markish had gone from him back to Simone, and in any case the doctor's hand came out, gripping Mullen's arm and drawing him back.

"It is all yours now, our restaurant," Markish said to Simone. "You will nourish it."

"I will nourish it with love," she said.

A small smile from Markish, an almost imperceptible, affirming, movement of the head.

"Yes, with love," he said. "And the garden also, with love."

"And the garden," she said.

He was still looking at her, with some question in his eyes, which now were seeing as well that horizon that was his alone.

"And you," she said, "I will nourish you with love."

To Mullen it was an unbelievable thing, and for him close to unbearable, to see how strong was the emotional force that glowed in the man's eyes.

"Yes. That's good," Ben Markish said. "Kiss me, sweetheart, and then just keep holding my hand."

Simone kissed him, very soft, on the lips and stroked his head with her free hand, and then his life left him. She wrapped her arms round his head and pressed his face to hers, as if she would hold him there for ever, and then she laid his head back on that improvised pillow of folded-up coat. She looked at his face and picked up again the hand she had held and looked at that, and then she let the hand lie on the bright tartan of the rug, and she came to her feet.

131

Her eyes left the doctor, who was confirming for himself that his patient was dead, and came up at Mullen.

All he could think to say was: "The garden?"

She smiled into her tears, and at him, as if he had said the best possible thing. "Yes," she said. "We have a cottage, an old mill near Vézelay. We have made the garden very beautiful."

They heard the clamour of emergency vehicles howling their way up the street, and Simone made a face.

"You must hold me," she said. "I think you know how to do that."

After what had passed between her and Markish, he was not so sure that he was a good enough man to be the one to hold her, but if she thought he would do, perhaps he was wrong.

The racket came to a stop outside and, as she hid her face in his shoulder, uniformed men with guns came through the door. He put one arm round her back and the other round her head, as if he was a roof over her.

"Nobody leaves," a voice yelled, settling matters for those whose imminent departures had been delayed by their respect, or whatever other forms their fascination took, for the scene between Markish and Simone.

The same voice, closer, said: "You should not have moved the body."

Mullen looked over Simone's head and saw the doctor light a cigarette and confront the man who had spoken, a tall, black-haired, narrow-faced, not merely thin but etiolated, plainclothes policeman in a black-leather coat, quite as if the Gestapo had never gone home.

"The body has not been moved," the doctor said, "since it became a body."

"Where is the owner?" the policeman said.

"Madame is the owner," the doctor said. "She should go up now to her apartment, which is above here. And when you are ready to interview her, I shall be present."

The lean face suddenly smiled, achieving the most remarkable transformation from quasi-military officialdom into human being.

"You are right," the policeman said. "I came expecting a gun-fight, you understand," and he looked at the pistol in his hand

and put it away, "Now I shall become calm again. You are a doctor: I can tell a doctor anywhere – just as you can tell a policeman, I dare say. He was shot?"

"Yes," the doctor said. "I was dining here. Two men came in, Algerians, I would say, and shot him from three tables away."

Pain swept through Roberto like a wave from the sea, so that he nearly drowned. "They shot me, too," he said. "Oh hell. Take her," he said to the policeman and moved Simone gently towards the man, who did indeed take her. The last thing Roberto saw as he went to his knees was the look of astonishment on the man's face.


The Dujardin-M'pofu team had parked the car three houses from number 27. It was beginning to seem a long time ago. It was a quiet street, and it was dark soon after they arrived. There had been no need to perform any manoeuvres to disguise what they were doing.

Sometimes one of them slept while the other watched. Once Dujardin grew restless and went for a walk. The hours had come and gone, but no light went on in Markish's apartment.

"Look," Dujardin said.

Two men were coming fast along the pavement. As they came to number 27 they slowed for a moment, looked at the house, exchanged a few words, and then came hurrying on past the car.

"Two Arabs," Toko said. "So what does that mean? Were they interested in his house?"

"It seemed like it," Dujardin said. "Something else, though. I saw their faces close up. They had a look on them . . . Wait, do you hear that?"

It was the whoop of a police car. Flashing blue lights went past at the far end of the street.

"Let's go and see," Dujardin said. "Nothing's happening here."

They came to the junction. "Yes," Dujardin said, "that's a crime scene if ever I saw one."

Down to the right were police cars with lights flashing, a small crowd was spilling into the road.

Dujardin pulled onto the main road and parked the car against the kerb. "I'll take a look," he said.

As he approached, he saw that the police activity was centred on a restaurant. Beside him a man and a woman were talking to a motorcyclist astride his machine.

"What's happened?" he said to them.

The man on the motorbike bent down to adjust something on the side away from Dujardin.

The man on the pavement answered: "A shooting. One man killed, they're saying, and another wounded. In the restaurant."

Dujardin went on to join the crowd, and to listen. Some of them had been dining in the restaurant and had run out after the shooting.

"Who was killed?" Dujardin asked.

"A man called Markish," he was told. "He was often there, always at the same table."

"And there's one wounded," another man said. "The ambulance is taking its time."

Dujardin went back, out of the crowd, past the two people talking to the motorcyclist.

He said as he got in: "Markish is dead, our man is wounded. There, that ambulance, that's for him."

The crowd was moved back to clear a way for the ambulancemen, who were out again almost at once. They put a stretcher into the back of the Citroën and went on their way with the siren ringing and lights flashing.

Dujardin followed. "This is good," he said. "We can stay well back and follow that light."

"Things are moving fast," Toko said. "The two Arabs, you think?"

"Sure of it," Dujardin said. "That's what I read on their faces."

The car ran on down the road after the ambulance. Well behind it, the man on the motorbike followed the car.

# 13

"Duncanson really was very sweet," Joanna said. "He was kind and sensible when he told me you'd been shot, so that I knew at once you were going to be all right."

After she said this she tossed her dark hair and gave him a rather tough look, as if to say there was nothing about being wounded that added any extra value to what she felt for him.

"And," she said, "about you being here, in France I mean. In the first place, he said we would deal with the Mullen escapade in two stages. Stage One is getting you well again, flying me over to see you and paying your hospital bill. Stage Two will be tearing you off a strip or sacking you, whatever seems appropriate."

She tossed the hair and gave him exactly the same look again. "About you and me having an affair," she said, "which is against his professional instincts, he was pretty good about that too."

"He was, was he?" Mullen said. "Bloody nice of him. You seem to have taken quite a shine to the old bugger."

"He's not old and he's not a bugger – at least I've never heard it suggested." Joanna said. "I think he's handled it extremely well, and I'm grateful to him."

He was propped up on a bundle of pillows and now he turned towards her, taking care not to let his face change as the pain bit into him; because the last thing he wanted, while her grey eyes confronted him with such straitness, was for her to think he was seeking sympathy as a way of avoiding the direct contact.

Even as he noticed this, he said to himself: this is not like you, Roberto Mullen. What's happened to the flip wisecrack that turneth away the serious stuff?

He loved Joanna's face. He was tired of love going up in smoke. He liked this woman who could talk straight to him when she

knew the bullet that had wounded him might have killed him –
would have killed him if it hadn't gone through two centimetres
of beechwood on the way. He liked the way she dealt with things
as they were, and didn't go off on some inappropriate emotional
ride about this shooting business.

"You're right about Duncanson," he said. "I take it back. He
could have sent Edward Raleigh over to handle things with the
cops. Raleigh would have read the Riot Act and prophesied doom
like a schoolmaster."

"Duncanson's not a schoolmaster," she said, "whatever else he
is. He's a big bad man with a good streak in him where it counts."

"You sound as if you fancy him," Roberto said.

"I do rather," Joanna said, "but that doesn't mean anything.
You're my fella."

"He's not pretty," Roberto said.

"He's ugly," Joanna said, "but that doesn't matter. It's true that
you don't look altogether like a piece of cheese, but on the other
hand you're unreliable, immature, uncentred and unaware, which
means you're hard to know and you make your life into total
chaos. It's just that, despite all of the chaos, you're my fella and I
love you."

The effects of being shot still showed on his face. It had lost its
colour and the eyes were shadowed by fatigue and pain. She knew
you did not have three ribs splintered by an already mushroomed
bullet without it hurting a lot. In his eyes, watching her eyes now
while they read each other, she saw a movement she could not
name, perhaps the beginning of a question.

"Duncanson said he was amazed at how long you kept on your
feet after the bullet hit you," she said.

"Did he?" Roberto said, as if he was still inside the moment that
had been there before she spoke. "I suppose it was the adrenaline –
to begin with, anyway. I didn't feel it much at first."

He went on watching her, wondering what was going on
behind that serene but deeply thinking countenance.

She said: "And then? After at first."

"And then," Mullen said, "Markish was dying. I couldn't, well,
I couldn't leave them. You'll understand that."

"I'm sure I will," she said, "but tell me more."

"When Markish was shot, he dropped his gun on the table," Roberto said, "and I grabbed it and ran out to the street, but they'd vanished. Not a sign of them. So I went back in again."

"When you went back to the restaurant," she said, "what happened then?"

"Simone was holding his hand," Roberto said. "He said the restaurant was all hers now, and she was to nourish it, and she said: 'Yes, with love'."

"With love," Joanna said. "Go on."

It was hard for her not to flinch, so hard was he searching her for whatever it was he was listening to in himself. She wasn't sure about the sense of this, but that was what it felt like. The main thing was to keep meeting him all she could, to be there, with her eyes and her face, and with what she said to him; to say just enough to help him bring it out.

"Yeah," Mullen said, "with love. They had a garden, too; he asked her to nourish that, with love. They loved the garden, they'd made the garden together, she said after. When he died, she asked me to hold her." He stopped for a long moment.

"I held her until the police came," he said, "then I lost it." Another pause. "When she asked me to hold her, she said I would know how to do it."

"She was right about that," Joanna said.

His face lightened a little, but wore a wary look as well. "Was she?" he asked.

"This is quite deep for you, isn't it?" she said.

"Quite deep," he said. "What about you?"

Joanna sat up and took in a breath. She felt that, until now, she had hardly breathed through this at all.

"Roberto, love," she said. "Are you beginning to go all grown-up on me?"

His face eased out and he shook his head at her. "Give me a cigarette," he said.

She lit it and gave it to him. She looked around for an ashtray.

"There's no ashtray," he said. "Smoking's not allowed."

She folded a tray out of some Kleenex and put it beside him. "Use that," she said, "and I'll wash the stub down the basin."

She felt suddenly radiant and leaned down and kissed him.

"Hey, Roberto," she said.

"Yeah," he said. "I know. Well, maybe I don't know, but . . ."

"Shut up," she said. "And she was right about that hug, right about you being the man for that."

He looked at her, and out of the sunny window, and at her, and she looked at him, and the cigarette burned his fingers. She took it from him and washed it down the handbasin.

"How do you feel, love?" she said. "Are you ready to see Harry Seddall?"

"Sure," he said. "I feel good."

"I don't think you want too many people at once," she said. "Besides, I don't suppose I'm cleared for everything you'll want to talk about. I'll come back afterwards. OK?"

"Do that," he said.

She went over and kissed him, her lips cool on his forehead.

"It's a puzzle, you know," he said.

"What is?"

"Me," he said.

"Roberto," she said. "You ain't whistlin' Dixie."


Harry Seddall came into the room wearing a hide coat that was either unstructured by design or destructured by use. Whatever the cause, the effect was to make it look so much at home on him that he might have been one of those nineteenth-century mountain men in North America who never came out of their clothes between winter and spring.

Out of one of its large pockets he produced a saucer and from the other he took cigarettes, a lighter, and a crumpled piece of paper.

"I hear you're a lucky man," he said, and gave Mullen a deprecating and ironic and amiable expression that was part smile, part leer.

Then he dumped everything except the bit of paper on the bedside table. "No smoking, I hear. Can't have that," he said. "Nicked the saucer from our coffee tray for an ashtray."

He put a finger to his lips.

He unfolded the paper and held it in front of Mullen. Scrawled on it were the words: "I assume this room bugged separately or together by an infinite number of French police and security outfits. Write anything we don't want overheard."

Something of that first smile was still on his face while he and Mullen assessed each other, but the face was changing. Mullen saw a man fifteen years or so ahead of him, of the same kind of middling height and build as himself; a man whose expression was moving to something hard and calculating, a man from whom he thought he felt some kindliness, but a kindliness which was not entire, and which was accompanied by a force of will that struck him – from the way the man stood there, his feet apart, his hands in the deep pockets of that hide coat, his round head a little forward and tilted to the side, his yellowish eyes cool and satirical – as being strong enough to be brutal.

Harry Seddall saw another of those lads, no longer young, who was still playing with life; a young middle-aged man, fetching to the women, but at least not one of those clean-cut types who believed his mirror, or saw himself as full of virtuous promise – therefore a man who would yet, perhaps, make himself into what he might be: a man full of a kid's piss and vinegar, but uncertain yet what it was there for. He saw, too, a man who'd just been near to his own death and next to another's; and you could say what you liked, but death always left its fear: not necessarily of itself, but fear of waste of life, waste of self, waste, if you acknowledged such a thing, of spirit.

Well, heigh-ho, and all that. He lit cigarettes for both of them and gave one to Mullen, and from one of the pockets he extracted a small writing pad, and from another a pen, and put them on the bedclothes.

"Tell me the tale," he said.

"Sure," Roberto said. "I was lucky all right. They meant to kill us both. I can see how an arms dealer like Markish could have guys who'd want to kill him. Why me, I don't know, except that I was there. If the furniture hadn't been so solid I'd be dead too."

Seddall picked up the pad and pen and wrote: "How this grab you? Could they have thought you to be Frankl?"

With his voice, he said: "Did you get a clear sight of them?"

Mullen took the pad.

139

He wrote: "If they knew Georg was to meet Markish, they might have assumed I was Frankl, but how could they know that?" He held up the pad for Seddall to see.

Aloud, he said: "Yes, I did have a clear sight of them, in the wall mirror before they blew it apart. A couple of small, wiry characters. North Africans was the popular view, I gather, but dust-ups like that, the French tend to think Algeria–Tunisia–Morocco, don't they, if the appearance fits. I mean, they could have been that, from what I saw. So why not?"

He tapped the writing pad, to signal a return to the Frankl question. "I think they were just out to get Markish and whoever was with him. Maybe they thought that would earn them a bonus."

"You could be right," Seddall said, "but when I'm doing my job and I get shot, I incline to think it has to do with me. Why don't you?"

The sun had come round to the window and Mullen squinted into its light. "I don't know," he said, "except that I shouldn't have been there in the first place."

"I've often been where I shouldn't have been in the first place," Harry said, "but I'd still think it was damn personal if I was shot for it. I think these things, when they happen, happen on purpose, with malice aforethought, directed at me."

That feel, that odd mixture of friendly interest with cold and even harsh comment behind it, came from him to Mullen. "You sound almost as if it had nothing to do with you, as if you don't take offence at being shot."

"I'll tell you something," Mullen said. "I was more interested in Markish dying with Simone holding his hand than I was in what it was all about, or in why I got in the way of a bullet myself."

"That's right," Seddall said. "That's right." The way he said it surprised Mullen. It came not at all from the sarcastic roughneck, but as if the man meant it.

Seddall went to the window and adjusted the blind to take the light off Mullen's eyes. "How would it be," he said, "if I asked you to tell me what they said, Markish and the woman, while he was holding her hand and dying?"

So Mullen told him, while Seddall sat himself on the foot of the bed and listened and thought things. When Mullen had finished, Seddall went and looked out of the window and then came to the bed, took the pad and wrote on it.

He showed the page to Mullen. "Markish said: 'Those CBRs of yours are real money'?"

It came back to Mullen that when he'd heard Markish say them, the words had reverberated in another part of his head than the place where he heard them. But that was all. He couldn't pin it down then and he couldn't pin it down now.

He nodded, but that wasn't enough for Seddall, who gave him the pad and the pen. Mullen wrote it out: "That's what he said."

He was about to return the pad when he drew it back from Seddall's reaching hand and wrote some more: "Of course they *are* real money. If you've got CBRs you can kill or threaten to kill millions. So?"

Seddall read this and then looked at him with a surly smile. He tore the pages they had used out of the pad, folded them over and tucked them away in the inner recesses of the hide jacket.

"Anything you need?" he said.

At this abrupt ending to their meeting, Mullen found that he was tolerably pissed off by the confusions that Seddall's ambiguous and altering manner caused in him.

"Not a thing," he said.

"Sure," Seddall said, as if he was used to people being riled by the way he behaved. "It was quite good that, playing substitute for our friend. The only thing is, we don't know where he's got to; all that money on him too. And then of course, there's a contract out on him, but I do rather believe that he'll have worked that out for himself. Especially if he gets to hear about how your dinner ended up."

On this parting shot, he smiled cheerfully. "Get well soon," he said, and went away.


The woman stood with the phone in her hand and looked out of the window over the evening lights of the city. "Where are you calling from?" she said.

"From the Opéra," Georg Frankl said. "Stunning building, resounding performance of *Les Troyens*. How goes it with you?"

"*Ça va,*" she said. "*Et toi?*"

"God, I miss you," he said.

"Me too," she said. "At least we're in the same city."

"What are you wearing?" he said.

"As a matter of fact," she said, "black thigh-boots. I've been shopping. They come right up."

"I know what you mean," he said. "What else?"

"Since you ask," she said, "nothing else. I haven't decided what to wear with them."

"What are you trying to do to me?" he said.

"I don't think I'm only trying," she said. "Am I?"

"No," he said. "Listen, I don't think you have to go back. I think we're starting."

There was a sighing sound down the line. "I'm glad you said that," she said. "I learned something today. I hope it doesn't make you change your mind."

"Tell me," he said.

She told him.

"Aiee," he said. "Give essential detail."

When she had done, she said: "Do you want me to go back?"

"No," he said, "absolutely not. You keep moving as planned, and I'll call tomorrow, also as planned."

"Take care."

"I do," he said. "You also."

"I love you," she said. "I long for you."

"Yes," he said. "I don't have to tell you."

"No," she said. "We'll talk tomorrow."

Frankl made his way through the aficionados waiting for the next act and out into the square. He was wearing a good pale-grey suit, so pale it was almost white, and a silk hand-painted tie with brushstrokes in red abstract shapes on a white background. A coat of dark-grey lightweight Cheviot cloth hung from his shoulders and he had a long daffodil-yellow muffler round his neck. He wore black Oxfords on his feet and carried a rolled umbrella. On his head he wore one of those classy grey fedoras with a broad black band that the Men Who Run New York City wear.

He looked tough, successful, elegant and full of energetic confidence. He knew what he was doing and where he was going,
both here, tonight in Paris, and, metaphorically, in the world. He
was not at all the man of that dinner party in England presided
over by Sir John Arkley.

He hailed a taxi and gave the name of a street in the seventh.
There was a perpetual smile on him, which sometimes showed on
his mouth and sometimes not, and when it did not show, the trace
of it lingered.

Since the driver of the cab was smoking, Frankl lit himself a
thin black cigar and lowered the window to let the smoke out.
The evening air was cold and brisk, no damp in it to speak of,
despite the river and the season. The streets were full of traffic
and the pavements of people. He was part of all this, vital and
energized by the people who were the pulse of the metropolis,
and giving his own share to the vitality.

The taxi stopped. Frankl walked a few streets and turned a few
corners, and went into a café-bar full of chatter, beating with rock
music, smoke drifting in the lights.

He walked straight through and up a flight of stairs into a large
double bedroom. Here he shed the coat, took off the suit and hung
it up carefully.

When he came out of the room again, he was wearing a
motorcyclist's black leathers and carrying a crash helmet. At the
foot of the stairs he did not go into the bar but turned left along
a passage. The door at the end opened onto a small courtyard
with an old Citroën DS standing in it and a motorcycle under a
tarpaulin.

A few minutes later, with the big engine of the BMW throbbing
under him, Frankl was heading west into the night.


Joanna came into the hotel dining room in a low-cut black mini-
dress with spaghetti straps at the shoulders, which flowered, bell-
shaped, into a black rose round her hips. She wore black fishnet
tights and high-heeled black shoes.

Sorrel, wearing blue denim street-scruff, said accusingly:
"You're looking radiant again."

143

"Well, it cheered Roberto quite a lot," Joanna said.

"He'd be in a really bad way if it hadn't," Harry said. "He doing all right this evening?"

Joanna gave him a dark look from behind the wing of hair that fell down the side of her face. "He was when I left," she said. "He wasn't liking you a lot."

Seddall was disgruntled at having to deal with this. "I didn't do him any harm," he said.

"You didn't do him any good," Joanna said.

"That's what you're for," he said.

"Why don't you two quarrel another time," Sorrel said. "Have a drink or something, Joanna, or do you want to start eating? We're halfway through already."

"I'm starved, actually," Joanna said. "More than anything I'd like steak and salad. Fast food, that is. Or ought to be."

When this had been arranged, Harry poured her a glass of wine. "I don't suppose," he said, "anything more came up with Roberto about the shooting, or Markish, or Frankl, or any of that?"

"Nothing important. At least, not that I can remember," Joanna said. "I don't suppose I can smoke in here?"

"Certainly you can smoke in here," Harry said, and produced the Gauloises. "But your steak'll come in a minute."

"I know," Joanna said, and let Harry light the cigarette. "It's this dress," she said, giving a kind of exhilarated shiver as she leaned towards him over the table, "it makes me feel like being bad."

"Think what it does to me," Harry said. "If smoking's all we can do about it, I'll have one too."

"You two are perfectly sick-making," Sorrel said. "Rowing one minute and making up to each other the next. And with poor Roberto pining away on his sickbed and Olivia on her own at Compiègne."

"Olivia's hardly pining," Harry said. "She's on her own at Compiègne because that's where she wants to be. All the same, I'd better phone her. She has no idea I'm here." He got up and left them.

"I think I rather like him, actually," Joanna said to Sorrel.

"Harry's all right," Sorrel said. "He's not perfect, and he has a

144

weird manner sometimes, but when the chips are down he's the man to have on your side."

"I suppose the chips are down, when you think about it, with our Roberto," Joanna said. "He may be wounded, but he's not a wounded hero, is he? He's a wounded absent-without-leave person. He said he couldn't make out whether Seddall was for him or against him."

"That's how it goes with Harry," Sorrel said. "Are you sure Roberto didn't come up with something? 'However insignificant it may have seemed to you at the time,' as the police say. That's what Harry wants, something to get his teeth into."

"He got his teeth into something when he was with Roberto," Joanna said. "He went all broody when Roberto told him about something Markish had said. I'm not allowed to know about it."

"I know about it," Sorrel said. "Harry's broody about it inside his head there, but he hasn't made sense of it yet, or if he has, he's not telling."

Joanna's steak arrived, and she fell upon it as if her protein count was dangerously low. "We need more wine," she said. "I do, anyway," and her grey eyes flashed at the wine waiter, which proved to be signal enough.

"While you're guzzling," Sorrel said, "go back over what Roberto said to you. Tell me if anything he said stopped you for a moment. It doesn't have to be important. Odd or surprising would do."

Joanna meditated while she chewed, and while she swallowed, and while she took in some of the blushful Hermitage.

"There was one thing," she said. "Hi, Harry. All well at home?"

As Harry sat down she forked a piece of steak and was about to put it in her mouth when Sorrel laid fingers on her arm.

"Joanna," she said.

"Oh, yes," Joanna said. "Wait a sec." She devoured the bloody gobbet at an indelicate speed.

"Right," she said. "It's truly nothing important," she said to Harry, "but Sorrel told me to think of anything the least bit odd, so I suppose . . ."

"Tell it, you hellish woman," Harry said. "Or I'll throw that luscious piece of meat on the floor."

"Which one of us do you mean?" Joanna said, and laughed like anything.

"It was only this," she said when she had calmed down, "but I hadn't heard it before. According to Roberto, Frankl has a terrific way with women. He seemed to have an absolute rapport with the woman who runs the safe house: Louise, that's the name. Really close, Roberto said.

"And then that nurse or companion who's got that very strange thing going with Arkley – I mean, he's so old, isn't he? Apparently Georg (I have to think of him as Georg, talking about him like this, though I don't *know* him) was playing footsie with her, in the drawing room after dinner, actually, not under the table at dinner, but where Arkley couldn't see. Roberto said it was amazingly sexual, considering that it was just feet and they were among all these mostly rather awful people. And they'd only just met, and she is Arkley's girlfriend, after all."

She went at the steak again.

"I'm afraid that's all it is," she said. "I can't see that it's going to help."

Seddall pushed his chair back and slouched low with his legs stretched along the side of the table, one ankle crossed over the other, and brushed ash off, or into, his shirt.

"I dunno," he said. "Why does nobody ever tell me anything?"

He lit a cigarette, and dropped his eyes to sight at the carpet between the toes of his shoes, and smoked.

Joanna swilled some wine.

"What does that mean?" she said to Sorrel.

"Search me, love," Sorrel said. "Only time will tell."

# 14

"Come in," Duncanson's wife, holding the door, said. "Colin will be down soon. He's having a bath."

She was a small woman with a tattered lived-in face, full of shapes and lines that had harassed what had once been lovely and without blemish, so that it was now lovely and tattered. Tilted up at him as it was – with pale-brown eyes on him, eyes with a translucence he had never seen before, eyes candid and scanning – it was compelling and forcefully attractive.

"I'm frightfully sorry to disturb you so late," Harry said. "I've interrupted him on his way to bed, have I?"

She had been making way for him to go into the house, but these remarks stopped her so that he was still held on the threshold.

"You're very English," she said.

He felt taken by surprise, as if he had asked her what on earth she meant by that.

"The fulsome apology," she explained, "which you may or may not mean, and then the question which breaks the ice for you but not for me. No, Colin wasn't on his way to bed. He's just having his bath, is what it is. Give me your coat."

She led him into the drawing room. "I've made you some sandwiches," she said. "Whisky or coffee? I'm having both."

"Whisky, please," he said. "This is bloody nice of you. Is it all right to say that?"

Her smile was an open and immediate smile, but it was for her, not for him.

"Sit down," she said. "I'll call you Harry. I don't like this business of playing around with surnames until you get there. My name's Maggie."

He sat down in one of those Italian-designed armchairs that surround you with functional form but fill you with comfort. There were two other chairs like it and a couch to match, a few low tables, lamps, and very little else: this in a large square room with a russet carpet like autumn leaves covering the floor, set off by two vases of chrysanthemums in corners, and a sense of peace in it that was not inert, not passive: a room with calm and energy together.

She put a plate with sandwiches on the table at his hand, and a napkin, and the whisky and soda.

Within reach of his left hand was a Scrabble board with a game about halfway through. Maggie Duncanson sat on the end of the couch on the other side of the board and said: "Eat away, and it's your move."

"Dear God," he said, "I hardly know how to play this game."

"Then you probably think it's only a question of coming up with obscure words to fit the spaces," she said.

"It isn't?" he said.

"Find out," she said. "Play. And do eat."

He ate. They were ham sandwiches, of a good size without being doorsteps, really good ham in them, well mustarded, and brown bread that was eatable as opposed to medicinal.

He ventured a word, and was rather proud of it: ETIOLOGY.

She put down two letters and scored three times what he had.

Seddall frowned at the board. He felt impeached in his intelligence and cunning, both of which were dear to him.

He made ANTHRAX, with a double word score, and felt better.

She put down all her letters, making XYLOPHONE and PUNK, and earning a huge score.

"Death and taxes," he said, enraged.

She smiled widely, this time at him. "It's a better game than you thought, isn't it?" she said.

"It's that all right," he said, glaring at the board.

He took his time now, fuelling himself with whisky and ham sandwich.

He put down three letters, making two words and his best score yet. She did better.

"This is very interesting," he said, seething gently.

"Tell me," she said.

"It's not just about knowing words and being clever with them," he said, "or even being intelligent. It's a question of concentrating on everything that's there and being quick-witted and, most of all, committing yourself to the game that's in play."

"The game that's in play?" she said, the light-brown eyes intent and translucent.

"Yeah," he said. "The game that's in play." He looked into those eyes of hers, but somewhere beyond them as well. "The game in which I am a player, as against the game in general – not the game before or the one after, but the game that I'm playing against you now: committing myself to that."

"This is something more than Scrabble you're talking about," she said.

"I think it is," he said. "Maybe it is."

"You're not saying experience of the game doesn't count?"

"Far from it," he said. "You're wiping the floor with me, and that's partly because of your experience of the game. What I'm saying is that my experience of the game is inadequate."

"I would say that up to now your experience of the game has simply been a long way from the top league," she said.

"Far from top league," he said, "but also, different. Played differently. That's what's interesting me just now."

Colin Duncanson came into the room. "Can I have one of these?" he said, and seized two of the sandwiches and sat down beside his wife. He looked at the score sheet. "You're still winning," he said, "but I suppose Seddall screwed it up anyway."

"Listen," Harry said. "In the words of General of the Army Douglas MacArthur, I shall return; and when I do, you two had better look out for yourselves."

"I'm going to play the piano," Maggie said. "If it distracts you, whichever of you dares can tell me so. You must come again," she said to Seddall, "and not on business. I'll get your address from Colin."

"Just one thing," Harry said as he stood up. "You're English yourself, aren't you?"

"Yes," she said. "I am. Goodnight."

149

When she had gone, Duncanson said: "What's up?"

"I don't know," Seddall said, "not up here," and he tapped the top of his head over the brain-pan, "but there's a lot going on inside me that my head won't grasp yet"

"That's a fancy way of talking about intuition," Duncanson said. "Have a sandwich. I'm going to. Maggie won't want any. She eats yoghurt and fruit and such. Gone vegetarian."

"Thanks," Seddall said. "I know what intuition is, it's a not very high-scoring word in Scrabble. There may . . ."

"Wastes a U, too," Duncanson said.

"What?"

"Intuition's got a U in it," Duncanson said. "Never know when you might want one to let you use a Q."

Seddall was tired, but his flash of impatience at this interruption vanished in a crooked and half-belligerent smile. "All right," he said, "I'm learning. Where was I? Duncanson," he said, "there's a whole lot of sub-text to this business. I can feel it, and I've had glimpses which tell me I'm being taken for a ride."

"That's very polite of you," Duncanson said. "You mean we're being taken for a ride."

"Yes," Harry said. "I do."

He became aware that for the last few minutes he had been listening to a beautifully played piano above him. "What's that?" he said.

"Schumann," Duncanson said. "*Waldszenen.*"

"God, she's lovely," Harry said.

"She's a great musician," Duncanson said. "She cut a tendon in the fourth finger of her left hand when she was a girl, or she'd have had a career at it."

"I didn't just mean her piano playing," Harry said.

"I know that," Duncanson said.

The articulated, lilting music came muted, but with its voice clear and unclouded by the image of that solitary woman at her piano in the lateness of the night.

"You keep late hours," Seddall said, when his thoughts had reached here, looking at Duncanson brisk from his bath and dressed in flannels and shirt and sweater, as fresh as if he were about to start the day.

"I'm an insomniac," Duncanson said. "Maggie keeps me company, often enough, and sleeps till noon."

Seddall thought that to leave this house tonight would be like leaving the theatre after a play that had struck into him. Time enough.

"This girl of Arkley's," he said, "this Anna, what do you know of her?"

"Oho," Duncanson said. "Sits the wind in that quarter? I know that she seems to have disappeared about thirty-six hours ago, and that Arkley's in a stew about it."

"Has she, by God?" Seddall said. "Well, I'll tell you something . . . No, first of all, what can you tell me about her?"

"She was a star recruit, if you can excuse a paradox like that, which I don't," Duncanson said. "She joined Arkley's team summer before last and they went mad about her. She pulled off some coup in Israel and was on Arkley's general staff – you know the way he runs things – in no time. She had everything to start with, too. A first at Oxford, modern history. It's not a tough subject, but a first's a first. Security-vetted sound as a bell, although by them of course, not by us. Jewish family, third generation, parents killed in car crash and left her well-provided for. When Arkley lost his leg he wanted her next to him and she took a course on how to look after a man with his mutilation" – Seddall stared at the word – "and the next thing you know, there they were, that old ruin and the beautiful child. Beauty and the beast."

He looked full at Seddall, that plug-ugly man with the beautiful wife upstairs, and looked up at the ceiling, and rubbed his face with both hands. "How it goes," he said. "What do you have to tell me?"

"I think she and Georg Frankl," Harry said, "are like that." He held a hand up with fore- and middle fingers crossed.

"Well, well, well," Duncanson said, and showed his teeth in a large grin. "It's terribly important," he said, "for men like you and me not to get excited at moments of revelation like this. But, Seddall, this is something."

He got up and left the room, and Seddall sat and listened to Schumann. At one point he went over to sniff the chrysanthemums and wander round the room, then came back to his chair, listening to Maggie Duncanson playing her piano.

Duncanson came back. "Just arranging a few standby things," he said.

He took almost the last of the sandwiches, fetched the whisky and the siphon and put them on the table beside the Scrabble board. "Help yourself," he said. "I'm a slow thinker. First Georg is off the scene and now Anna's off the scene. Vanished, out of sight, beyond our ken."

Seddall said: "What kind of a stew is Arkley in about Anna disappearing?"

"What do you mean, what kind of a stew?" Duncanson said.

"Well, in the first place," Seddall said, "what is so 'disappeared' about her not being around for a day or so? Can't a girl go off on her own if she feels like it? Miss a day at work, too, without its being a crisis of some kind?"

"I think that's exactly it," Duncanson said. "Arkley's got the two mixed up. It's a hell of a thing for a man like Arkley to have a popsie like that, you know, a girl less than half his age. I wouldn't care for it myself. A girl's not a woman, you know, or not often; doesn't make a companion for a man who's seen life. She may even be of a nature more mature than the man's, but her lack of experience makes her seem silly to him at the same time that the old man's childishness seems foolish to her. Why am I talking like this?"

"I don't know," Seddall said. "Don't stop, anyway."

Upstairs, the piano, which had fallen briefly silent, embarked on music of considerable dramatic force.

"What's that?" Harry said.

"Brahms," Duncanson said without thought; without moving his mind from what he had been saying. "Opus 79 No. 2."

"I suppose," Seddall said, "you know her whole repertoire."

"What an extraordinarily banal thing to say," Duncanson was annoyed. "What does that mean: her whole repertoire? She's a pianist, she plays anything she wants to. I play the fiddle, myself. Not anything like she plays the piano. But I know music."

"Do you play duets, then?" Seddall said. "That sort of thing?"

Duncanson stared at him out of that slab-meat face. The look began as one of outrage then turned into laughter.

"Seddall, can this be you?" Duncanson said. "Will you please have the decency, to yourself if not to me, to abort this sentimental view you are developing about my marital relationship. You know nothing about Maggie and me, and I find this kind of stuff extremely picayune."

Harry looked to be much shocked by himself, and deeply embarrassed. "Is that what it sounded like?" he said. "What's happening to me?"

"It's this Olivia of yours," Duncanson said. "She's a tough woman, I hear, and she's French, so that it comes out differently from what you're used to. You probably think she's hard. There are places where Englishmen are soft in the gut, you know, and they like that to be catered for, however tough they may be themselves. It can make them mistake toughness in women for lack of feeling. Don't be such an idiot about it. Toughness joined with generosity of feeling, when they come together in the one human being, is a combination hard to meet." He nodded to the ceiling above which the music played. "Like in her," he said.

Seddall lit a Gauloise, looked at Duncanson and thought. "Yeah," he said. "Well, we don't think any of this is what's happening with Arkley and his Anna, do we?"

Duncanson looked suspicious. "Have you been doing this on purpose?" he said. "To suss out my credentials as a commentator on Arkley and his girl?"

Seddall gave a deprecating grin. "I should like to think so," he said. "If I was, I learned more than I bargained for. Where do you get off, Duncanson, being so guru-like about human nature?"

"That I am not," Duncanson said. "But I'm in charge of this country's security. Human nature is one of the things I'm supposed to know a little bit about."

"Oh, sure," Harry said. "But did they know you thought like this when they appointed you? I mean, it's all very close to introspection, Duncanson; the way you look at people. It means you look at yourself. It's not the kind of quality they used to go for, appointing the head of MI5."

"I'm a master of disguise, laddie," Duncanson said. "Out there in the jungle I'm an in-fighting Whitehall warrior who's connected in all the right places."

"I'm lucky to be talking to you," Harry said.

"That's right," Duncanson said. "You are."

"Is Arkley nervous that he may have lost his girl," Harry said, "or did he think there was something funny about her before this, and if so, is he nervous because he sees a plan he had designed slipping out of his fingers . . ."

"You know your Arkley, don't you?" Duncanson said: interrupting exactly as he had at that conference.

". . . and the girl slipping away too? Thus he's lost control of both, the two biggest things in his life right now, so that the effect on him is exponential? Is he in a really boiling stew, or is he just simmering?"

"I would never have thought," Duncanson said, "of seeking to divine Arkley's state of mind by way of culinary distinctions. I don't know, is the answer to that. Let me share what I do know. Have a dram."

He poured them both some Scotch. Seddall hoped he was to hear nothing this night that would stop him getting at least a few hours' sleep. After the kind of day he had been having, the whisky would begin, and quite soon, to act like a soporific.

"After," Duncanson said, "our historic meeting, that is to say, between the time Arkley left home and his arrival at his place of business – because, you will remember, he came straight to our meeting from his breakfast – the girl Anna went off the map. Is that clear?"

"Oddly enough, yes," Harry said, "but the syntax was muddled."

"Bugger the syntax," Duncanson said.

One of us is getting a little pickled, Harry thought, without being at all sure which of them it was.

"So there she was," Duncanson said, "either smiling at him over the cornflakes, or saying bye-bye all drowsy from the pillow, and the next thing Arkley knows is that she ain't at the office as anticipated and she's not at home either. Along about lunch-time she has still not turned up at the office, and you might suppose she's gone on a bender, or a shopping spree. But then, when she is not home for dinner – this is last night, you apprehend – darker counsels begin to prevail in what is left of the Arkley household. Maxton, Arkley's own personal gunsel, is called in to be briefed

154

and consulted. He emerges looking grave and ready to be seriously active."

"Gunsel?" Harry said.

"I like those old B movies," Duncanson said. "My one weakness."

"How do you know all this?" Harry said.

"The how is mine," Duncanson said. "The why is because it's my business to know."

Harry said: "I don't know Maxton personally, but I know a lot about him. He's another who came into Arkley's inner circle in this last year or so."

"As with Anna?" Duncanson said. "Yes, he is. What is more, Seddall, it is only in this last year or so that Arkley has had an inner circle. Before that, he was his own inner circle, centre and circumference, all in himself."

"You're being meaningful," Harry said.

"Sign of weakness?" Duncanson said. "Sign of age? Of impending dotage? Seen it before with power-mongers like Arkley. History's full of it. Roman emperors, medieval kings, Renaissance princes, inexplicably either lose their confidence in themselves or get paranoid and change the people who've seen them right these ten or twenty years past for new and often untrustworthy people."

"You are questioning Arkley's state of mind?" Harry said.

"I do not say so at all," Duncanson said. "I merely speculate, now at this late hour in the night, over a few drinks, on the nature of power and the progression it makes with those who grapple it to them with hoops of steel, as if it were a friend."

"It's not?" Harry said.

"No," Duncanson said. "It's an enemy."

"*Tout court?*" Harry said.

"*Tout court,*" Duncanson said.

"How bloody interesting," Harry said, "coming from a man in your position."

"I have not said that I dislike having power," Duncanson said, "assuming that's what I do have. This too: if I have power and it is my enemy, I can perhaps be on terms with my enemy."

"You're a great logic-chopper, aren't you?" Harry said.

"Arkley," Duncanson said. "Let's deal with one problem at a time. Arkley is our problem just now, not me."

"Problem is not logic-chopping," Harry said. "Now you're saying that Sir John Arkley, director of MI6, loaded with reputation and the authority of years in office, doyen of his peers, is a problem."

"My, you're a percipient wee man," Duncanson said.

"Don't go all Scotch on me, for heaven's sake," Harry said. "Since you are talking straight at last, it would be awfully obliging of you to do it in English."

Duncanson said: "You make us sound like a couple of subalterns of the North-West Frontier Force. Here goes. Arkley arranges to kill Frankl, and you and I and Quick from the Cabinet Secretariat go all pale at the thought. Arkley says it's for reasons of State, and that he regards Frankl as a risk he can't evaluate to our joint campaign to find these CBRs and have them out of Africa before they are let loose to the slaughter of innocent thousands, even millions – in any case, to the detriment of the British Government's standing in the world, since they're British and no one will believe we didn't have a hand in it."

"Right so far," Harry said.

"Well," Duncanson said. "I don't believe it. It's not that I think Arkley would flinch at killing a man for no better reason than that, with no more certainty than that. I'm sure he's done it often enough. It's just that I didn't believe him when he was telling us that was why he'd arranged for Frankl to be killed."

"Why not?" Harry said.

"What I heard in his voice," Duncanson said, "and what I saw in him, was Arkley plotting. Besides, there's something up, I know there is for a fact, between Arkley and that general, General Tinsley."

"I don't know Tinsley, really," Harry said. "He's just another general to me."

"I'll tell you this about Tinsley," Duncanson said. "When the generals were meeting and caballing and pulling out everything they could to save the Army from being shrunk down in the Defence cuts, Tinsley was not among those present."

He offered Seddall a long, significant look, with his bushy eyebrows arched, until the question came.

"All right," Harry said. "What was Tinsley doing?"

"Tinsley," Duncanson said, "was doing his very best, with the cunning, conniving mind that lurks behind that honest boy-soldier's face of his, to see that the Defence cuts did not put a crimp in our chemical and bacteriological effort. He didn't give a shit about regiments being amalgamated, or how many of the new Challenger tanks were ordered, or whether the lads were going to be armed with Tower muskets, or told to start a census of yew trees because longbows were going to be it from now on. Chemical warfare and bacteria are what give Tinsley a buzz. Toxic gas and the Black Death, that's where Tinsley sees the defence of the realm. He's not even a scientist. He was just an infantryman with a good career record, doing well in action when there was any, putting in some good work at the Ministry and as attaché in New Delhi, making his way up at a good fast trot until he was put on some committee that was set up to evaluate the military usefulness of Porton Down. When he got there he decided that Boffinland was where it was at. That's who Tinsley is."

There was a silence while Seddall and Duncanson looked at each other. After a while Seddall sighed. "You shouldn't have given me so much whisky," he said. "Here we are up to our necks and Arkley has *carte blanche* from Downing Street to sort it out the quickest way, and you're saying there is an axis between Arkley and Tinsley, and that Tinsley is a CBR freak from way back."

"Not from very far back," Duncanson said pedantically, "but for the rest, yes, that's what I'm saying."

"What do you make of it?" Harry said.

"I don't have enough to go on to say this," Duncanson said. "But I make of it that Arkley and Tinsley are into something. I don't mean into something for profit or gain, or something disloyal or unpatriotic – excuse the concepts. I think perhaps they're using their initiative, maybe in response to the defence cuts and the cooling-off of the Cold War, and that they may have got carried away."

He watched Seddall listening to this and taking it in. "What are you thinking?" he asked.

"Power," Seddall said.

"I know," Duncanson said. "It might just be. One of them has had it for a long time and knows he's going to have to leave it soon because he'll be old. The other may have got the taste for it and likes what feeding on it does to him. And they may not be on their own."

"What do you mean?" Harry said. "Can you name names?"

"Yes, but I won't," Duncanson said. "Not to you, old boy. Need to know, and all that. But what it means is that there are always people around in high places who want to save the country in spite of itself. And when they start stirring they make very murky waters indeed."

Duncanson went off into a rapt and private state. After a while he came to himself and from that marvellously ill-made face produced a smile of great warmth. It reminded Harry of that smile of Maggie Duncanson's, which had been for herself, not for him. This was a private smile of Duncanson's, emerging from that private state.

"Do you remember, when you were a very small boy," Duncanson said, "that the actual colours, the red, white and blue of the Union Jack, exhilarated you when you saw them en masse at some great event?"

"As a matter of fact," Harry said, "no."

"I do," Duncanson said. "It was a childish thing. As good as fireworks it was for me. I think some men keep that inside them when they've grown up, hidden inside them, hidden even from themselves. Then, when they become men, they attach to the flag the ideas of honour and glory and patriotism, which can be healthy enough, *dulce et decorum est pro patria mori*. Edith Cavell made it work, if you like. But there are men who get it wrong, you see, as well. Times change on them, and the world changes, and the country changes, and they think – they believe deeply – that the moral fibre's gone, or going, or will go if it does not get help. They are the guardians of the country's honour, is what they come to think. They believe there's only a shred of honour left, and that they are its upholders. Like a tattered Battle Honour in a cathedral or a military chapel, with just a glimmer of colour left; and they represent, they are, the glimmer of colour."

158

He smiled that smile again. "I think that's what we're up against."

"A shred of honour," Harry said.

"Yes," Duncanson said. "Have some whisky. Just a wee deoch an doris."

"What's that?" Harry said.

"It's what we call a wee dram tae speed ye on your way," Duncanson said. "Although it's hellish late, and you're welcome to sleep here."

"Do you ever think," Harry said, "that you're an upholder of the shred of honour yourself?"

"You're asking me that," Duncanson said, "because you've just lost an illusion. That's an idea you've had about yourself without knowing it, and now you don't like it."

Seddall gave him a smile of his own. "I'll take your wee deoch and whatever," he said. "And I'm truly grateful for your offer of a bed, but I simply couldn't handle all this perception at breakfast."

He looked up at the ceiling. "The music's stopped."

"A while ago," Duncanson said. "Maggie's taken herself to bed."

Seddall accepted the wee dram.

"You never answered my question," he said.

"No," Duncanson said. "I didn't."

"You're not going to," Seddall said.

"That's right," the head of the Security Service said. "Top Secret. Divulge on Need to Know Basis Only."

# 15

The ringing of the phone wakened him, but by the time John Murphy put his head round the door all Seddall had managed to do was turn over in bed and become aware of the day, outside the window, into which he had now been called. It looked grey; possibly wet.

"Morning," Murphy said. "Mrs Lyon wants you on the phone."

"Tell her I'll call back in five minutes," Seddall said.

"Can't," Murphy said. "I'm holding the other end of Patrick's ladder. Papering the drawing room today."

Seddall wrapped himself in a dressing-gown and went to speak to Mrs Lyon. "What's up?" he said.

"Not you, by the sound of it," she said, full of fun.

"Mrs Lyon," he said, "I was drinking whisky with a Scotchman last night, and I'm regretting it like anything now. If you're going to be all witty and Scotch on me, I'll put the phone down."

"Scots," she said, "and Scotsman, not Scotch. That's what ye were drinking, and ye'll get nae sympathy from me. And your good leddy away and all."

"What's that got to do with anything?" he said.

"Weel ye ken," Mrs Lyon said, as if Harry had been cutting a swathe through all the fleshpots of London. "The dug's no weel," she said.

"What's wrong with him?" Harry said.

"Now, dinna fash yersel'," she said. "He's aff his food and winna leave his basket, and his nose is het. I've called the veterinary surgeon" – English, and full out, Harry noticed: the old fraud – "and he'll be here in an hour, once he's put the wee Carver girl's pony oot o' its misery, for it's broken its leg, puir beastie, and the puir wee girl too, for I've nae doot she'll be greetin' sair."

Seddall's head began to ache. "Olivia and I will be there for the weekend," he said, "if I get this bit of business I've got on hand finished by then. You're remembering that?"

"I'm minding it fine," Mrs Lyon said. "She was on the phone tae me yesterday telling me whit tae get in the way o' food for ye tae eat. And a Mr Frankl phoned." The headache vanished in a flash. Frankl? Frankl! Why on earth would he phone the house in Somerset?

"Oh, yes," Harry said, "and what did he want?"

"He left me a number for ye tae call him," Mrs Lyon said. "I have it here, if ye'll get your paper and pencil. He said he wants tae talk tae ye aboot the wandering boy, whatever that means."

"Nothing to me," Harry said.

"Aye, that'll be right," she said sceptically. "Are ye ready wi' your bit o' paper?"

"Fire away," Harry said.

It was a French phone number, which was hardly surprising.

They exchanged goodbyes in their two languages, and hung up.

The phone rang instantly. "Seddall," he said, wondering what to do about breakfast. Eat out, this morning.

"Sorrel," the phone said. "We've got a crisis," she said. "Roberto Mullen's been kidnapped. Joanna's in the most dreadful state."

"The wandering boy," Harry said. "No doubt of it."

"Is that a sort of joke?" Sorrel said.

"No, no," Harry said. "Something else. That boy was in no state to be kidnapped. How was it done?"

"They broke into the hospital and lowered him out the corridor window on a rope – block and tackle, the works. They left the gear behind. From the way they'd rigged it, it looks as if they may have let him down on a stretcher. So they may be looking after him, up to a point. What was that wandering-boy remark in aid of?"

Harry told her about Frankl's message, as relayed by Mrs Lyon.

"Do you want me to call the number?" Sorrel said.

"I'll call him first," Harry said, "and then I'll call you back. Where are you?"

"In my room at the hotel," Sorrel said. "Joanna's with me."

"This is hard for you both," he said.

"Yes," Sorrel said. There was a pause. "If when you phone Frankl you find there's a follow-up to be done and you want me to do it . . ."

She let it hang there, and he thought furiously. He knew he was supposed to work out what she would have said if Joanna had not been with her.

"You're worried about leaving Joanna on her own?" he said.

"Yes," she said, "and with nothing . . ."

". . . to do," he said.

"Spot on," Sorrel said.

"And you have an answer to that one, I'll be bound."

"Yes," Sorrel said.

"If there's a job for you, you want to bring her in on the action."

"Exactly," Sorrel said.

"Hell," he said. "Is she any good? I don't want you going into enemy country with an amateur holding onto your skirts. Mullen's halfway up the spout already. I don't want you to get hurt unless you need to."

Sorrel gave a light, slightly too light, laugh. "That was nicely put," she said.

"Listen," Harry said. "You know bloody well I don't want a hair of your head hurt, just as I know bloody well you'd be furious if I didn't let you go into a tight place if that's what's needed."

"You're right," Sorrel said. "I was playing silly buggers, and I apologize. Joanna's gone to the bathroom," she said in a lowered voice. "Tact or pee, I don't know. You asked if she's any good: she's tough, young, fit, sensible and quick on the uptake; and she's a senior secretary, so I've no idea what use she'll be if we get into a war. I'll give her the low-down, that's all I can do. Say yes."

"She could always act as a runner," Harry said. "So, yes. It all depends on what Frankl has to say. There may be nothing for you to do at all. I'll call you back as soon as I've spoken with him."

Georg Frankl sat in the bar of the Boeuf Couronné in Chartres and wondered which of them would arrive first, Anna or this woman Sorrel Blake.

There was a strong charge of whimsy in Georg today, as there

162

might well be in a man who had come out alive from being shot off the road on his motorcycle, with nothing but a grazed face and a bruised side to show for it. The whimsy gave him to speculate about Harry Seddall, who seemed to Georg to be in some ways as a rogue animal, a survival beyond his species; though what precisely the species might have been it was hard to say.

Seddall would have belonged in the century before, as a commander of irregular cavalry: Seddall's Horse, Frankl thought, that would have been it. Which made Sorrel Blake, even now galloping to the rescue, a detached squadron, or a flying column, in that evocative phrase. He knew it was not all whimsy. There was something not contemporary about Harry Seddall, just as there was something ancient about Georg Frankl.

"We succeed sometimes because of it," Frankl said.

The girl behind the bar gave him another glass of wine, as if she had thought the words were a request.

"Time past is present in time future," Frankl said. "It's an essential idea." He was still thinking about himself and Seddall, but he wondered also what the words would bring. Peanuts, maybe.

"*Je ne comprends pas,*" the girl said.

"*Le temps . . .,*" Frankl began helpfully.

"Yes, yes, I know what it means," the girl said in English. "I understand it with my head, that's not difficult. *Mais pas dans l'esprit.*"

"Work on it," Frankl said. "It's worth it."

"Perhaps," she said. "*Un de ces jours, peut-être.*"

A polite way of saying, Frankl thought, that she might do it when she was as old as he was – forty-two years old is old? – and had, therefore, nothing better to do.

He hoped Anna would come first, before the Flying Column. He had loved Anna well, deeply, with joy when they were last together, but a lot had happened since, to put it euphemistically.

He looked forward to their meeting, not as the child behind the bar would do to a meeting with her lover – with ardour and unsullied optimism – but with a mixture of curiosity, intense interest, a protective shield of amusement, and the hope – since one should always hope unless the odds were annihilating – of happiness. How could he know what he would feel? What she would feel?

A warm kiss fell on the nape of his neck, and he closed his eyes and hunched up his shoulders and shuddered as it moved through him. When the kiss ended, he threw his head back and opened his eyes and revolved on his stool.

Anna: beautiful and ordinary and real in dark jeans and a navy sweater. Anna, wearing also solemn eyes and a smile at once immediate and profound.

Frankl wrapped all of this in his arms with intense interest and unsullied ardour, thus combining – though his mind was too over-whelmed by his feelings to notice this – the states he had attributed both to himself and to the girl behind the bar.

"Ah, Georg!" she said, not lifting her face to meet him; talking into his shoulder. "Is it going to be all right? Is it going to be good again?"

"I think it is," he said. "I think it is."

"Despite Arkley . . ." she said.

"Shut up," he said quickly. "Let it be. I think it's going to be all right."

"And good again?" she said.

When she lifted her face, there was a lustre of tears in those luminous eyes.

"I think that too," he said. "And good again."

He knew, though, as he said it, that each of them doubted and that she heard his doubt as clearly as she had told him hers.

"We'll see what happens," he said. "What else can we do?"

He was going to kiss her, but the kiss would have had an elegiac quality. Surely a moment of fear could not kill what had been between him and Anna, but certainly, if it could, this might be such a moment, and a kiss now, a real kiss now, would find it out. He put his lips, therefore, only to her forehead and her eyes, kissing the tears there as you kiss the hurt on a child to make it better.

"Next year in Jerusalem," she said.

"Jerusalem?" he said. "Jerusalem? We're not doing this to be in Jerusalem."

"That was my joke," she said. "We rather need one."

"All right," he said, like an American. "Let's go over here and talk," and he put an arm round her waist and went to a table on the far side of the room.

When they had drinks in front of them, Anna said: "So, Dujardin is in this."

"Yes," he said. "And the Zulu girl, M'pofu."

"I understand she's a singer in a boîte."

"Yes," he said. "Well, it turns out she can go up and down the walls of hospitals like a cat burglar, and also that she can shoot. She is more than a singer in a boîte. She shot my bike off the road from the back of a moving van with a sub-machine-gun of some kind. We were going fast and I was not close. It was good shooting."

Anna said: "His last two jobs before the Peruvians put him in prison: he had an accomplice, not identified. You think it was her?"

"I think it likely," Frankl said.

Anna thought. "Dujardin," she said. "He was in a military prison, awaiting trial. Do you think they just let him go?"

"Not for a moment," Frankl said. "He killed the youngest colonel in their army, and he got to be colonel because he was the one man who was putting it over on the Shining Path. He'd just about cleared them from his sector. They'd not let Dujardin just walk away from that one."

"Sendero Luminoso broke him out of jail?" Anna said. "That's what you think?"

"Maybe," Frankl said. "But it's not Sendero he's working for now, is it? Taking Roberto Mullen out of that hospital – and doing it because they thought he was me. That's nothing to do with Sendero. If they broke him out of jail, I would say it was because someone else gave them a contribution to their war chest. Someone who wanted to use Dujardin."

"So they took Mullen because he was the man with Markish," Anna said, working it through. "That was how you were to be fingered for Dujardin – you were to be with Markish. Then Mullen voted himself in to substitute for you, so when Dujardin saw Mullen having dinner with Markish, he thought Mullen was Georg Frankl."

Frankl nodded.

"Which means," Anna said, "that John set you up to meet Markish, and you were to be shot?"

A movement as if he had been galvanized by an electric shock went through Frankl. "Don't call him John!" he said. "I can't take that. Call him Arkley."

165

Anna stared into his eyes, a long stare. "Arkley," she said. "Yes, I'll call him Arkley. So Arkley arranged for you to be shot by Dujardin. But it was not Dujardin who shot Markish and Mullen. The French think it was North Africans, don't they?"

"That's right," Frankl said. "Dujardin and M'pofu arrived on the scene just after the shooting and followed Mullen's ambulance to the hospital. I wonder why they didn't just kill him there? They must want something from him. They went to a lot of trouble to sneak him out of that hospital. It was a pleasure to watch them work."

Anna put her elbows on the table, held her face between her hands, and stared at Georg again, another of those long stares. "You didn't, by any chance, have anything to do with these gunmen turning up at the restaurant to shoot Markish? After all, you have a special interest in those crates. You might not want Roberto to learn too much of what Markish could tell him."

Frankl became withdrawn. "Why do you say that?"

"Because I know when you're being evasive," she said. "And because you want to rescue Roberto Mullen, even though that's nothing to do with the operation. That's not like you. I think it could be guilt about Mullen."

"Since it's what I'm doing," he said, "it is like me. Reassure yourself, all the same. I plan to get a deal out of it."

"All right," Anna said. "That's more like it, and more like you. You've called in Seddall to help. Is that wise?"

"Oh yes," Georg said. "That's wise. It's very wise. If Seddall makes a deal, he'll stick to it."

Anna liked the look on his face. She liked the way his body was: alert, and relaxed with it, ready for action.

"Tell me," she said.


"That's the deal?" Sorrel Blake said. "That's the whole deal? That's absolutely all you want?"

"That's the deal," Frankl said. "The whole deal."

"It doesn't seem an awful lot," Sorrel said.

"It's personal with me," Frankl said. "I want the personal satisfaction."

166

"I hear you say so," Sorrel said, "and that's about as noncommittal as I can get."

"Sure," Frankl said, looking comfortable and well composed in the pale-grey suit and a dark sweatshirt: looking intelligent, assured, up-to-something, confident, on the *qui vive,* content, expectant, and comfortable.

Sorrel was wearing leather trousers, which felt good on her in France, with the autumn moving into winter. They were the colour of light cognac. She wore Chelsea boots and a white sweater, and a mass of short golden curls and eyes like the summer sky. To Frankl, she looked beautiful, tough, competent, and seriously intelligent.

"I don't know if we can arrange it," she said. "I don't know if Colonel Seddall can bring it off. It's quite a tall order." She stretched out a leg and looked down the length of it to the toe of her boot, and then across the table at Frankl again. "Well, you know that. An armed raid into a foreign country is not just one of those things. And it means overflying other Sahara countries to get there. Altogether it will be quite a piratical exercise. I know Mossad is used to this kind of exercise, but we find it all rather madcap and reckless."

"That's why it's such a nice deal for you," Frankl said. "You get Mullen back in one piece – with a bit of luck, anyway. You get the map reference for the rendezvous of this desert caravan. And all that is required of Seddall is his promise to do his best to keep his side of the deal."

Past Frankl's head, over some roofs, she saw the twin spires of Chartres Cathedral, where Anna and Joanna had gone while Frankl and Sorrel negotiated.

"I'm not going as a tourist. I'm going to pray for Roberto," Joanna had said. "It would be time for someone to pray for him, whether he'd been kidnapped or not."

Joanna was doing pretty well, Sorrel thought, but she was getting taut and strung-out by this time. If this deal was to be struck and Mullen rescued, the quicker the better. It's up to you, Sorrel. Don't hang about. Do it.

"You've got a deal," she said to Frankl. "What's this hunch of yours about where they're hiding Mullen?"

This took the imperturbable Frankl she'd been meeting today by surprise. "How can I have a deal?" he said. "You haven't spoken to Seddall yet."

"We're in a hurry," she said. "Assume I'm plenipotentiary. You're banking on Seddall keeping his word, you quaint old-fashioned ex-Mossad thing you, and that's all you're banking on. If I give you my word, that will be to him as if he'd given his own. How can you fault that?"

Frankl examined this. He said: "You're right. That is what I'm doing. You give me your word?"

"I give you my word," Sorrel said formally. "And if it helps: I may be only a weak and feeble woman, but I have the heart of a prince."

"You quoted that because you're embarrassed. Giving your word of honour – such an anachronism," Frankl said.

"Why don't you put that where the sun don't shine," Sorrel said. "Stop trying to prove how cunning you are at understanding people, especially women. Just tell me where Dujardin's taken Mullen. This may come as a shock to you: it's not relevant and I don't justify it, but I don't much like you. Perhaps if we have the air clear, we'll get on faster."

On the surface, at least, Frankl kept his cool. "What was all that about?" he said.

"Oh, come on," Sorrel said. "You must know yourself at least a little. With you that kind of personal remark is second nature. We're talking business. Let's keep to first natures. What about Dujardin?"

"I expect the wound will heal," Frankl said. "All right: Dujardin. He inherited a house from his mother, fifty or so kilometres from here. He didn't sell it, he kept it. Dujardin had quite a thing about his mother, obsessive, probably . . ."

As he gestured behind him to the north-west, Sorrel broke in. "How do you know all this?" she asked.

"Ah," Frankl said. "Dujardin is known. Even you people have a little dossier on Dujardin. When you have a dossier on a man like Dujardin, Mossad has a biography."

"The idea about him and his mother," Sorrel said. "How did you come up with that?"

"That's my department," Frankl said, "or I should say, that

was my department. With professional assassins, we like to know what makes them tick, we like to know their weaknesses."

Sorrel looked at him coldly. "You're saying we're gifted amateurs."

"In fact no, I'm not," Frankl said, "or I wouldn't confide myself to Seddall and to you in the way that I am doing. Your MI6 does the same sort of thing, and I have reservations about their quality. The CIA does it too, of course. In your terms, I should call them ungifted professionals. But maybe I'm ego-boosting. Maybe it is just that we in Israel are what you would think a little paranoid. And then again, you do not live among your enemies in the way Israel does." He stood up. "I think the sun is over the yard arm, as your gifted amateurs used to say. Do you want a beer, or would you prefer wine?"

When he came back with the glasses, he said: "I think you should phone Seddall now, and get him started. You need to know the address of that house. It's near Verneuil. You need French police cooperation and you will want British presence."

"You're right," Sorrel said. "You could run this operation as well as anyone." She stood up.

"Better than most," he said, with an unblinking eye, "but I don't know that I want to be there."


Seddall had driven over the plain to Chartres often enough, both when the corn was high and when it had been cut, and his memory was of a landscape, whether of grain or stubble, gilded and lit by the sun.

He had never been out here in the rain and wind and dark of a November night, and the sense of the flat, wet land stretching away for miles around him oppressed his spirit.

He trudged back to the car and got in.

"It looks to me," he said, "as if the best thing to do is to go back to the crossroads."

"We have a signpost for St Luc?" Sorrel said.

"Well no," Seddall said. "What we have is a signpost for Bourg-Achard. If I'm right about our general position we should find St Luc between us and Bourg-Achard. If we proceed in the direction of the said Bourg-Achard, then with any luck we'll come across a signpost saying St Luc."

"And if we are the recipients of unimaginable good fortune," Sorrel said, "we shall come across St Luc itself."

"That is how it seems," he said.

"And meanwhile I have to back fifty yards down this bloody road in the dark," Sorrel said, "in which the margin of this presumably unclassified road and the fields seem as one. So if we get bogged down, don't blame me."

"I could walk down the middle of the road with a torch," Joanna said from the back. "Give you an aiming point."

"No, love," Sorrel said. "I'm exaggerating, because Harry's made such a lousy job of map-reading."

"Look," Seddall said. "It's a lousy map for this kind of work, the scale's far too small. And we have time in hand. Let's not get flustered."

"Flustered?" Sorrel said. "Who's flustered?"

She thought that if it went on any longer, this by-play between the two of them, whose object was to distract Joanna from fretting about Roberto, would become increasingly forced.

"Hang tight," she said. "Here we go."

She went into reverse, put her head out of the window and ran the car back down the road with her tongue between her teeth and the gear whining like a banshee.

There was only one bad moment, when the car wound about as if it was taking a chicane back-end first, and then she was past the crossroads.

"Road to the right?" she said.

"Road to the right," Seddall said. "Wherever it is, it's less than ten kilometres away. So we don't actually need to go as fast forward as you like to go backwards."

However obscurely expressed, this was a kind of compliment, so Sorrel let it go. "I can't, anyway," she said. "There's mist rising now as well."

"I wonder what Frankl's up to," Seddall said. "I wonder what Arkley's doing this minute. I wonder if your boyfriend will bring it off. I wonder if Olivia can swing it for us. I wonder if the Tuareg have fallen upon the caravan and opened Pandora's box."

"The Tuareg?" Sorrel said. "I know they're on the go these days, and I don't blame them either, but that far south?"

"Certainly that far south," Seddall said. "I wonder if Duncanson's keeping an eye on that general."

"Did he say he would?" Sorrel said.

"No. Why would he say so, even if he was?" Seddall said. "That's his business."

"Was that a signpost?" Sorrel said.

"Only to a farm," Joanna said.

"I wonder," Seddall said, "all these things, and I feel like a spider at the centre of a web which everyone is weaving away at except me."

"A sort of cuckoo spider," Joanna said.

"A doleful image, but sort of," Seddall said. "Also, I wonder how the dog is."

Sorrel drove half a kilometre and Joanna and Seddall said as one: "St Luc."

"Where, where?" Sorrel said, and braked to a stop and extinguished the lights.

"Well, here," Seddall said. He delivered himself of a strenuous sigh. "If Joanna could help you park off the road so that you don't have to use your lights, and if you can do it with no engine noise at all – none of which is going to be easy – I shall go a-stalking," he said. "Wait here till I come back."

He left them to it and set off.

He was glad to be out of the car, glad to be done with navigating blindly into the terra incognita in front, and with the child Joanna behind him, giving off, however hard she might have tried not to, the fear she felt for her Roberto.

It was one of those nights in which the violence of the wind and the tranquillity of the mist went oddly together, as if nature was out of joint. The wind, at its whim, blew the rain into his face and down his neck, and the mist kept St Luc out of sight.

What he was looking for was not, in the first instance, St Luc itself, but the force of French police that had been sent to rescue Mullen and deal, one way or the other, with his kidnappers.

He was walking silent and watchful along the road. The relieving force would be lurking quietly in its chosen station, or according to dispositions already made: in conditions like these, he might very well pass through them without making contact.

Between the gusts of wind each sound came as preternaturally loud. His feet squelched loud and lonely on the road. A magpie, nocturnal or dreaming, chattered and was still. A rabbit squealed, and doubtless died, to the weasel or polecat that had met it on the way. Somewhere to the north a train howled, faint and distant.

Though it rose and fell, the blowing of the wind did not cease. At a pelting of rain onto his face Seddall turned his head aside and saw a long bar of light.

He went towards it, and it became the bar of light under a door. It took longer to get there than he expected, and as he went he found himself walking among houses that seemed asleep. When he drew near to it, the bar of light was revealed as lying under the double doors of a carriage gateway.

Out of nowhere he was seized from behind. One arm was twisted up high behind his back so that he was forced forward, and at the same time a man in uniform appeared before him, holding a pistol to his face.

"By the living God," Seddall said in fury. "Take your hands off me!"

"*C'est un anglais,*" the man behind him said, maintaining his hold.

"*Oui, c'est un anglais,*" Seddall said. "*C'est un colonel anglais qui va vous jeter dans la chiasse.* Let me go, damn your eyes."

"*C'est un colonel anglais enragé,*" the man with the pistol said, showing no signs of respect for rank. "*Suivez-moi, mon colonel,*" he said.

He went to the gates and murmured a word, and they opened to let through the frog-marched Seddall and his captors.

Once released from the armlock, Seddall blinked in the light. He did a curious thing. He turned and studied the man who had held him, a heavy six-footer with a square face and a red moustache, but little hair. Seddall ignored the presence of other men standing around, and studied him for something like thirty seconds.

The man turned his face away at last as if he was shy.

Seddall faced the man with the pistol. A smaller man, with

polished black hair and a sallow face that gleamed in the light, and black, bad eyes. He began to turn away at once, holstering his pistol.

Seddall said: "Wait," and gripped him by the arm.

The man averted his face with chin up, full of suspicion, as Seddall surveyed him in his turn.

Seddall let him go.

"What was that about?" a voice said.

Seddall took in that he was in a barn-like building full of men and vehicles, what had perhaps been a small mill or factory at one time. Beyond a group of identical white vehicles – those small buses the police use – he had glimpses of farm machinery, so that presumably it was either being used, or had been used most recently, as a store or repair shop.

The three or four men round him, now that the two thug-like guards had gone, were watching him. He recognized only one, the man who had spoken: a tall, lean man, in beautifully made tweed, with the worn-out face of one in the penultimate stage of mortal illness; with grey hair and moustache cut like a soldier's, and grey eyes as cold as night on the Eiger. It was not in fact the case that Henri de Gailhan was dying. He had looked like that ever since Seddall had known him.

"Hallo, Henri," Seddall said.

De Gailhan and Seddall shook hands. "You may want to shake hands with this one," de Gailhan said. "Seddall; Commissaire Nogent, from the rue des Saussaies."

Nogent was one of those straightforwardly handsome men who looked as if he had been a debonair rugby player until life had poured a coat of shellac over him.

"The other two," de Gailhan said, "you need not shake hands with. We are among the *canaille* here."

Seddall had dished out some rough insults in his time, but he had never heard anything like this, and it showed on his face.

"Look at the vans," de Gailhan said.

Seddall went to the nearest vehicle. There was a shield on it, and lettering, blue and red on the white coachwork. The words on the shield were POLICE NATIONALE: CRS.

As he came back to de Gailhan and Nogent, the two men were

passing him. If there was expression in the look they gave him, it was of that indifference which shows itself as contempt for those outside the club.

"Henri," Seddall said. "What is this? We want to get our man out alive."

"Well, my friend," de Gailhan said, "it seems you've been asking favours of us in more than one quarter and the CRS got to hear about this one. They volunteered with insistence, and the Interior Ministry assigned them here."

"What's it to them, for God's sake?" Seddall said. "There's no finesse in these people, Henri, you know that as well as I do. They're not trained for this job, they're riot police."

De Gailhan gestured at Nogent, and left the answer to him.

"You're right," Nogent said. "They're not trained for this. Unfortunately this man Dujardin brutalized a man of theirs once in a fight, a senior officer. A personal fight, over a woman. The man is crippled now, out of the service. They took no legal proceedings. They look after their own, is how they put it. It is my Minister who assigned them. It is not what I would wish. We must do what we can. I have two men with me, but we are here only to give a colour of normal police activity to the affair. We cannot take part. The commandant," he meant de Gailhan, "has a few men also. Perhaps he will make his own discretion, but what he can do I don't know."

"Be there," de Gailhan said. "That's what we can do, and try to save something from this mess. These idiots will go at the house like blitzkrieg. That's how it stands, Seddall."

"I guess we'll have to do what we can here," Seddall said. "How far away is this house?"

De Gailhan looked over Seddall's shoulder and said: "Map."

The map was brought by a young giant wearing unmarked overalls, a trooper of the heavy brigade if ever Seddall had seen one.

He and Nogent and de Gailhan went to a bench against the wall, under a strong light, and bowed their heads over the map.

# 16

It was a red-brick, well-off farmer's house on three floors, with the dormer windows of a third floor breaking the line of the steeply pitched roof. The front of the house made the cross of a T and the stalk ran out behind to a narrow belt of trees that sheltered the house from the north wind.

After the trees, the agrarian plain stretched for miles to the forest that ran almost to the River Seine, though there was no suggestion of that vista left now. Only the immediate area of the house showed, ringed by the arc lights of the CRS, and ringed beyond that by the night.

The lights had been on for an hour now. Nothing else had happened. Behind the lights the CRS waited: behind the hedge at the edge of the lawn that fronted the house; behind the walls that bound the vegetable garden on one side of the house and the old stable yard on the other; under the trees at the back of the house.

Skeins of mist hung in the searing light. Images of lost souls drifting in the scudding rain, they answered the violence of the wind to a sorrowful rhythm of their own, as if they floated on the long, slow waves of an invisible sea.

Bathed in the light but swathed also in the mist, the tall house stood astounded at this confounding of nature by the intrusion of man into the darkness of the night; a large but tame and friendly creature, staring blind from its startled windows into the hostile glare that had sprung up round it, fearful of what this strangeness must portend.

There had only been the shock of the brilliant ring of light flaring suddenly upon the house, and after that the silence.

No voice called to the house from outside the ring of light. No loudspeaker had demanded the surrender of those inside the house. No human figure had shown itself.

The effect was of implacable fate arriving out of nowhere to pronounce the doom of those within. Despite herself, Toko felt the atavistic fear, and shivered.

"How are you doing?" she said to Mullen.

"Not too bad, I think," he said. "I didn't like the ride in the van much, but you've fixed me up well here."

"Well, I know how to change a dressing, at least," Toko said.

"You know a bit more than that," Mullen said. "You knew enough to rig that thing." He moved his head to indicate the needle running the intravenous drip in his arm.

"I trained for a year when I was a kid," Toko said, "and I learned a bit more when I was fighting with Frelimo in Mozambique. I know practical things like gunshot wounds."

"And you know enough not to give the patient an overdose of painkillers," Mullen said.

"Now come on," she said, and put her hand on his forehead, and then felt his pulse. "Do you really want more, or are you kidding me?"

"I'm just joshing you," Mullen said. "I'd sooner wait until the going gets rough and know we have something in reserve."

"Attaboy," Toko said. "God, this gives me the creeps."

She went back to her post. The room in which Mullen lay on the neatly made bed, and in which Toko stood now peering out through one of the cracks in the shutters, was illumined enough by the light that broke in through these gaps to have the ghostly effect of a false dawn.

"I'm glad you turned out not to be Georg Frankl," she said.

"Why?" Mullen said. "If I'd been Georg Frankl you'd have had your fifty-thousand quid out of him."

"Maybe." Toko shrugged. "I guess. I'm glad you're not him because we were going to kill him, and I've got to like you."

"You quite like me," Mullen said, "but I think you might kill me yet."

Toko looked at him.

They heard the swift movement of Dujardin on the bare boards

176

of the floor above. Mullen moved his head at the ceiling. "If he told you to shoot me, you'd shoot me," he said.

Toko looked out through the crack. "Why would he do that now?" she said.

"Maybe he's a sore loser," Mullen said. "Maybe he just likes to tidy up. Maybe he thinks there's still a chance he can escape from here, that these guys don't know who he is. That might mean it would be safer for him if I were dead."

The silence came back, broken only by the creak of the boards as Dujardin kept up his patrol of the house.

"I wonder who these guys out there are," Toko said. "They have a strange way of doing things."

"I don't know," Mullen said. "It has its psychological effect. Perhaps they're going to wait till morning, now that they've got you trapped."

"Well, lover," Toko said angrily, "none of this is part of the procedure for trying to get kidnappers and their hostages out alive, so you'd better hope they're thinking at least of getting *you* out alive."

Mullen tried to ease himself up on the bed and pain struck into his back and through his body. Toko heard the in-draw of breath and went to him.

"You hurting?" she said.

"I tried to sit myself up more," Mullen said. "I think I'll wait before I have another go."

"You just ask me," Toko said. "I'll hoist you up when you want to move."

"All right," Mullen said.

The burst of pain and its reminder of his utter helplessness were feeding his irritation. He wished the woman would make up her mind whether she was his captor or his nurse.

"Lie still for a bit now," Toko said. "Do you want some water?"

"No," Mullen said, and went quiet on her.

Mullen was in a chaotic and divided state. He could hear himself talking away, saying these things to her in a calm voice, but if they came from a calm place it was hanging in there by the skin of its teeth.

177

Fear flowed again like a running tide. Helpless from the wound in his back and weakened by it, he was weakened more deeply by the actual fact of it – for Mullen had never been shot before, and to the trauma of the wound was added this persistently recurring aftershock of panic that his whole self should be so violated.

Here, in this ghostlike room in this deserted house, he knew himself fallen apart. He felt all fragmented within and, at the same time, disintegrating into the emptiness around him. He was terrorized by the sense that he and unreality had become one: that he was no more now than a shadow, who had once been a human life; that he belonged in this dimness with this woman who would lay her kind hand to his brow one moment and might kill him the next: that the place to which his life had been travelling and where its journey was already ending was here, with that madman running about upstairs as if he could fight off an army, and with that blind, messageless cordon of light peering at him through the shutters.

So he lay, waiting for nothing, not waiting, a suspension of atoms hanging like dust in the cosmos, and tears came unbidden to his eyes.

Down in this desolation of self-pity something stirred. He sensed it with nothing more than the sense a fisherman has that a trout is sleeping in a pool. He stared at the dimness of the ceiling that was his sky, and waited.

After a while he frowned, for the first sign had come to him and it was a whisper of shame. He did not care for that. What was he supposed to do? How was he supposed to feel, in such a situation as this? He couldn't even sit upright in this bloody bed, never mind run around in small ingenious circles, devising a brilliant manoeuvre to get himself out of here.

He felt his mouth twitch at that, at "small ingenious circles". That was comic, and fatuous too, which to Mullen made it all the funnier. What was he going to do about the bookie and that frightener, Starker? Was he really going to put all he could raise on the horse at Brighton? Christ, what was he thinking about that for? He had as much chance of laying that bet as . . .

His mind stopped and his eyes went to Toko, standing by the

shuttered window, to the glimpses of light at the cracks of the shutters, and then back to the ceiling.

It seemed to him that he might execute a little scheme to make Toko grateful to him, which would at least give him some chance of not being shot by her simply because Dujardin told her to do it.

"Can you lift me up a bit?" he said.

She came to him across the ghostly room and eased him up on the pillows.

"Ah," he said, as the pain bit, but not as fiercely as it had done before.

"How's that?" she said.

"It's good," he said. "Thanks. Suppose you were trying escape, what are the ways out of this house?"

"I can't let you go, Roberto," she said, "and even if I did, you couldn't move anywhere. What are you talking about?"

"I'm talking about you," he said. "Not me."

"Huh," she said, a sound with a bit of laugh in it, but not a very successful bit of laugh. "I'm not going out of here. What do you think they've got behind those lights? Bows and arrows? I'll bet you there's about two hundred thousand rounds of nine-millimetre out there, with plenty of weapons to fire them and men to fire the weapons. I'd guess they've got enough there to shoot the house down."

"Then why don't they start doing it?" he said.

"I don't know," she said. "I sure to God don't know. Maybe they're waiting for our nerve to crack. Maybe they're waiting for daylight. I don't know why they haven't *said* anything. I don't know why they haven't asked us to hand you over, promised we won't be harmed, all that, gone into the usual dialogue. I mean, this is *odd,* you know?"

"Yes, it's odd," he said. "So tell me, what would your escape route be if there were no lights outside? If it was dark?"

"Just me on my own," Toko said, "slipping out of here?" He heard in her voice what a beautiful idea this was to her. In her own great want to live she had forgotten Dujardin for a moment. He knew the link between her and Dujardin was strong, but he didn't know how deep it was. He let himself believe, for a moment, that he had begun to separate her from the Frenchman and went on with his little game.

"Yes," he said. "Just you."

They heard the sound of Dujardin scuttling about above them like a huge rat, and Toko lifted her head to the house above. Mullen abated himself, unbreathing, till she spoke.

She spoke, still looking towards the sounds Dujardin made, following them. "There's a skylight in the roof of this part of the house," she said, "at the back. I'd try for that. Out of the skylight, down onto the roof over the kitchen – it stretches out at the back, you know, and there's a tree I think I could jump into, a big oak that reaches out to the kitchen chimney on the end there."

"The gable end," Mullen said.

"Right," Toko said. "There's a whole bunch of trees there. I'd work past them as fast as I could – maybe stay up there, go from tree to tree. Oh, I looked for my way out as soon as I was here, once we'd got you fixed up."

"And then?" Mullen said.

"Then I'd run out," she said. "You've never seen me run, but once I was away they'd never catch me. I can run all day, man. And I know how to hide. Out there? Out there I could make myself invisible."

Then she was silent. She pulled gently at the top of the sheet and smoothed it, and went back to her window.

"What I think," Mullen said, "is that they're not waiting for daylight. I think what they'll do, either because they've planned it already or because they'll think of it, is put the lights out suddenly and attack slam-bang as soon as they've done it, because they'll hope you're blinded for the first few moments after the lights go out."

"Well, so I will be," Toko said.

"If you're looking into the light when it goes out, then yes, you'll be blinded," Mullen said. "And you probably will be looking into the light. So as a defender of this house you'll have had it. These people won't have been looking into the light and they'll come in with the infra-red, seeing like cats in the dark. You won't see a thing. You'll be dead red meat before your safety's off."

"My safety's off now," Toko said, "but you're right. Did you have to say 'red'? You could leave a girl something."

"I am leaving a girl something," Mullen said. "You know your way round this house by now, and you can get to your skylight without having to see too well, and by the time you get there you'll have your sight back. So it goes like this. Lights out and you run at once for that door, up the stairs, one flight, two flights, hand on the rail. Out the skylight and into the night and go bush. If I wasn't so tired I'd do it myself just for the buzz."

"You would, huh?" Toko said, but she was thinking about it all right, he could feel it across the room.

All of a sudden she ran to the doorway and stood with one hand on the jamb, looking at the foot of the staircase in the hall.

"Yeah," she said, and went back to her lookout at the window.

"So what's in it for you?" she said. "You're not doing this for the sake of my pretty face."

"That is strange but true," Mullen said. "One, if this room's not defended it ups my chance of not being shot to pieces. Two, it halves the defence force and shortens the battle, which also improves my chances. But the main thing is the hope that you'll be so grateful that you won't bump me off even if lover-boy up there tells you to kill the poor unfortunate hostage."

"I don't know why . . ." Toko began.

"It happens all the time," Mullen said. "I don't suppose the bloody kidnappers know why they do it. Even when they have a cause I don't think it's the cause they do it for. It's something to do with bloodlust and gunfire, and going down to death yourself. The current theory would probably be about bonding between killer and killed, and you could fill a whole spectrum with garbage from that to making a sacrifice to propitiate the gods, or sending a slave before you into the afterlife to have the beds aired when you arrive, but who cares? All I know is that kidnappers whack hostages and I have so many expectations of being whacked one way or the other, I'll look at anything that changes the odds. I'll take that water now, please."

He was exhausted, but at least he'd done something for Roberto Mullen instead of just moping and bewailing his lot – except that moping and bewailing were not big enough words to describe the

181

state he'd been in back there. Even as he repeated the words, he felt himself shy away from the terror of where he had been back there. That wasn't gone. That was waiting for him. Keep away from that, Roberto old son, he told himself.

He took the glass of water from Toko, who hadn't said anything since his little speech about kidnappers sending their hostages before them. He swallowed, two or three gulps, and gave back the glass.

"Do you want to go down," he said, "in Dujardin's last stand? He'll expect it of you. It's the state he's in. Do you want to die young for nothing?"

She filled the glass again and laid it on the table she'd put beside the bed. He felt like a figure in a painting. Man on bed, empty room, light ultra-dim and spooky, black female beside bed. What's it about?

"I've seen you and Dujardin," he said. "It's not Romeo and Juliet with you two. It's something strong, but it's not that. You don't need to go down into the tomb together. He'd leave you. Look at it that you're leaving him, that's all. And it's not deserting him. He's not thinking of fighting his way out of here. He's going to go down fighting, that's all it is with him."

"That's not what you said earlier," Toko said.

"What did I say earlier?"

"You said maybe he thought there was a way out of here yet. That he'd want you killed because you can identify him," Toko said, "in case these people don't already know who he is."

Get out of this argument fast, Mullen thought. "I wish to God I knew who these people out there are," he said. "They're not behaving like cops and they're not behaving like trained counter-terrorist army either: saying nothing, doing nothing, being invisible."

She went quickly to the window again, as if she'd remembered her duty, but he knew he had awakened fear, or memory, in her.

He watched her and waited. He watched her peer out into the light and then glance at the doorway, a quick and furtive glance, the bars of light flickering on her face and body when she moved, as if she was on the screen in an old silent film.

It was working on her, all right. Mullen decided he'd said

enough, that he should quit while he was ahead. It might turn out to be of no advantage to him at all, even if she did take it on the lam – and always supposing they did put the goddamn lights out and pour in their attack according to his game plan.

From her station by the window Toko spoke at last. "I think it's the CRS. You know about the CRS?"

"Jesus Christ on a bicycle," Mullen said. "Yes, I know about the CRS. If there's anybody I don't want out there, it's that mob."

"Yeah," Toko said. "I know how you feel." She drifted towards him as if she had given up her function in the defence of this insufficient fortress. "The CRS have got it in for Dujardin. He wrecked one of their men. They won't want him alive. How do these things work? Will there be no one but CRS out there? Does it make a difference?"

"Probably not," Mullen said. "They won't want any survivors to tell the tale. It begins to look, Toko, that whatever happens, your Roberto is going to be screwed. I hope to God there are some responsible cops or some sane types out there."

He was damned if he was going to slide back to the desolation he had been in before, all the same. "What are you going to do?" he said to her.

Toko stood there, adrift in the middle of the room. But she'd made her mind up. "I'm going to leave you here. I'm going to get the fuck out as soon as the action starts. If I can."

Mullen smiled to himself.

"Is that a smile?" Toko said, coming closer. "Why are you smiling?"

"You're going to leave me here," Mullen said. "You're not leaving Dujardin."

"It's true in a way," Toko said. "I'll leave Dujardin later. If I get out of this, and he gets killed, I'll do my leaving later. It will be bad times then for me, but that will be the time: later. I can't do it now."

She came right up to the bed. "I'd like to take you with me. I'd like to make you safe, too, but there's no way to do that now."

"Don't get maudlin," Mullen said. "I still think you might shoot me if the man wants it."

Toko took his hand. "If you say so," she said. "What's up with you all of a sudden. Why do you sound so chirpy?"

Mullen said: "They say gamblers like losing as much as winning. Maybe I know my stake's down and I'm riding the bet. Hell, the Interior Ministry couldn't let the CRS loose on this without having a responsible fellow from the police or the army there too. I have to think like that, don't I, when the stakes are so high?"

They heard Dujardin's feet move along the passage overhead and come running down the stairs. He loomed like a giant in the doorway.

"Get to the window," he said to Toko, his voice an enraged whisper, a muted roar of fury.

"Don't be so excited," Toko said, but doing what he ordered. "We're all going to get shot to fuck anyway."

"How's he?" Dujardin said. "Is he giving you trouble?"

"I like that," Mullen said. "Why should I give her trouble? This is the nicest place I've ever been in."

Dujardin came a step into the room. "Shut your mouth," he said.

"*Mort pour la France,*" Mullen said, though he was feeling that fatigue again, and the fear of the fear that went with it.

"What does that mean?" Dujardin said.

"Forget it," Mullen said.

Dujardin came to the bedside in a movement so swift you would think he had leapt across the space. He was huge in the dimness and to Mullen seemed enlarged by energy suppressed in him that he wanted to use.

Mullen thought: this is it, he can't strike at those invisible enemies out there, so he'll destroy me. The forces compressed and frustrated in the Frenchman struck at Mullen like an actual blow; but that was all. Dujardin stood over him, breathing fast, as if he had run a race, one fist clenched and the other gripping the sub-machine-gun slung on his shoulder. Then he turned to Toko at the window.

"He has a quick lip, this one," he said to her. "Watch him. Don't let him talk you into anything."

"Into what, for God's sake?" Toko said. "What else can happen now except the last firefight. The last one, Dujardin."

"Yes," he said. "I know." He went closer to her but not close enough to touch her. "God, to get out of here!" he whispered. "God, to get that swine Arkley! Just that would do me."

"Forget it," Toko said. She turned from the window and on her face, criss-crossed by the bars of light through the shutter, Mullen wondered if he saw contempt. "Die like a man, Dujardin," she said. "That's all that's left for you to do."

Dujardin's back and shoulders and the hold of his head gave him the look of a wild creature turned suddenly clumsy and lumbering by being caught in a net. Of the three of them in that room, each of them alone in the imminence of death, he became more alone than any.

"Like a man?" he said. "Like a rat in a trap."

"And me?" Toko said.

"And you," Dujardin said. "Yes, you." He nodded his head at this, over and over. "You," he said. "Well then. Good luck," he said, and went from the room, and his feet ran upstairs into the emptiness there.

From the top of the stairs his voice burst through the silence. "M'pofu," he yelled. "Shoot him before the end. Kill him."

Then they heard him resume his endless patrol from end to end, back and forth, along the house.

Toko came to the bed and laid a hand on Mullen's cheek. He knew she felt driven to do it, to do what Dujardin wanted her to do, that part of her was given to that, and part of her opposing it.

Mullen called on the last of his resilience. "Gosh, Toko," he said. "What's a nice girl like you doing in a job like this?"

Her hand stayed on his face and she shook her head at him. "Roberto," she said. "Roberto, what a . . ."

The lights went out.

# 17

With her hand still on Mullen's cheek, Toko took one glance at the windows to be sure, and then was out of the room and running upwards with no more thoughts in her mind, nothing but the instinct to escape.

As she went, she heard the clatter of automatic fire from all around, a tremendous noise that broke open the night and shook her to the heart and lifted her on and up to the top of the house. She had a glimpse of Dujardin as she went, illumined by the flash of his own gunfire, just one moment of him caught through a door crouched at a window with the shutter thrown back, and beyond him streaks of fire and muzzle flash coming from everywhere, and then she was on the top landing at the skylight. She threw it back and lifted herself through on her arms, letting the Heckler and Koch drop behind her as she went, no more than an encumbrance for her now, where she was going.

It was black night out there on the roof, and she slid down towards the slates of the kitchen block two floors below; towards, but with luck – with all the luck she had ever needed – not down into the Armageddon that was flailing at the house, and did seem manic enough to keep on and on until the building crumbled to the ground.

She reached the guttering and hardly slowed, slipping down on her belly and hanging to the edge for only the split second that would check the speed of her descent, and she let herself go into the dark through the hail of fire crashing into the upper wall and then was on the kitchen roof running and sliding on all fours for the chimney at the far end.

She reached it shuddering, hearing slates of the roof she had passed explode behind her. Not knowing whether it was random fire or whether it had been aimed at her, she took no refuge in the illusory shelter of the heavy stone chimney stack, but went up onto it. Like a diver flying from a rock, she threw herself at the faint mass of the tree that was out there, its branches reaching for the house.

She took a hard blow on the face and another on the thigh and was in among leaves and twigs, her hands desperate for anything to hold to and falling now – the gamble failed – when her arm went round a solid branch and her foot broke through another, taking some of her weight before it broke, so that her arm got its purchase and she was coiling up onto it, moving into the tree. From this tree to the next, and then the next, that had been her wild plan, but it had become too wild for her now, hopeless in the dark even if it could be done by day.

There was a break in the intensity of the firing now, as magazines were emptied and replaced, emptied and replaced. She could sense it in them that they would move in on the house now: it was the inevitable impulse after venting such a wild discharge, feeling the guns grow hot in their hands, roused by the sound and smell and fireworks of that fury of destruction they had unleashed.

And it came: the incredible quiet which still left what had gone before it ringing in her ears. Quiet, and then shouts, orders issued, the sounds of men moving in the dark, followed by voices below coming towards her as they moved in for the kill.

She felt for the knife in her boot: it was there. She reassured herself that the pistol, the Auto-Mag, was in the pistol-pocket of her overalls. She lay quivering in the tree like a panther waiting for the hunters to pass.

She looked up through the twigs and branches and half-shed foliage of the oak tree and saw that the moon was out, only a sliver of a moon, which was just as well, for the mist that had hung about the house was thinning away: no cloak to hide her now.

They stopped under her tree, three or four of them. She did not look to see, for eyes shine in the dark, but lay still with her face on her arm and listened.

"*Il n'y a personne qui vive là maintenant, dans cette maison,*" one of them said, low but clear.

"*Peut-être*," said a cautious one.

"*Personne!*" the first man said.

"*Et l'otage?*" said another.

"*Bouf,*" was all the answer he got.

"*Allons,*" said the first one, still softly, but merrily. "*Au piste!*"

There were metallic sounds: weapons being checked. Then they moved on up the side of the kitchen. Another group called quietly to them and moved up the far side.

It was time. There could be lights again at any moment.

Toko listened and listened, peering down now through the tree to see her way, to guess her way, for the waning moon and the stars showed her little.

She felt her way down with her feet and found a place for one of them and came off the branch. Another branch took the other foot and she was in the quoin of the tree. She had a sense of the drop, about twelve feet. She slung herself down held by two hands, then by one, and let herself go.

The ground was soft and she met it with a thud and a squelch as she landed safe, only to slip and fall her length. She lay with her hand on the pistol, her ears as alert as any insect's antennae.

All she heard were voices from the perimeter far to her right and from the far side of the farmhouse, from the front, as if it was all over there.

She came up and went on through the copse of trees, wondering how many men they had left on the perimeter, whether there were dogs, what gauntlet she had yet to run.

The copse ended at a stone wall, breast-high. Nothing on the other side of the wall that she could make out: no bulk, still or moving, in the dark, nothing to hear. Then she heard a creak to her right and saw the bulk of a vehicle, and supposed a man climbing in or out of it. Logic made her look left, and there was another, and on top of it, sure enough, the shape of some equipment that must be those scarifying lights. No troops here at the end of the copse, since they would have been wasted on the trees.

Straight ahead, she said to herself. She went over the wall and found herself on stubble. Instead of crawling or running over it in a crouch, she simply walked forward, northward into the darkness of the plain.

No one called out, no guns fired. Nothing happened.

She walked on and on across the field, a big field, and over the ditch and across the narrow road that bordered it, and onto the next field. It was the same as the last, a flat field of stubble.

She bent down and put her hands on her knees and let her breathing come back to her, and then she set off running, not fast, a gentle lope so that if she fell her fall would not be heard, and with which she could run all night.


The Forlorn Hope – the four paras of the First Spahis led by Commandant Henri de Gailhan, with H. Seddall, colonel of Lancers, assigned to bring up the rear as not being a member of the familiar team and in any case not properly equipped with body armour, stun grenades, and the rest of the appropriate personal arsenal, never mind top-line physique and reflexes – went into the wood the instant the general assault started.

When the CRS chief was making his dispositions, five and sometimes six men and a heavy machine-gun to each van with its rack of lights on top, he had said: "There will be no van at the end of the wood, since the effect of the lights would be wasted. Therefore . . ."

"I'll take the wood," de Gailhan said.

The CRS man crossed eyes with him. He saw nothing there but death: nothing sinister or duplicitous. Nothing to make him doubt, except that the wood was what de Gailhan had chosen.

"Very well," he said. "The Spahis will take the wood. And you, Gilbert, will be behind them as a reserve."

On their advance, now, through the copse, the racket of the machine-guns and the smaller arms was accompanied by the occasional whack of bullets into the trees about them as the firing went wild. Shards of wood and once a severed branch fell about them, splinters and ricochets whined in their ears.

A little dicey, Seddall thought; with luck it will make young Gilbert take his instruction to act as reserve more literally than was intended. The event was so like real warfare that it seemed odd not to be wearing the gear. Following on after these fellows in his old leather coat, with nothing more than a pistol in his hand, gave him the sense of being an irregular, an obsolete military figure like a partisan.

They came to the end of the wood and the team of Spahis spread a little, dropping to one knee like runners poised for the gun at the start of a race. Not that they'd have heard it. He took the same stance, putting himself behind de Gailhan. The firing seemed to have intensified. This close to the house the impact of the immense discharge of bullets on the brickwork could either be felt or heard, Harry was not sure which, so chaotic was the effect of the noise.

Hellish dark, he thought, being unequipped with night glasses. The mist had cleared in the last hour or so, and he looked up at the sickle moon. For a moment he had the illusion that an animal had sailed through the air into the tree beside him, but as he looked down and blinked, de Gailhan and the team sprang forward and he went with them.

De Gailhan had it sussed. He threw himself straight in at the kitchen door which had been shot to nothing, and the rest followed.

"Done it," Seddall thought. Then the man before him went down.

Seddall fell over him, going his length in the mud. The air above him filled with the hail of fire and the chips of brickwork which exploded off the wall a few feet away from him, bullets and debris thudding into the ground about him. He got the wounded man under the armpits and dragged him through the space where the door had been, and was promptly pulled out of the line of fire and thrown into a corner while the Spahis brought in their comrade.

They laid him on the floor. As Seddall got to his feet he heard the injured one gasp and say: "Go, go. I'm all right."

De Gailhan bent over him and a torch found the blood on the man's leg. A knife slashed open the trouser leg, revealing the wound: a hole on one side of the thigh and a messy pit on the other where it had passed through.

The commandant lifted a hand and a treated dressing was put into it. He put it to the exit wound and another went on the entry.

At that moment the fusillade fell away and stopped.

"You're wasting time," the wounded man said quietly into the sudden, resounding, silence. "Give me my pistol in case you flush them out this way, then go!"

De Gailhan said: "We've been five seconds. Take care." He stood up and, in his turn, said: "Go!"

There were no more orders. The survivors of the team went in their own orchestrated pattern through the house to the front, forming and reforming. Seddall held back, not being party to what was second nature to them. From the front hall they went in pairs to rooms that opened off it.

Seddall, standing in the hall and staring up the staircase into the dark, heard distinctly across the still unnatural silence a muffled voice from the room not yet entered by the Spahis.

"Christ," it said.

The next second, shots crashed into the front door of the house and he leapt towards the voice.

Again the silence. He edged into the room. "Mullen?" he said. "Roberto Mullen?"

"Here," the muffled voice said. "Over here, under the fucking mattress!"

"De Gailhan," Seddall shouted. "In here! *Le voici! Vite! Vite!*"

"*J'arrive,*" de Gailhan roared.

At the moment Seddall found the mattress with Mullen underneath it, there was a stampede of boots in the hall as the CRS came in at the front, followed by cries and shots as they ran into de Gailhan and his men crossing the hall.

Some genius found a light switch and the shooting abruptly stopped.

The *éclaircissement* taking place in the hall illuminated, also, the situation of Roberto Mullen. He had got himself off the bed and brought the mattress down on top of him.

Not a bad effort, Harry thought, taking in the state of the room, its walls holed and disintegrating, the window shutters blown away and the floor covered with debris of wood, plaster from the ceiling and chunks of brick mysteriously hurled into the room by the violence of the gunfire.

Throughout this appalling onslaught Mullen had lain there under the mattress, waiting to be torn apart when fate caused this or that machine-gunner to traverse his weapon a fraction of an inch this way or that.

Alive he obviously was, but God knew what state he would be in.

De Gailhan was in the room now. He and Seddall bent to the white face which was all that showed itself from under the improvised shelter Mullen had made for himself.

"Ambulance outside. Medic's on his way," de Gailhan said in English. "How many of them were there, your kidnappers?"

"Only one left," Mullen said. His voice was very dry and small. "He's up there, upstairs."

De Gailhan made a signal to the soldier behind him and the man went off to impart this news to the others.

"How d'you feel?" Seddall asked.

"Oh, boy," Mullen said, and cracked a grin. "Mafeking has been relieved."

The boots of the relieving force thumped on the floors overhead as they sought their prey. But even as Seddall and de Gailhan lifted the tattered mattress from him, Mullen lifted a freed arm to point upwards.

They lifted their eyes and saw the blood drip slowly from the exposed boards where the ceiling had been shot away, then fall onto a pile of rubble and plaster below.

From the CRS men in that room above came a mixed chorus of triumph and baffled rage: Dujardin's requiem.


Some miles north of the house, the moon looked down from a racing sky on a small and alien figure shivering in the wind. The sky, clear now of all except the flying clouds, was full of stars.

She stood leaning against the wall in the lee of a barn and thought. She had been running steady and the sweat was chilling on her, but she paid no attention to that.

Thought was the wrong word for what she was doing. She was listening to herself, to a voice inside her. She looked at the sky. The stars were a pale imitation of African stars. She remembered herself and where she came from, and she remembered Dujardin.

She pushed off from the wall of the barn, and ran back the way she had come.


"So far, so good," the chairman of the meeting said gloomily. The chairman was Harry Seddall and the chair he sat in was at the head of the dining-room table in Olivia's house near Compiègne. He was also, in fact, the meeting, since the others had gone for a walk in the forest. He was using the house either as a communications centre or a command post: the definition would be decided by the extent to which he found himself to be in control of events.

The house was a good hundred and sixty kilometres from Chartres. Those of them who had been at the taking of the farmhouse at St Luc had been carried here the next morning – the morning of this day which was now upon its evening – by French army helicopters.

Seddall was, in fact, slightly bewildered by the cooperation he was receiving from the French. Mullen had been whisked away to a French military hospital, where a room had been provided for Joanna Harvey so that she could attend on her beloved. This was good behaviour, and did not surprise him. What did surprise him was the equability with which the French civil and military bureaucracies were lending themselves to the mounting of the illegal expedition that he and de Gailhan had planned to lead into Africa.

Now, however, only de Gailhan was going to lead it.

Seddall had come up against too many invisible obstacles. Sorrel's beloved SAS bloke and half a dozen of his friends at Hereford had, all within the space of twenty-four hours, been granted leave and had it cancelled. No amount of finagling on the old-boy telephone network had brought support for an irregular operation.

Seddall had, at last, called Duncanson.

"The fix is in," Duncanson said. "You're a good fixer, but you've met your match. And you know who your match is at that game."

There was a pause, then: "Be careful," Duncanson said.

"Be careful," Seddall repeated. "What is there to be careful about?"

"You're getting close," Duncanson said. "That's all it can mean. And it means you're getting close to the top."

"There's a specific thing you're not saying," Seddall said. "Say it."

He held the phone for so long without getting a response that he began to think Duncanson might have walked quietly away and gone to lunch.

"Don't go to Africa," Duncanson said. "If you go to Africa on this raid, they'll have you."

"It's not a raid," Seddall said.

"Be your age," Duncanson said. "Of course it's a raid. It might never get into the papers, but you'd be taking a risk the Government would never sanction if it knew beforehand. The thing could blow up in their faces. And yes, I know we are used to operating on the basis of not telling the Government how we do what they want done, but the times are changing, Seddall. Those days are going, perhaps gone. And yes, it's ironic that the man who's putting the boot in on that account is the game-player, the fixer we've just referred to, since he's done more dirty work with a blind eye to the telescope than any of us. If you want to beat him, though, don't go to Africa. The French can do it. It's their sphere of influence, as one used to say, that part of Africa. Let the French do it. They don't need you."

For a while after that, Seddall sulked.

Olivia found him on the terrace, staring moodily at the carp in the pond. "You look as if you were going to jump in and end it all," she said. "What's wrong with you?"

She was vibrant. She stood over him poised springily on those long legs, her body exuberant with exercise, her beautiful face glowing and her brown eyes strong with life. If ever there was a woman whose very existence was a reproach to self-indulgent morosity, it was Olivia.

He stood up and she walked into him. "Nothing's wrong," he said.

"You want to go with de Gailhan," she said.

"I wanted to play at Beau Geste," he said. "That's all it was."

"You've done that kind of thing," she said, "and Henri will do this one as well as you. Also, I like you being here for this, using my house for it. I like to see these outward signs on you of the invisible process going on inside. You're very sinister, like a spider at the centre of his web."

"I'm nothing of the sort," he said. "I'm a straightforward Englishman."

"There is no such creature," she said, "And certainly not you."

"You're right in one way," he said. "The centre of the web is not in Africa, and the invisible process inside me is beginning to say that it's in France, not England. So this is where I should be. But I want you to know, light of my life, that the real reason I'm not going with de Gailhan is that I'm frightened. Duncanson tells me that They – you know who I mean by They – are just waiting for me to go, so that they can pull the rug out."

"I don't know what pulling out rugs has to do with it," Olivia said. "But I'm glad you're too frightened to walk into a trap. Perhaps you are growing up at last."

She ran her hand slowly down his face.

"Let's go and feed Henri," she said, "before he sets off for Fort Zinderneuf."

# 18

In the centre of the Sahel, about halfway down what was once French Equatorial Africa and some way north of where the Sudan–Chad border meets the northern frontier of the Central African Republic, the caravan that had crossed the desert from the Red Sea took its ease.

To men and animals, after that journey, the gorge of al Hala was as a paradise of nature: miraculously, this year the rains had come. There had been rain from al Hala to the Ennedi mountains. Instead of a river bed there was a river; the trees lived and the grazing land to the west was green.

The place was well chosen. It was only a little way into Chad, a country where war was either recurrent or continuous, but al Hala, far out on the eastern margin, had no military value in fighting that was endemically between north and south.

No one came here except the herders, but when they knew the strength of the caravan they kept their goats and cattle, and themselves, well away. This was a caravan that a handful of men could have managed, yet here were more than a score, armed to the teeth with modern weapons for all the world as if they were soldiers themselves.

They were not soldiers, but they served under a hard discipline. Once on the journey a man had tried to open one of the cases to see what they carried; and once here, in the gorge, where the cases had been stacked carefully on a shelf of rock, two men had tried it.

All three had been shot out of hand by their chief.

On the first day after their arrival they had rested, and for the next two days they had been put to work, patrolling the flat sand-sheet east of the camp which had been the last stage of their desert cross-ing, in contrast to which the lushness of the gorge had opened to them like a paradise. They had removed any object that was bigger than a pebble: stones, the mummified carcase of a camel, the skeletons of a few smaller animals, wild and domestic; an old rifle stock, a small patch of scrub and a few isolated bushes. When that was done they set out, on each side of the ground they had cleared, oil flares in metal pots that wanted only to be lit to mark out the strip at night. Now they simply waited, trapping hare and hunting gazelle and killing lice for want of anything better to do.

Another day had passed. They sat round their fires and boasted of fights they had fought, men they had killed and women they had bedded.

At last the camp settled down to sleep. The sentinels at their posts sat under the blazing stars and soon the only sound in the night was the breathing of men and camels. To them, it was just another night.

But for Abd el Sudi, their leader, in his chosen place beside the stacked boxes that had been taken from the crates on the beach over a thousand miles away, it was not just another night. It was more than one night too many.

He sat awake while his two lieutenants slept nearby, wondering what the man Markish thought he was doing, leaving him stuck out here for days on end. The leader was increasingly aware that though al Hala was a place of no importance and therefore, on the basis of chance, safe enough for a short while, nevertheless an extended stay here built up the risk that a Chad army patrol might come this way.

He was a lean man, a man near the end of his fifties, who had carried salt across this land until both the desert and its markets began to fail. He had then turned to making a living for himself and his followers in ways that were, for him, both more rewarding and more fulfilling. He was a man of his hands, but he had a good business mind as well, and a rising account in a Cairo bank.

Markish had told him what was in those boxes. Though he was a man who feared nothing, he had begun to find this business of sitting watch on them testing to the nerves. It was hard to believe, waiting here in the presence of so much immanent evil, that it would not hatch out and escape of itself. He wanted two things: he wanted to be away from here and he wanted the balance of his fee.

He came to his feet and picked up his automatic rifle, touching one of his lieutenants on the shoulder. "Watch till I return," he said, when the man woke. "I am going out to the airstrip."

He climbed lithely out of the gorge, moving easily from rock to rock like a man half his age. Near the top he called out to the man posted there, to warn him of his coming. He passed him and strode out across the thin layer of sand, feeling the hardness beneath his feet.

He had begun to have the thought that Markish would not come, that he would be left here, the possessor of that pile of innocent-looking boxes with the lead cylinders inside them which held enough disease to wipe out he knew not how many tribes; left here to confront the question of what was to be done with them.

How could a man answer such a question? How could he walk away from it? What must he do? Take it to a place where no human being had ever been? Where was there such a place? Was he to wander Africa while his camels died and his men slipped away one by one, until only he was left, doomed to be the perpetual guardian of this evil?

"I am not a messenger of God!" he shouted to the Pleiades above his head. "I am only my father's son. I am not fit for this."

Even as the shout died, he heard the aircraft.

He was released into action as if he had been reborn.

He fired three short bursts from his automatic rifle over the gorge while running for the flare pots on the farther side of the strip. He lit one, then another, and another. Soon he saw flares light up on the other side of the strip, followed by the flares on this side, starting at the far end. Then a man came and took his place.

The plane was circling now, but with no lights on. He glimpsed it as it passed, a shape against the stars.

Finally it swung away, and he knew it was preparing for the landing run. All the flares were lit, and he grabbed one of his men and told him to pass the word to clear the airstrip. "Every man to that side, beyond the flares," he said, pointing to the gorge.

He made his way there slowly, feeling the release in him, feeling it even in his walk, in his bones and sinews. It was as if a hand that had been inside his breast, clutching at his heart, had loosed its hold.

198

He passed through the line of flares as the others ran off the strip to stand behind him. He quelled their excited chatter with a wave of the arm, and waited.

The sound of the plane had gone altogether, and for a few moments he almost doubted, but then he heard it again on the run-in. As it approached the airstrip, its landing lights flashed on, and at that moment it was to him as if he had achieved a triumph.

The plane touched ground as light as a feather and was down, running towards them, running past them with sand flying up from its wheels, then slowing and coming at last to a stop.

Its lights went out, and the first of the flares had burnt out too. In twos and threes the rest of the flares died. The plane stood there, no more than a shape in the dark, its engines silent. Nothing happened for so long that at last he went towards it, thinking belatedly that this was perhaps the courteous thing to do, instead of waiting with dignity for the fliers to come to him. He did not know what was the custom among airmen.

When he and his men reached the plane, lights came on, a door opened and a ladder came down. Three men emerged, clear in the light of moon and stars.

He heard the French accent in the Arabic of the man who spoke. "Greetings," the Frenchman said. "In the name of Allah, the Merciful, the Compassionate."

Before there was a chance to reply in kind, the Frenchman went on: "Listen to me. Believe what I say. Any man of you who makes a bad move will be dead. There are guns behind you which fire three times faster than those you have."

It was unbelievable, but he believed it. In that instant he knew it was too much to hope that none of his men would make a rash move.

There was a bark of automatic fire behind him to his right and a man fell and lay there with blood on his chest. One of the two men with the Frenchman went at once to tend him.

El Sudi called out: "Do not die for nothing. These traitors have tricked us. We will do what they require of us."

The Frenchman said: "I'm sorry that this man is hurt, since all we wish is for you to take your camels and go where you will. We shall ask you for your weapons, but if you want to go a day's journey away and then return, you will find them here."

The leader said: "Where is Ben Markish?"

"Markish was killed," the Frenchman said, "and not by us."

"Ah," the leader said. "So that is what has happened."

He turned round in the most natural manner in the world, as if there were no danger in doing so, and saw the line of men standing there armed with sub-machine-guns. "Well," he said. "We shall not give you our rifles, but since you wish it, we shall lend you our ammunition for a day and a night."

The Frenchman came closer. The two men saw that they were much alike, except that the Arab had faith and the Frenchman had none.

"We do not know each other," the Frenchman said. "But if you will agree to an armed truce, no fighting for a night and a day, then it does not seem to me that I shall need either your ammunition or your weapons. You have been idling here some time, have you not? Perhaps it would be a pleasure to you to take a day's journey to the east, to remind your camels, before they grow fat and slothful, that their life is in the desert."

One of the others who had come from the plane, a smaller man, said in French: "But this is ridiculous. To risk so much on trust."

"Not on trust," the Arab said to him. "On honour."

He had sensed the temper of his men and knew that they were pleased with the Frenchman's solution, not only because it left them their weapons – which it would be a disgrace to surrender – but because he had both invoked the principle of honour, which recognized that though they were mercenary scoundrels they were also men of family, and shown himself nimble-witted in making his proposal for a truce.

"My name is Abd el Sudi," he said. "I accept the truce."

"I know that name," the Frenchman said after a moment. "It is a famous name."

"Not on me," the Arab said. "But it has been famous."

"Mine also," the Frenchman said. "My name is de Gailhan."

El Sudi bowed. "I have indeed heard it," he lied politely. Then, with no more than sufficient irony: "My camp is yours," he said. "Come."

While still it was dark, Abd el Sudi and his camel train and his men left the gorge of al Hala and struck into the desert under the stars.


"What now? Do we load up?" asked Percier.

"No, Sergeant, we don't," Captain Giron said. "We wait for sunrise. I don't know what the devil is in those boxes, but Major de Gailhan regards them with enormous respect and says we will not move them up that rockery until we can see what we're doing. So: I want two men at the aircraft; two patrolling round and on the airstrip – and by patrolling I mean moving all the time, you understand; and two more on the far side of the gorge, in place, watching and listening. The rest will remain here."

"Do you expect trouble?" the sergeant said.

"I expect nothing," the captain said, "and therefore I expect anything. You know the score. It is forbidden to open fire. Incoming elements of whatever kind, whether they are two nomads and a camel or a whole tank corps, are to be reported to me or the major at once. I shall remain here beside these mysterious terrors," he jerked his head at the boxes stacked on their stone platform, "till morning."

The sergeant looked at them. "I wonder what is in them," he said.

"Don't wonder," the captain said. "Simply know that the major said if we drop one it will be as the end of the world."

In these unsettling terms the invaders, in and around the encampment that had belonged to el Sudi, prepared to pass the remainder of the night. They kept one fire going and let the rest subside into embers.

"You are at home in the desert," de Gailhan said to Georg Frankl.

"I like three things," Frankl said. "The desert, a metropolis, and a beach in the sun."

"You are fortunate," de Gailhan said. "I like only the desert, and I have little chance to see it."

"You could leave the service," Frankl said, "and make your life in the desert."

"I am not a romantic," de Gailhan said. "I do not wish to become an imitation Arab. What I like is army service in the desert. I was born fifty years too late."

"Major," Anna said. "Do you not think that if you had been born fifty years earlier, you would still have been born fifty years too late?"

"Such percipience!" de Gailhan said. "Yes, it is true."

"That is why you trust el Sudi and his men to keep their word," Frankl said. "It is all you have left, your idea of honour."

"I noticed," de Gailhan said, "that you set little store by it, up there."

"Ask the scientist how much store he sets by it," Frankl said.

"Well, Bernoux?" de Gailhan said.

"If you mean do I trust the Arabs to keep their word," Bernoux said, "yes, I do. What I do not trust is those boxes. I want to look at those boxes now. I do not want to wait till morning."

Bernoux was a slight man with a toothbrush moustache and a clear handsome face. He had a self-confidence that belonged to himself as well as to his expertise. It appeared to make no difference to him whether he was in his laboratory or part of an illegal incursion into the territory of a warlike state.

"No," de Gailhan said. "What if they were open and there was a surprise attack? In daylight we can see for miles and be pre-warned. I can't take the risk, Bernoux."

"Bah," Bernoux said. "If we are attacked, you will fight off the attackers. That is your job."

"My dear Bernoux," de Gailhan said, "if we are attacked, we shall very likely be overwhelmed. This is a country which, when it is not at war, may be at war again at any moment, and its military are more likely to move in companies than squads the size of ours. What is more, I am ordered not to engage with any troops of the territory."

Bernoux came out with a sound like an impatient growl, but he produced cigarettes and offered one to de Gailhan. "If we are afraid of being attacked," he said, "why are we allowed this bonfire to warm ourselves?"

"Obviously," Anna said, "because the people who live over there," and she waved westward, "have grown used to el Sudi's camp being here, and Major de Gailhan does not want to signal to them that anything has changed."

"You know this country?" de Gailhan asked her.

"No," Anna said, "but there are books about Africa in Olivia's house. I read a little while we were waiting there."

"Of course," de Gailhan said. "You and Frankl knew of this rendezvous before I did."

People like us, Frankl thought, are all the same. De Gailhan does not have it in his conscious mind yet, but he will soon be suspicious of us because of that little fact.

Silence descended on them. They settled into various postures, more or less easeful, to pass the time of waiting. Frankl lay on his side with his head pillowed on his arm and gazed past de Gailhan down the gorge. De Gailhan sat upright, his back straight and his head alert, as if he were the very eyes and ears of the night.

The cars, when they came, advanced slowly up the gorge. Only the lead vehicle had its lights on. When they had climbed to the level patch of ground that held the encampment, about a hundred metres away, the first car continued but the others – how many: two or three? – could be heard moving off to either flank, and then all mechanical sound diminished, as if the vehicles had, like the lead car, stopped with their engines ticking over. The lights on the lead car went out. Where it had stopped, on the farthest edge of the firelight, they made out the shape of the heavy machine-gun aimed at them, from which they could conjecture at least two or three others.

At the first sound of the cars, de Gailhan had risen and hailed two of his men. "Make the rounds," he said. "All weapons here out of sight. Tell every single man on outpost duty to stay there. Unless a firefight starts, they are to stay at their posts and do what they are there for. I will handle this." The men went off into the dark.

Frankl knew, or hoped he knew, what de Gailhan was thinking. It was an open advance, so either the incomers were innocuous or they were Chad military. Possibly Sudanese, strayed over the border. The French were forbidden to fire on either. It was a time for words. De Gailhan was good with words. He would handle it. On the other hand, Frankl was good with words, but he did not see how, if he had been in de Gailhan's shoes, he could have explained their presence away.

An officer with two soldiers approached the camp fire. The soldiers drifted off to either edge of the firelight.

No time was spent on courtesies. The officer was young and in his element; sure of his ground, with a strong force to back him and right on his side.

"Well, well," he said in English. "Europeans." His eye rested on Georg Frankl. "Mostly," he added. "Who are you? What are you doing here?"

"Famine relief," de Gailhan said. "The fuel supply on our aircraft failed. We made a forced landing. The plane's up there. The aircrew are working on it."

"So," the officer said. "You're French. Famine relief here, in Chad?"

"I was afraid of that," de Gailhan said. "The pilot said he thought we'd crossed the border."

"You have indeed," the young man said.

He passed between the Chadean soldier on his left and the campfire, moving slowly, considering what he saw, taking in de Gailhan and the people with him. Frankl, who was now sitting up with his hands round his knees. Anna, who had come to her feet. Bernoux, who stood beside her, lighting a cigarette with his hands cupped round the flame.

"You, monsieur," he said to Bernoux. "What do you do?"

"My profession?" Bernoux said. "I'm a scientist. I specialize in disease. Cholera, that sort of thing." He smiled a little. "Disease prevention, actually, is my chief interest."

"And you," he said, standing over Frankl. "What do you specialize in?"

"I'm an assessor," Frankl said, "and a dietitian. I estimate what food is needed, and what kind."

"And you are an Israeli," the officer said, his hand on his pistol.

He lifted his arm and gestured with the pistol. The lead car came closer, until it was level with the sinister pile of stacked boxes and the men gathered there. The Chadean soldiers on either side fell back a little.

With these movements the atmosphere between the two groups changed to one of outright confrontation; antagonism and the imminence of violence hung in the air.

"You," the officer said to de Gailhan. "Bring those men over here."

"Why me?" de Gailhan asked.

"Do it," the officer said. "Don't play games."

De Gailhan called to the others. The captain, the sergeant and the other half-dozen men still in the camp joined him and stood in a loose group.

"Interesting," the officer said. "Except for the Israeli, the scientist and the woman, any one of you looks fit and tough enough to be a soldier."

"Famine-relief workers have to be tough," de Gailhan said.

"The diet in the West," said Frankl the nutritionist, "builds strong men."

"Ah, yes," the young officer said. "The Israeli. You and the woman will show me what is in the boxes piled over there."

A general but almost imperceptible movement, as if a breeze had moved lightly over wheat in a field, passed among the French. De Gailhan looked down at his feet, saying silently, in as marked a way as he could, that he wanted no impetuous moves to be made. Whatever he made of this, the young Chadean certainly noticed it. "The rest of you," he said. "Stand in a line on that side of the fire. With your backs to it." It was the side farthest from the lead patrol car, where they would be well illuminated for the car's machine-gunner.

Bernoux said: "But this is insufferable."

The officer turned on him. "My dear sir," he said. "You have not travelled much in the world. This is perfectly sufferable, I assure you. Have I harmed you? Have I arrested you? Have I even reproached you with entering my country illegally? All I have done so far is to protect myself and my men from you and your friends, whose story I do not believe for a moment."

His teeth flashed suddenly in the firelight. "And it is also true," he said, "that power comes out of the barrel of a gun. So stop behaving like an idiot and get over there."

Bernoux looked at him gravely, as if he had returned to his professional persona and accepted the logic of what he heard. Nevertheless, he had not been silenced. "I should warn you," he said, "that these boxes contain specimens of virulent disease which I have been taking in the Southern Sudan. They are highly contagious."

He joined the line of undoubtedly humiliated Spahis. Like them, he turned his back to the fire and to the machine-gun.

"Come," the officer said to Frankl and Anna, and together they went over to the boxes, which had travelled so far and had such a history, and whose existence had driven to heights of anxiety men whose lives were so distant from each other as Abd el Sudi and Sir John Arkley.

The officer reached into the back of the patrol car and pulled out a small crowbar, which he handed to Frankl. "Let's make sure," he said.

Frankl levered the top off the box. Inside was a metal case with a built-in lock. "Look at this," he said.

The officer looked at it and became thoughtful.

He gestured with the pistol. "Do you think this would do it?" he said.

"Nine mil," Frankl said. "It might. It might simply jam the lock. We have to make sure. Anything might have happened between here and the Gulf."

The officer spoke to the car's driver, who brought the vehicle round until it was sideways to the fire and the line of men beyond it. The gunner swivelled his weapon as the car came round, so that it still covered its putative target.

The pistol fired once and the lid of the metal case flew open. The bullet whined off into the night.

The men under the machine-gun reacted variously. Some turned round, others turned their heads; one jerked forward as if he was going to run and then stopped to the pull of de Gailhan's hand on his shoulder.

"Yes," Frankl said. "OK?" he said to the Chadean.

"OK," the man said.

It took five shots to open two more boxes, the third being stubborn. They heard shouts from up above the gorge, which were answered from the other side.

"We agreed on three," Frankl said. "It's all we need. All we wanted."

"Time to go," the officer said.

They put the three boxes in the cab of the patrol car and climbed aboard. A burst of fire came from the airstrip side of the gorge, but the aim was high, and the car's machine-gunner had the sense not to return fire.

The driver completed the turn he had started when he put the vehicle broadside to the camp and set off down the gorge, which took a sharp bend almost at once. He took his time, driving without lights. The other cars fell in behind. Once round the corner the convoy put their lights on. When the foot of the canyon had been reached, they ran out into the open land before them until the camp was miles behind.

Then the lead car slowed to a halt and the others drew up beside it. There were only two of them, and only two men in each.

The machine-gunner, the driver, and the other two men of the crew got out of the lead car and lit cigarettes. The men from the other cars joined them.

"Well done," the officer said. He went from man to man, handing over bundles of money. "And a little extra," he said.

He shook hands with each man and they made their farewells.

The eight men got into the two cars that had followed and set off across country to the West. The three who were left watched them go.

Then there was a silence, as sometimes in the theatre after a play that has seized the audience utter quiet comes before the applause.

"I can hardly believe it," the officer said.

Anna threw her arms round him. "God, Taif," she said. "You were wonderful."

Frankl stood apart, looking to the east, which threw the first gleam of daylight over his face.

Anna went to him. "What is that smile?" she said. "What is that particular smile?"

"I was thinking," Frankl said, "it was a good gamble. Three million, or thereabouts. A professional gamble. Mullen would have liked it."

"Are you growing sentimental, Georg?" Anna said.

"Maybe," Frankl said. "Just a little, maybe."

"Just a little," Anna said, "and only very occasionally, would suit you."

"Only very occasionally," Georg said, "is all I could manage. Every time I win a gamble like this."

The three millionaires got into the car and drove north.

# 19

Seddall was thunderstruck.

Duncanson, when he was told, was thunderstruck.

"Money?" he said. "Cash money?"

"Yes," Seddall said. "Dollars, sterling, Deutschmarks, French francs, Swiss francs. Between six and eight million, sterling equivalent."

"And biological weapons?" Duncanson said.

"Not a trace," Harry said. "As soon as Frankl and the girl had gone, Bernoux, the French government's scientific expert, insisted on examining the cases. Nothing but currency."

"I have one thought," Duncanson said.

"That's more than I have," Seddall said.

"Nowadays," Duncanson said, "if you want to move large quantities of money around so that it's untraceable, banks are no good – not in this age of computers. Everything's traceable with computers. But camels with banknotes in their saddlebags, that's different."

"Not bad," Seddall said.

"Other than that, I've got to think," Duncanson said. "I'll talk to you later." But he did not, at once, put the phone down. "I say, Seddall," he said, "are you still there?"

"Yes," Seddall said.

"Frankl," Duncanson said. "What an operator."

"Oh, sure," Seddall said. "He's that all right."

Roberto Mullen, who was coming along nicely in the French army hospital, was thunderstruck too. "Christ Almighty!" he said. "I've gone over the whole bloody story with you, and the French cops, and French Intelligence once they got interested, not to mention that blithering idiot Raleigh who Duncanson sent over. Now you want me to do it again?"

"That's the spirit," Seddall said, quite as if Mullen had volunteered for some arduous duty. "Joanna, can you work this rather classy tape recorder? At least, I hope it's classy, the price I paid for it."

"Of course I can," Joanna said.

The room was large, bright and cheerful, good enough for a Marshal of France. The walls were a version of that pale green to which superior clinics are prone, but it was a very pleasant version. Deep bronze chrysanthemums, rich dark lilies and blithe yellow freesias decorated it. Mullen was sitting up in bed, drip-free at last, wearing crimson silk pyjamas; Joanna was elegant in a Prussian-blue suit whose skirt came almost to the knee, and Seddall was still looking quite respectable, it being too early in the day for his suit to have gone distraught on him and for his tie to start wandering round his neck.

"Listen, Mullen," Seddall said. "The caravan turns out to have been loaded with money, nothing else. But those CBRs have vanished from the Gulf and they've gone somewhere. You're the only line I've got. If there's a clue to where they are it may be inside you. Now drink your nice coffee, stop complaining, and talk."

So Mullen went over the whole story once again, from the start of his journey to Paris with Georg Frankl until the moment when Seddall found him on the floor in the farmhouse at St Luc. It took a long time because there was a lot to tell, and though Roberto was much stronger than he had been, he was far from restored to health and had little energy in him. Twice, therefore, before lunch the tape recorder was switched off and Joanna and Seddall left him to rest.

They walked the hospital grounds, it being a sparkling late-autumn day. They kicked the carpet of beech leaves on the grass in amiable silence and talked idly now and then.

"I love the sense of renewal a crisp autumn brings," Joanna said. "Autumn's fresh start time for me. Is it with you?"

"Yes, it is," Seddall said. "I always feel like striking out on some sort of expedition in the autumn. Sometimes I do it. What do you put it down to?"

"Not sure," Joanna said. "School years start then, maybe that's it."

"I think it's more ancient," Seddall said. "Harvest's in. Time for mischief. With reference to mischief," he said, "fresh start time doesn't mean you're thinking of splitting from Roberto, does it?"

"Wow," Joanna said. "Do you know me well enough to ask me that? And if I did, it'd be because I needed to or chose to, or both. I don't like you calling it mischief. I like a bit of mischief, God knows I do, but I wouldn't leave Roberto just for mischief."

"I stand corrected," Seddall said.

"Yes, you do," Joanna said.

"Time to go back, I think," Seddall said.


On their second walk, Joanna said: "A lot's been happening with Roberto, you know. He's been a pretty screwed-up guy since I've known him, and I knew him long enough at work before I took up with him. The shooting and then the kidnapping, that was rough on him."

"I know this," Seddall said. "Why are you telling me?"

"Because he's too calm, too ordinary about it," Joanna said. "I don't know what's going on inside him. It's not real, after being put through so much, is it?"

Seddall thought about it. "No," he said. "I wouldn't be as calm as he is. You're right. You still haven't said why you're telling me."

"I don't know what might happen, what he might do," Joanna said. "And I quite trust you, in some ways."

Seddall thought about this too. "That seems reasonable, actually," he said.

In the afternoon, Seddall drove off with the tape on the seat beside him and by six o'clock he was back at Olivia's house near Compiègne. He found two notes waiting for him. The first was from Olivia: she had gone to Somerset, where she looked forward to seeing him at the weekend, and Mrs Lyon had phoned to say that the dog Bayard was better. The other note was from Sorrel and said she had gone into the woods with a gun.

"What kind of people are these?" Seddall asked himself. "I come home from a hard day at the office and instead of the welcome drink, the slippers and the footstool for the feet, there's all this gadding about."

All the same, by the time he'd got his own drink and made himself comfortable by the fire in the drawing-room, he was so content with his own company that he was hard put to get down to listening to the Mullen tapes. After fifteen minutes of this, he stood up and went to work.

Sorrel came back to find him at the dining room table, listening through earphones for better concentration.

"Got a partridge," she said. "But I was too close."

The bird was lacerated. "You certainly were," Seddall said. "Go away."

"It was a lovely walk, though," Sorrel said, not one whit abashed, since she knew this mood. The Genius was thinking. "I'll make dinner."

"No," he said. "I don't want dinner. When I'm hungry I'll rummage. Goodnight."

It was not yet half-past seven.

In the middle of the night he woke her up. "What? Who is it?" she said, and switched on the bedside light. Seddall was wearing his dressing-gown and, so far as she could see, nothing else but a leer.

"Be your age," she said. "You and I stopped doing this years ago."

"Don't be a twit! Get up, come downstairs. I think I've got a glimmer. I'll put the kettle on for coffee," he said encouragingly. He had moved the tape recorder and his notes to the kitchen at some time during the night. Sorrel sat at the table and sipped coffee, and listened.

"There are three elements to this," he said. "First, when Markish was dying, he said this thing to his woman that Roberto found very moving. He said that the restaurant was all hers now, and that she should nourish it with love. And then he smiled – I think that's important, the smile – and said she should nourish the garden with love, too. After Markish died, she told Mullen the garden was at their weekend cottage, an old mill near Vézelay."

He looked at her. If his eyes had not been bleary with mental and general fatigue it might have been the kind of look called piercing. As it was, from a face that could have done with a shave, and a head where the hair had been rumpled with cogitation until it was all over the place, it was more like the kind of look called manic.

"You've got that?" he asked her.

"I've got it," Sorrel said. "Go on."

"Next," Seddall said. "During that dinner with Markish, they drank Gevrey-Chambertin. Of that great burgundy year when the Japanese bought just about the whole Gevrey-Chambertin vintage to lay it down as an investment."

"Roberto knows this kind of thing?" Sorrel said. "I've never seen him as a wine buff."

"Markish told him," Seddall said. "So remember: the garden at Vézelay, all Simone's now, to be nourished by her with love, right? And this business of laying down good wine as a copper-bottomed incremental investment."

"I'm remembering," Sorrel said. She got up to get the coffee pot off the stove, not so much because she wanted the coffee as to get away from being the focus of that over-active mind, to have a break from being stared at by those red-rimmed eyes out of that wild face.

She remained standing at the stove, the coffee mug in her hand. Seddall went on talking at the chair she had been sitting in, as if he was too involved with what was going on in himself to respond to extraneous events.

"Now," he said. "While Roberto was a prisoner in that house, the woman M'pofu told him that when Dujardin was in prison in Peru they held him in solitary confinement for months. To keep himself from cracking up, Dujardin had various ploys. Isometric exercises, recalling the strategy of historic campaigns and tactics in famous battles, and this: he would think of a painting by Van Gogh and recall everything he could about it, until he knew there was nothing left in his memory of it to bring before his mind's eye, and then go on to another one."

"God, that's good," Sorrel said. "I do like that in him. What a shame he was such a thug."

"Well, he was," Seddall said, and turned in his chair now to face her again. "He was a case-hardened killer and that's that. Anyway, the last Van Gogh he was looking at, so to speak, before the jail was blown open and he escaped, was that painting of the fishing boats lying on the beach. He always liked to remember not only the painting itself but where he had seen it, what gallery it was in.

"Before the explosion blew down the wall he was getting upset that he couldn't remember where on earth he had seen that painting. And the answer was, he told M'pofu, that of course he couldn't remember, because it's in a private collection. He had only seen reproductions of it."

Seddall appeared suddenly to be smaller than he was. He could no longer have been called manic, only tired, baffled and anxious.

"That's all," he said, and looked away, chewing his lip.

Sorrel knew she had to come up with something. She hadn't the faintest idea what he was trying to convey to her, but she mulled over what he had told her.

"Collectors," she said. "Wine, for example, and art. And the garden at Vézelay, Markish telling Simone to nourish it."

Instantly his face came to life again. "Well," he said, "it's possible. Collectors: some of them are hoarders more than they are art lovers, or in the case of the Chambertin, hoarders rather than connoisseurs of wine. They get hold of the best available in their chosen field and store it away till they want to put it on the market."

Sorrel had a horrible glimpse of where he was going. "Markish was in the arms market," she said.

"Yes," he said. "Here," he went past her to the coffee pot and poured some into her mug, which was more than half full already, and then into his own. He emptied the ashtray into the bin and lit himself another cigarette.

He was becoming the ebullient Seddall again. "It's a thought. We mustn't go off half-cocked, but it's a thought and it's all we've got. I mean, Markish was handling the CBRs for Arkley and General Tinsley; Markish was the entrepreneur. God knows how that camel train came to be carrying millions of pounds in cash across the desert, but the CBRs must have gone somewhere."

Sorrel, standing in that big, sane, country kitchen with its old stove, garlands of dried herbs, garlic and wild mushrooms hanging from the walls, and shelves lined with various pots, pans and crockery, felt something fade inside her as she thought of a man called Markish who might have been so carried away by his trade that he laid up a store of biological weaponry to wait for the market to be ready. Laid it up in his garden, to be nourished with love.

"It's a hellish idea," she said.

Seddall, who was walking around now on the other side of the room, stopped. "Oh, yes," he said. "It's an enormity of an idea. It's monstrous. And I don't think that Markish was keeping it for the furtherance of trade. I don't think he could have been that monstrous, from what we know of him. I think he had some colour of legitimacy for storing it – if indeed he was storing it. I think he was storing it for Arkley and the general."

"Why?" she said. "Assuming you and I have not gone off our trolleys, why would they want that?"

"I want Duncanson here," he said. "I can't talk on the phone to him about this, however safe the line. No line is safe enough for this. And I'm not leaving France, not when the answer seems to be here."

"Well," she said, "we know he's an insomniac. We can call him now. If he's willing to come without being told why you want him, except that it's excruciatingly vital, he'll be here for breakfast."


He was there for a late breakfast. He flew into a military airport north of Paris. Sorrel met him and drove him back to the house, though Duncanson had three men with him and a car waiting, which followed on behind.

At the house, two of the men began prowling the gardens and the third settled himself in the library.

There was a moment, as Seddall was laying out his theory, in which Duncanson's marred face cast itself abruptly into the lines of some gargoyle stricken with the fear of too much knowledge of evil. Then he settled back again, his bushy eyebrows up, and listened to the end.

"That woman makes good coffee," he said.

"I'll ask her for some more," Seddall said.

When the gaunt-visaged Stephanie had brought the coffee and departed, Duncanson said: "It's not impossible. It's not impossible at all. Officially, we have no biological warfare substances in a product state. Officially, we have them at Porton Down for research purposes, purely to learn how to counter them. But damn it, we know it ain't so."

"And Arkley's gone megalomaniac," Seddall said. "He's in that limpid state old men in positions of power reach when they believe they alone see clearly and think well."

"It's a thing he could do," Duncanson said. "I can't quite figure why. I can conjecture: he knows the world is no safer now than it was during the Cold War; that the Army is being shrunk; that the Navy is hardly shipped or equipped for war; that the traditional Western Powers are growing weaker and less warlike while others are growing more bellicose; that danger always comes on your blind side when you're not ready, and that we may be faced with a war we can't win with conventional weapons. It's all there, I could parrot that line of thought for ages."

"If it's there," Seddall said, "there must be a specially prepared store. What does it need? Air-conditioned space, refrigeration?"

"Well," Duncanson said, "that brings us to General Tinsley, who went boffo on biological warfare. That's the chemistry, isn't it. You put these two men together and that's where the chemistry starts. Tinsley would know what kind of bunker they'd need to make to store the stuff. I'd put it underground. Under, if you're right, that garden at Vézelay that was to be nourished with love. What a rotten thought."

Sorrel was suddenly impatient. "It doesn't take that long to get used to," she said. "We know there are mad people in the world, and foul and evil people. So, what's next? There's no point sitting here pulling long faces and making appropriate noises to tell ourselves our hearts are in the right place. Markish is dead; Arkley knows that. Arkley knows his camel train's been hijacked, or at least its cargo has, so he knows that's blown. But is he not going to think that if he can clear out that bunker or store or whatever it is which may very well, because that's what it feels like now, be under that garden at Vézelay, then everything will still be explainable one way or another and he'll be as safe as houses?"

"Oh, yes," Duncanson said, "when he gets the right signal, that's what he'll do."

"If I know Arkley," Seddall said, "he'll stay away from that one. He'll get the general to do it. I can see that from their point of view one of them will have to be there, to be sure it's done and to be sure no one else breaks their secret, and to be sure where the stuff is taken to now. But Arkley won't do it himself when he can get the general to do it for him."

"I have a strong hunch," Duncanson said, "that the general won't be around to do it for him."

Sorrel hated this kind of heavily allusive talk; indeed, any talk that didn't tell you outright what it meant.

"Mr Duncanson," she said formally, feeling as if she was usurping more than one mantle of Queen Victoria: the minatory, the imperious and the morally rectitudinous for starters. "What have you to tell us?"

"Miss Blake," he said. "General Sir Arthur Reginald Craye Tinsley put a bullet through his head at his house near Goudhurst in Kent this night past. He had certainly heard the result of de Gailhan's expedition and, not having Arkley's megalomaniac certainties, he knew the jig was up."

"Damn and blast," Seddall said callously. "Then Arkley will lie low."

"I doubt that," Duncanson said. "I was the first to hear of it. I have had a team on Tinsley. He was alone in the house. His housekeeper lived in the village and came in daily, his manservant was on leave. I got the call not long after I spoke to you."

"Yes?" Seddall said. "So what did you do?"

"I got second team down there as quick as light," Duncanson said. "They put the bomb together as they went, to the familiar pattern. As far as the world will know, General Tinsley will have been blown up by the IRA."

"Will Arkley believe that?" Sorrel asked him.

"I rather think he will," Duncanson said. "Tinsley did the IRA some real harm when he was in Ulster. In fact, his name was on an IRA hit-list the police found last summer. It all fits together very sweetly. I'm pretty certain Arkley will go for it. I imagine Tinsley's death will positively impel him into action.

"If you're right about Vézelay, I believe we may expect Arkley to make his move very soon."

"Good," Seddall said, but his voice was flat.

Sorrel wondered if he had the same feeling she had: that General Tinsley's death fitted too sweetly to be true.

Duncanson rose to his height. He had withdrawn to a place within himself, and his eyes hardly touched them before he moved to the end of the long room and stood facing out on the lawn strewn with fallen leaves, on the trees, half-bare, which traced stark outlines on the pale sky.

He spoke with his back to them. "You'll need to bring the French in on this," he said. "We're watching Arkley and that praetorian entourage of his. I'll let you know if they move." He amended this: "*When* they move. It's going to happen," he said. "I feel it in my bones."

He went to the door, and gave that sudden rictus of a smile, and left them.

Sorrel could not tell if the contempt he had shown was for their horror of a thing he had done, or if it sprang from anger that they should suppose he had done it.

# 20

There were some roses still; patches of pink and white cinquefoil between bushes; colours deep and elegiac where clumps of herbaceous flowers lamented the summer. The garden had a desolate air, almost mournful in the damp day. In the eye of the beholder, Seddall thought – or rather the binoculars thereof, for he was well away from the mill where Markish and Simone had nourished their love, and the garden with which they had enriched it. At the ambiguity of the word enriched, his lip curled in disgust. Love took many forms, but some of them were beyond his understanding. He put the glasses away and went back down the little hill to the car to wait. There were other eyes watching the mill and its garden; they would watch until Arkley's people came.

Arkley's people had certainly set out for France, led by the gunsel Maxton, but of Arkley himself Duncanson's watchers had lost track a full twenty-four hours ago. So the trap was set. There was no expectation that the wait would be a long one. Maxton's team had no cause to play about; the job they had to do was best done quick and neat.

In Paris, Sorrel had unhappily betaken herself to a solitary dinner at Simone's restaurant at Neuilly, so that she could give news of any development there.

There was nothing to do now but wait, probably until the night had settled in. Perhaps till tomorrow. Perhaps until the next night, but surely no longer than that.

And as for Arkley: well, Arkley was who he was, and he would have every kind of resource at his disposal. Unknown houses, cars garaged all over, waiting for his need. Arkley could cross the Channel in disguise, or by private plane or motor-cruiser.

Seddall knew Arkley. He knew that however the devious Sir

John had arranged for this operation to be conducted, the man himself would be close by. For all his gifts as an intriguer, Arkley was a man who could not stay away when the stake was personal. That the game was at its height and the risk at its pitch would add lustre to the fascination of the lure.

A car came bumping up the track behind him and stopped. A man got out of the passenger seat and spoke through Seddall's open window.

"Edward Raleigh," he said. "Duncanson's office. Mind if I get in?"

"Sure," Seddall said.

Raleigh got in, a man in his early forties, of conflicting smells: the musky richness of his aftershave fought the brisk aromatics of his new tweed coat. He was also, Seddall recalled, Mullen's *bête-noire*.

"So it's there," Raleigh said.

"Something's there," Seddall said. "There's a concrete store, all right. We don't know what's in it."

"Under the grass," Raleigh said. "Can't be there for fun."

"No," Seddall said.

"So we're in at the kill, eh?" Raleigh said with relish, as if he'd kept up with the hounds all morning.

"What did you say?" Seddall said, looking at this curious individual, all brisk and sharp-chinned and pointy-nosed; all go, not a lot of fun to be with.

"Mind if I smoke?" Raleigh said.

"No," Seddall said.

Raleigh spent a moment trying to work this out and gave up. His cigarettes stayed in his pocket.

"Let me explain to you," Seddall said, "there are a lot of aspects to this job I don't like. Arkley's never been a friend of mine, but I've held him in some respect, some of the time. I hate this. I hate what's coming."

Raleigh listened to this and to his credit, as far as Seddall was concerned, absent-mindedly lit a cigarette. He opened the window beside him and let smoke out. "Got you. Sorry," he said. "Want one?" He held out the cigarettes.

Seddall took one, Raleigh's lighter lit it.

"Right then," Raleigh said. "Duncanson's worked it out about the money. Asked me to tell you."

"Asked you?" Seddall said.

"Asked me what?" Raleigh said, baffled again.

"Put it this way," Seddall said, "is MI5 a service, or is it a family?"

Raleigh apparently took this to be rather friendly. "Bit of both," he said. "Anyway, about all that money that was trekked across the desert. Goes like this, Duncanson says – I wonder if we could have the engine on for a bit, give the heater a blast?"

"Get on with it," Seddall said. "The money."

"Same as the other, in a way, so they were killing two birds with one stone," Raleigh said. "you know that A. got *carte blanche* from The Top—"

"A.?" Seddall said.

"Sir J. A.," Raleigh said, and redeemed a great deal by blushing very red. "I have this problem," he said. "I find it hard to use his name. It's such an extraordinarily wrong thing to have happened, to be happening."

"In at the kill," Seddall said unpleasantly.

"Well, yes," Raleigh said. "That sort of talk helps, that's all."

Seddall started the engine and turned on the heater fan. "Now finish telling me about the money," he said. "As brief as you can."

Raleigh said: "Sir J." – he looked at Seddall to see if this diction was acceptable – "got *carte blanche* from The Top to get hold of these CBRs. You knew that, Duncanson said. Duncanson said you didn't know Sir J. also got a blank cheque. Said if the CBRs were out there in the market he might have to buy them back. I mean, one way and another Sir J. was at both ends of the deal himself. He knew where the CBRs were."

Raleigh rolled down the window and threw out his cigarette, jerking his head up the hill whose far side overlooked the mill. "He knew he wouldn't have to spend a penny. He pretty well drained the Secret Fund. Not for himself – he's got pots of money, and what would he spend all that on? No: it's on the same programme as the CBR lark. The Cold War ends, country thinks peace is here for ever. With Defence spending down, Sir J. sees Secret Intelligence Service being cut to the bone."

He shivered and rolled up the window again. The sun was gone and the cold day turning to a chill evening. "So," Raleigh said, "he got all this cash together and was going to put it aside for a rainy day. He might even have planned to confide it to his successor. Who can say?"

"Why Africa?" Seddall said.

"My very question," Raleigh said. "Why not Africa? That's what Duncanson said. The money has still to be laundered, to make a clean entry into banks somewhere. Plenty of guys in Africa know how to do that. Take their commission, owe Arkley a favour, both maybe. I called him Arkley," he said. "Must be getting it together."

They were quiet, watching the sky darken.

"Awful mistake," Raleigh said.

"Well, yes," Seddall said, "but what in particular?"

"Trying to change the course of history," Raleigh said. "Feel I must get back to the warm. That nice little house the gendarmes have commandeered. Will you mind? Are you staying out here?"

"I don't know," Seddall said. "For a while. Thanks, Raleigh."

"Not at all," Raleigh said.

He left the car, shut the door firmly but not with a bang, and returned to the vehicle from which he had come. It turned out over the grass and went back down the track.

Seddall turned the engine off and got out of the car. He went up the slope of the hill and found the place behind the hedge where he had looked down on the mill and its garden. So quickly had the dusk drawn in that he could see nothing down there. He lifted his eyes and saw lights where Vézelay itself lay, but the tower of its church was invisible now against the sky. The cold was damp and penetrating and he wound the muffler round his neck and turned up the collar of his coat. He went aimlessly back down the hill again and wished himself away from here. If the moon had been out it would have seen a humourless and bitter smile pass across his face. It had struck him that Arkley, however deluded, or however clear-sighted and therefore desperate, was having a better time than he was.

The thought, however, lifted some of the sombreness out of him. He got back into the car and, abandoning his self-imposed and solitary vigil, went down to that nice little house where Raleigh and those who did not have to be out lurking in the bushes were warming themselves.


John Arkley thought that only a French engineer would have agreed to do it, and the man had done a marvellous job.

The car was a cream and black Delage drophead tourer. Of all his cars it was Arkley's favourite. He had kept it at St Quentin for the last decade, using it for three journeys in all those years, twice to Italy and once to Spain. The auto engineer at St Quentin had laboured for months to adapt it to the fact that its owner now had an artificial leg. To Arkley, the cost to him and the man's labour and skill had been well spent.

He dropped down to Vézelay under a cold and glittering sky, sticking to real roads, avoiding the autoroute. He wore the pale-blue tweed with a white fleck and a white cashmere scarf bundled up round his neck, for though the hood was up it let in draughts and though the heater worked it was not wonderful.

He did not know what he would do at Vézelay, only that he had decided to go. It would be more true to say that he found he had decided to go, because the decision had been made not by his mind but inside him. It was in his blood that he had to go to Vézelay.

He had no interest now in what brought him here. He had always fought to the last to wrest triumph from defeat, and mostly he had won. Whether he won or lost, he knew this would prove to have been his last battle. So how, that being so, could it matter to him where victory lay?

He had a sense that the tide of this battle had turned irrevocably against him, and yet there was no less exhilaration in him than if he was carrying all before him. He knew himself for a champion. If, now, his was the losing side, for all that he was no less a man than Bayard had been at Marignancy.

The sun, low now, a white orb climbing down the sky on his right, yet threw a gleam onto the long bonnet of the car. A smile of unsullied pleasure curled the mouth under the piebald moustache. He would not go to the mill that had belonged to Markish.

If Ennis and Maxton came away unscathed, well and good. If the whole affair went to hell on a handcart, so be it. Whatever happened, the events at the mill would be banal. He would get them to give him a good dinner at that hotel, the one where they knew how to cook, and then he would see. A stroll to the church, maybe, in the moonlight – if the moon came out.

Beyond that, he did not speculate.

He put his foot down and the road ran to meet him, the car sang to him with the zest of being put to its full use; for a moment a vision of Don Quixote hovered on the edge of his mind's eye, but it went away again before he saw it.

Maxton drove the hired Citroën, the big new one, only seven thousand klicks on the clock, a magnificent beast to drive. Ennis sat beside him stiff with excitement and quite unaware that he ought to be scared shitless. Maxton tipped back his leather sombrero with a forefinger and grinned like a mad dog. What a demented expedition this was. But it was no great matter to him. He had no idea whether the mill at Vézelay and its nasty little secret was blown or not. The great thing was that he was part of Arkley's household staff, he was not in government service. Ennis was, and the poor bugger's career would go up in smoke if there was a welcoming party.

He had seen in Arkley's eye that there was a dicey side to this one, and Arkley knew he had seen it. But the old villain had given him a bundle for it, to add to previous bundles. They knew where they stood with one another, without having to spell it out.

Behind them came the van, driven by MacFall and with Hooker, he of the hair-trigger and officer-like qualities, in what he would think of as command. As to the men with them who had been co-opted to do the menial work, shifting whatever was in the dump into the van, Maxton would not have risked his neck with that bunch if all they had to do was put out a fire in a dog kennel.

Maxton knew the way. He had driven here alone in the afternoon to reconnoitre. Enormous church, big hotels and the rest pretty-pretty. This bit of country did not thrill him.

He slowed the car. "Getting there," he said.

223

Ennis sat even more upright against his seat belt and peered into the headlights for the Cheyenne to show themselves.

Maxton pulled the car into the verge and stopped. "Out you get," he said, and squeezed out himself between the car and the steep grass bank. He went back to the van.

"Fifty paces up on your right," he said to MacFall. "Turn in at the white-painted fence. Drive straight past the house to the back and you'll see the lawn in your headlights. Get to it."

"Headlights?" Hooker said. "Are you mad?"

"What's your problem?" Maxton said. "If there's a welcoming party, they'll know you're there, with or without headlights. If there isn't, headlights out here in the middle of nowhere are not going to cause a ruckus."

All this went right by Hooker. "And just what are you doing, anyway?" he said.

"What does it look like?" Maxton said. "I'm standing here in the road talking to you."

"I mean, I take it you're going to lead us in?" Hooker said.

"Blow it out of your shorts," Maxton said. "Drive on," he said across Hooker to MacFall. "Wait," he said, as he found that Ennis was beside him. "Take in Mr Ennis. Up you go," he said, opening the door with one hand and giving Ennis a boost with the other. He slammed the door.

Ennis looked nervous and lonely as the van drove away. Maxton watched its lights vanish off the road to the house and ambled after it. He found a place where he could lean on the fence and see what was going on, so he lit a cigarette and watched.

MacFall manoeuvred the van until its lights shone onto the lawn. Hooker galloped around giving orders, returning always to stand beside Ennis, the man – technically, at least – in authority.

A crowbar was let into the grass until it found resistance, and this went on until the area where resistance was met was identified. Turf was cut and piled. The digging began. Maxton strolled away down the road past the Citroën and strolled back to lean on the fence again.

"*Vous vous promenez très tard ce soir, monsieur,*" a voice said.

Maxton did not look round. "Hallo," he said.

"Hallo, Maxton," another voice said. "Where's Arkley?"

224

"I know that voice," Maxton said, and came away from the fence. "Yes," he said, "the young Raleigh."

"I've been to school, Maxton," Raleigh said. "That one's not new."

Three other men stood around Raleigh. *Les flics,* Maxton told himself, or something like.

"Come on," Maxton said confusingly. "Let's go and see what's happening," and he set off up the driveway.

The diggers had exposed the door of the vault and their whole party was focused on Ennis, stooping over it with the keys in his hand, when the Commissaire Nogent's men walked quietly into their midst.

Harry Seddall was drifting after them when a man came running up behind him. "I have a Mademoiselle Blake on the telephone in the car for you, mon colonel," he said.

Seddall stood poised, this way and that dividing his swift mind. "Tell her – implore her – to hold for just two minutes," he said.

He went up to the site of the digging. Nogent had had the evildoers herded to the end of the lawn. Ennis, who had half-fainted, was carried there and laid down with a coat over him. Nobody, in either the home or the away team, gave a damn about Ennis. They wanted to know what was in the vault.

Nogent offered the key to Seddall, who shook his head. Nogent fitted and turned one key, then another, and gave a heave. The metal door swung up and fell with a thud onto the grass.

"Heavy," Nogent said, pleased with himself. A policeman shone a torch into the cavity. He and Nogent and Seddall saw a short metal ladder fixed to a concrete wall.

"Colonel," Nogent said, "I insist," and gestured to Seddall.

Seddall took off his coat and put it on Nogent's arm before clambering into the hole. He went down the ladder and stood on the concrete floor, then reached his arm up for the torch. The policeman stretched down and gave it to him.

Seddall shone the torch about and began, against his will, to smile. "It's too much," he said to himself. "Too much."

He went up a few rungs of the ladder and leaned his arms on the damp grass, where he met the eyes of Commissaire Nogent, who was kneeling to hear his news.

225

"Well?" the Commissaire said. "What is in there?"

"An awful lot," Seddall said, "of Gevrey-Chambertin."

He emerged from the hole. "I have to take a phone call," he said.


Seddall stood in the cellar of the restaurant at Neuilly and looked at the empty bin space.

"Thing upon thing," he said. "Here till yesterday. Missed it by a hair's-breadth. What's the scoop? No, is there somewhere we can sit down?" He had driven like the wind to Neuilly. With all that had gone on in the last twenty-four hours, he was fast running out of steam.

"Of course," Simone said.

He followed the two women out of the cellar and up another stair to Simone's flat. He sank into a plump couch covered in green velvet which was matched by two armchairs. He didn't much like the look of her furniture, but its comfort made up for it.

"Tell me about yesterday," he said to Simone.

She shrugged. "What is there to tell?" she said. "I knew what Ben's business was. I didn't like having him store a batch of armaments here, but he said it was only this once. We moved his precious Chambertin out and we put other wine all around it."

"Why hide it?" Seddall asked. "His business was legal."

"Don't be naïve," she said in anger. "You know quite well that some arms-dealing is not legal. I am almost sure this was not. He became nervous about keeping it at the mill and said he would move it on from here in a few days; as soon as he could. He wanted rid of it, he said. He wished he'd never got into it."

"And you have no idea what it was?" Seddall said.

"None. And for my part I'm glad it's gone," she said. "It's what killed him, isn't it?"

"I honestly don't know," he said.

"Mademoiselle Blake will tell you what happened yesterday," she said. "You must excuse me. I am crying again. If I don't go to work I shall break down, and I am so tired of doing that."

She went out, a woman growing used to sorrow, but in whom

the loss had come up once more like one of those overwhelming seventh waves in a storm at sea.

"It was a straightforward collection of freight," Sorrel said. "They had all the paperwork, and it matched the paperwork and the numbers on the boxes. Two men and a truck. Yesterday afternoon, when the restaurant was closed. They brought it round the back, loaded it up, took a drink and drove off. It was a Belgian truck and they spoke French like Belgians."

Seddall got up and went to a window and looked down on the street. Late diners were leaving down there, getting into cars and going home.

Sorrel came up beside him. "What now?" she said.

"I don't know," he said. "We've come right up a blind alley."

"Pause for thought," she said.

"Yes, that would be the best thing. Well," he said, with a bullish if rueful smile, a man gathering his forces after defeat, "it's the only thing. Tomorrow's Friday. Olivia's in Somerset. What's your weekend? Why don't you come down soon?"

"Let me play it by ear," she said. "I think I'll want to be at home. I feel as if I haven't been there for ages." Her attention fixed suddenly on the street below her. "I know that man."

So did Seddall, who focused just in time to see the figure vanish from sight into the restaurant. "This is a surprise," he said. "That's Raleigh."

Soon there came a knock at the front door of the flat, and Seddall went to open it.

Raleigh came in. He looked twice at Sorrel. "Hallo," he said, and to both her and Seddall: "Sorry to crash in on you like this, but it's quite important."

"You're not crashing in on anything," Seddall said. "What's up?"

"Duncanson told me to tell you in person," Raleigh said. The weight of the message silenced him for a moment.

"Well, then," Seddall said irritably. "Tell me."

"The biological materiel," Raleigh said. "The CBR. It's all back where it belongs, at the Government Research Laboratories at Porton Down."

"No, no," Seddall said. The thing was so monstrously unlikely

227

that he could not believe what his ears had told him. "It can't be. It's not possible. It's a trick of some kind. Duncanson's up to something."

Raleigh stood his ground and that furious blush came onto his face. "I can't hear that," he said. "And I don't want to hear you say it, so I'd better go."

Where the colour had come up in Raleigh's face, it had left Seddall's. He looked round him and sat down violently in the green armchair at his side. His arms lay loose on the arms of the chair and his hands were shaking.

Sorrel went to the drinks table, poured cognac into a glass and gave it to him.

"Come on," Sorrel said to Raleigh. "Let me see you out."

At the foot of the stairs Raleigh said to her: "Why is he so upset? I know he's been working flat out the last few days, and Vézelay was a bit of a disappointment, but that was a hell of a reaction."

"I don't know why," Sorrel said. "Perhaps he doesn't know why. But I think that he knows why at the bottom of his mind and it's too much for him to take in, so the easiest thing was to find it incredible."

Raleigh studied her during this speech and for a moment after. "You know what goes on in people," he said.

"Don't be absurd!" Sorrel said. "That was hardly earth-shattering. I know Harry, that's all."

Raleigh was not blushing, but he was pink. "When we're back in London," he said, "I'll ask you to dinner."

"All right," Sorrel said. "I'd like that."

When she got back upstairs, she found that Seddall had taken himself at his word. He lay fast asleep in the chair with the glass lying at his feet.

# 21

Arkley's dinner began with pâté de foie of duck, served hot with a sauce whose tang and purity of taste, in alliance with the richness of what it dressed, amazed him: so that for a moment his mouth became still and he gazed into an invisible distance beyond the walls of the dining room.

He was not a gourmet, but there came to him the idea that if food could bring happiness, this dining room would be paradise. It was, certainly, an extraordinarily well-run dining room. He was served by five different men, none of whom was ever in the way of another; whose economy of movement was such, and who presented themselves so sparingly at his table, that he was left in the contentment which he had desired, of dining alone.

Only the ceremony that went with the arrival of each course, in which the lifting of the cover from the plate was followed by a recitation of what now lay before him – and the mandatory encouragement to appetite – enforced response from him, but it was done so briskly and with such absence of self-consciousness that the little moment of social engagement was an addition to the enjoyment of the meal. Besides, all that was called for was an inclination of the head, or a movement of the muscles of the face.

He had sole, he had chicken done in the style of Bresse, he had a sorbet, he had Roquefort. As to the wine, he had reversed the chromatic order, having a few mouthfuls of a young Hermitage with the pâté de foie, and proceeding to a Pouilly-Fumé.

He had coffee and on an impulse, since everything had been so perfectly in balance, he asked if they had a rough brandy, which was found in the kitchen and wracked his throat as if the drink had been infiltrated with nettle stings.

He left the dining room surrounded by the sense that he had been loved by the waiters and, leaning a little heavily on his stick, for it had been a long day, went out into the night.

The Delage gleamed in the moonlight, or to be less romantic, in the lights of the hotel, and over there was the church.

He was drawn to it. He would have wished to go inside, but it was too late for that. Still, he was drawn to it, so he crossed the wide expanse, a solitary, limping figure, and stood before its façade. He stood before it with his head lifted, perceiving it not with any aesthetic sense, and with no recognizable attribute of worship in him.

He simply held himself there, under the power of that created bulk of stone, under the weight of the age it had stood there, held by its stillness and by its representation of eternity, which lay not only in the fact that it was a signature of divinity but in its illusion of permanence.

He started down the north side and had taken but a few paces when a woman's arm went lightly round his waist. He looked down and saw a black tousled head and a black face. He felt the light prick of the knife in his side.

"Ah," he said. "It is you."

"You don't know me," she said.

"I know you, and why you are here," he said. "I know you. I know you are Zulu and that your mother is of the Bakwena tribe of the Tswana people of the Bantu, and where she lives. And I know where you live and I know where you sing, and I know the Pole you work for. And I know how many people you have killed. I knew I would have a meeting here, but I did not know it would be with you."

"I am tired of killing," she said.

"But not yet," he said. "We are all tired of killing."

"No," she said. "Not yet."

The knife pricked him again. "Walk along a little," she said. "I have opened a door."

"But this is a delight," he said. "I had wished to go inside."

"Stop here," she said. "Do you want to look a moment at the stars?"

"You would. But I don't. In any case," he said as they went up the few steps and passed into the great church, "I would hardly see them. I see something else now."

Her arm left him and she pushed shut the door and ran a bolt across. Doing this, she turned her back, either trusting or filled with the certitude of mission or indifferent to what he might do.

They were in a giant cave, lit only by altar candles, so that its far end was a mystery of darkness.

"If you do not see the stars," she said, "what is this something else you see?"

"I see a flat, dark place in front of me to the horizon," he said. "The horizon is not far off. I could walk it in a morning. Even I could walk it in a morning."

"What is at the horizon?" she said.

"Well then," he said, "so you have seen it too, in your time."

The silence between them grew in that great space until it was too much to be borne.

"The horizon comes close," he said, "for you as well as me. You feel it?"

"I feel it," she said.

He looked up at the barred stonework of the arches, which he had never seen before in candlelight alone.

Then he looked at the woman. "Show me the knife," he said. "Good," he said, for the blade was nine inches long and would do its work without bungling.

"Where?" she said.

"In the heart," he said, "if you have a strong arm."

"It is strong," she said.

"Good," he said again. His bright old eyes looked into her gleaming young ones. "It is for Dujardin?"

"Yes," she said.

"I'll sit down and look at the candles," he said.

She nodded.

He sat down and she moved out of sight behind him.

He leaned his head to the side and closed his eyes until only the candle flames glimmered in his vision.

There was a moment of terror, in which he saw that there had been a moment of peace, and then a shock which broke into him as if he were a baby in the cradle as the horizon rushed towards him.

231

# 22

When Seddall found Duncanson, the head of MI5 was at his club lunching with, of all people, Sir Oliver Quick.

"How good," Seddall said, from behind them both. "Why don't I join you?" and moved forward to become visible.

"It most unfortunately happens . . ." Duncanson said, beginning the rejection.

Seddall, however, had already sat himself down.

"I'll have the claret, please, Johnson," he said to the steward, "and some of those biscuits please."

Duncanson and Quick were halfway through their steak pie. Quick, after greeting Seddall politely, had the indifference or the guile to continue with his as if there was nothing disconcerting about this new arrival; but Duncanson first cast a look round the room as if to assure himself there were plenty of places elsewhere to which Seddall could remove himself, then lifted and dropped a hand in the gesture which meant he gave up on that one.

"You belong here too, then," he said. "Don't remember seeing you here."

"Don't come here much," Seddall said. "A pity about Arkley," he said.

"A pity?" Quick said. "That's a bit offhand, surely."

"My goodness," Seddall said to Duncanson. "Doesn't he know what Arkley was up to?"

"Arkley had a long and distinguished career as a servant of the state," Quick said without blinking an eye.

Seddall's claret arrived, and with it the biscuits. He broke one and nibbled at it, saying nothing.

Quick dealt with the last of the meat, the sprouts and the potatoes on his plate. Duncanson, seized by whatever perplexities

Seddall's being there had raised in him, fell behind, and then abandoned the business of eating.

As if he had been waiting for this, Seddall said: "I think the American phrase for it is a sting, is that not right? When the forces of law and order," and he smiled unpleasantly at Quick when he said it, "assist a man into crime in order to do him down."

"I thought that was what you were about," Quick said. "We can't deal with it here. We'll want a room. I'm not going to miss my cheese either. We'll have it sent up."

He arranged this in the twinkling of an eye, and the three of them left the dining room: Quick and Duncanson walking together, both wearing lots of blue suit, and Seddall following along in rumpled tweed just up from the country, carrying his decanter and glass with him, knowing quite well that this was a showing-off thing to do, but wanting to feel as different as possible from the two who went before him.

"How do you see it?" Quick said, when they were ensconced round a table in a private room and the Stilton had been proved to be satisfactory.

"I see it in any number of ways," Seddall said. "I see that you wanted it known, but known only where it counted, that we had CBRs in the Gulf so that the enemy could be discouraged from using theirs. I see this as being done covertly, since officially we don't have them except in minute quantities for research. I see it, therefore, as being done behind the back of the command in the field, because you can't have a thing like that known at army HQ and hope to keep it top-secret. I see it as being the special preserve of General Tinsley."

When he mentioned Tinsley's name his hand was on the neck of the decanter and he shot his eyes up in time to see Quick's mouth tighten. "I see," Seddall said. "Tinsley died for his country. That's what I thought."

Duncanson had been sitting immobile, his face as still as stone. Now when he spoke, only his lips moved.

"This is dangerous for you, Seddall," he said.

Harry felt the sour smile on his face. He put his hand into his tweed suit. Onto that table, with its decanters, glasses, plates, silver and ripe Stilton, he laid a .38 Smith & Wesson.

233

"Do it," he said.

Quick's calm was impenetrable. He looked at the revolver and took some more cheese, and said: "You people are so damned melodramatic. Can I ask you to put that away, Seddall. The smell of the gun oil, you know. It doesn't go with the Dow's.

"And Duncanson," Quick said. "This is not dangerous for Seddall. I advise you to understand that. Do you want to go on, Seddall?"

"I don't know at what level Tinsley managed to get endorsement for having his CBRs on the ground in the Gulf," Seddall said. "I suppose it to have been finessed past a Minister by some Secret Warfare Committee with Arkley on it, and perhaps Duncanson, too. Once done, though, it came to a Minister's knowledge, and then you were all in a mess up there."

He nodded through the wall at Downing Street. "And then Tinsley and Arkley went strange on you. It is fascinating, is it not, Sir Oliver, how the heads of services like Arkley's and Duncanson's go strange in their old age? No wonder we have the thirty-year rule about access to Government archives. What you read in the papers about their predecessors must make your hair curl."

He watched Duncanson's hand, lying loosely on the polished table, tighten into a fist and shake with the pressure of his anger.

"Well, we know all this," Seddall said. "We know the CBRs were spirited out of the Gulf and your masters, Sir Oliver, who are also ours," he smiled at the rigid Duncanson, "were petrified by the possible consequences when they learned about it. At least, that was the story."

Quick had finished with his Stilton. He consulted the watch on his wrist and pushed his chair back a little.

"You've signed the Act," he said to Seddall. "Now hear the news: I know what a sting is, Seddall, and you're talking rubbish. Yes, we knew Arkley was doing something odd. Duncanson became aware of it soon after it was initiated, but you know perfectly well that the man in Arkley's job has an extraordinary imperium, of which no one but he has the map.

"Also, it was hard to believe that Arkley, having no fiat from on high, could have embarked on such a venture as this appeared to be. Arkley was a past master at dissimulation and, in the modern phrase, disinformation; witness the proposition that these materials were destined for some woman of power in West or Central Asia. If ever a red herring wasted the time of trained and informed minds, that one did.

"It is thanks to Duncanson that the outcome has been as fortunate as it has. He was able to track enough of the course that Arkley's scheme followed to pursue it through the labyrinth, and we had the advantage that Arkley was obliged from time to time to report on the actions he was taking. As to whether his reports were half-truths or falsehoods, Duncanson could make his deductions. We had to let it run, however, to see precisely where Arkley was going. Conjecture and, later, likelihood were not enough."

"Give a man enough rope," Harry said.

"And hang him," Quick finished agreeably. "Indeed. And why not? In a curious way, Seddall, you gave us the same kind of help that Arkley did. Even when your ideas led up blind alleys, nevertheless they helped to clear the picture for us."

He allowed his countenance a tentative flirtation with the cordial. "You are known for your strokes of intuition. It is simply that this was in its essence so mechanically intricate an operation and counter-operation that working in the dark, as you were, one could only go so far. And I do assure you, Seddall, that at as early a stage as possible, Duncanson had the CBR materiel replaced with harmless substances."

Quick consulted his watch again, and you could see him deciding that he would let another appointment go, that Seddall must not leave this room without being content with what he had heard in it.

"I think we might have coffee," Quick said. He went to a bell on the wall and then put his back to them, looking down on the street.

Seddall saw that Duncanson's hand had relaxed and lay limp on the table. When the girl brought the coffee, Duncanson said to her: "I shall pour it." He went so far, now, passing coffee across the table, as to let his eyes meet Seddall's, though they were so wary as for any expression in them to be meaningless.

Quick came back and took his seat.

"You used a phrase," Seddall said.

235

"I know," Quick said. "It was careless."

"A fiat from on high," Seddall said.

"Yes," Quick said.

"I think there was one," Seddall said.

"We live in a world on the brink of chaos," Quick said. "There is continuous war or civil war across the globe, in South America, Central America, Africa, Europe, Eurasia, the Middle East, the sub-continent, the Far East.

"It is a world in which the developed nations fear the growth of the Third World at the same time that they must encourage it for their own economic growth, and at the same time that they exploit the finite assets of the earth to the detriment of the Third World. And the Third World is well aware of this.

"It's a world where the Western nations take the temperature of their economies, which means in the end their stability, by the measure of stock markets, money markets, exchange rates, inflation rates, as if these were true guides to health. In fact, they say nothing about the patient at all, only that the life-support machine is functioning in such and such a way; or, to be even more sceptical, that the life-support machine appears to be functioning, because our knowledge of how it functions is not much higher than ignorance."

He sipped at his coffee and finding it not over-warm, drained the cup and filled it again from the pot.

"There are tyrannies, governmental corruption, countries out of control of their governments. There are increasingly insurmountable social problems, ranging from famine in unfortunate countries to inexorably rising unemployment and growth of poverty in fortunate countries. None of this is going to diminish.

"These are all practical matters, if you like. I have said nothing of national and nationalist passions, which inevitably controvert the same passions in other nations. There are national ambitions. There are hegemonies in dissolution and others in the making: the European Community, for example. What is that, in the last instance, but a psychological protection against fear of the unknown without?"

Quick broke off. He leaned towards Seddall and said: "I'm making quite a speech, or perhaps I've almost finished it now."

Where another man might have smiled on saying this, deprecating himself, he became, if anything, more serious.

"This is my vision of the real world," he said. "It is not the one you derive from the newspapers, where treaties are signed, international debts waived, help provided by the World Bank, hopeful policies announced, remedies proposed at the United Nations, millions raised for Oxfam."

He emptied, once more at a single draught, the cup of coffee before him.

"That is the real world in which this country lives," he said. "Entirely because of the condition of this world – and without making comment on any human being alive, it is a hostile world. To every nation on this planet, it is a hostile world because there is not enough in it for us all and because of the needs and nature of humankind.

"It is a world in which we in this country are not now strong enough to act militarily in every conceivable contingency. We never were so, in fact, but now we are much less so.

"Therefore," Sir Oliver Quick said, sitting back, upright and removed, "if, during the recent conflict, biological warfare materiel existed and was sent to the Gulf, if it was thought to have served its purpose in preventing the enemy from resorting to biological warfare, and if, in the aftermath of war, it occurred to some group in government that it should be secretly conserved against politicians more sanguine than they coming into power; or if it occurred only to Arkley and Tinsley on their own; then, Seddall, what do I say?

"I say to myself that in a hostile and chaotic and unpredictable world, however many of these suppositions may be true, I could understand them. I tell myself that the outcome has been fortunate. And I find in myself no need to lay bare a history that is, with the unhappy deaths of Arkley and Tinsley, already buried."

Seddall, who had been much taken with the greater part of this speech, found the end of it hard to swallow. He became conscious that he was staring at Sir Oliver as if to see that he was really there.

He was there all right. He was the same fleshy article with the high-coloured fat face, macho moustache and short clenched jaw.

237

He was still the man who liked himself enough to use no social or personal devices to put himself across.

He met Seddall's scrutiny with no more difficulty than if the man sitting across from him had been a painted effigy.

"You can live with that?" Seddall asked him. "What is that? Is it patriotism?"

"Certainly I can live with it and, more to the point, I do," Quick said. "Patriotism? Perhaps it is. Different from yours, I think."

He came to his feet and said: "Patriotism can be a tattered old flag." Suddenly Harry felt himself looked into, examined within. "I think perhaps that you try to get your stability from the past, Seddall. But the world we live in now is the world as it is."

For a brief space he maintained that close look, and it almost seemed to Harry as if there was a kindness in it, as if he thought Seddall could not bear to look at the world the way he saw it himself.

"Well," Quick said. "I believe that was a useful encounter. Good afternoon to you both." And he was gone.


Duncanson was at ease with himself now, since whatever he had done or not done it was endorsed by the powers that were. The eyes in the slabbed face met Seddall calmly.

"Did you kill Tinsley?" Seddall asked him.

For all answer, Duncanson widened his eyes for a moment.

"Did you get Arkley into this?" Seddall said.

Duncanson leaned his head a little to the side and said nothing, keeping his eyes silent.

"That was a good speech Quick made," Seddall said. "Good words in it like 'conceivable' and 'sanguine' and 'aftermath'. But its the short words in among the big words that score at Scrabble, isn't it, Duncanson? Words like 'kill' and 'lie' and 'fix'. Your wife taught me that. I would have liked to meet her again."

"You might do a lot with fix," Duncanson said. "As to the other two: was it someone in *Moby Dick* who said, 'Don't be so goddamn confident about your goddamn surmises'? I hope that leaves you in the dark, Seddall. Seddall in the dark, waving his tattered flag. Nice picture."

In a little while, Seddall went out too. He left the room, went downstairs and uplifted his coat and hat. In the street he hailed a taxi to take him back to Sumner Place, where he had left the car.

"Who can I believe, if not myself?" This ran in his head like an unwanted tune that won't leave you alone.

He was full of doubts and of something like fear. Seddall in the dark, waving his tattered flag.

He went into the house to see if the cat was there, which she was not, and out into the street again. He wanted Sacha's company on the drive back to Somerset, if she would agree to this. He found her just down the road, pretending to hunt in Onslow Gardens, for the night was her true hunting time.

She ran towards him until she remembered herself, then sat down and wiped a paw a few times over her nose and looked enigmatic.

"I'm going back to the country," Seddall said, "if you want to come."

He walked back to the car and she followed. When he opened the back door and she saw that Bayard's blanket was in the back seat, she closed her eyes and jumped in.

She was better in the car than she used to be, but failing the dog himself his blanket was enough to make the alien world of the car tolerable.

So they left London, two creatures who considered themselves capable of dealing with their own world, but full of uncertainties about this one.

# 23

"How's Roberto?" Sorrel said.

"He's fine in general, but right this minute he's in an absolute lather," Joanna said, "and you're going to have to help."

"What with?" Sorrel said.

"Come on, you'll find out," Joanna said.

Roberto's flat was a room and a bedroom, but the living room was high and airy and lit by two good-sized windows. The furniture was a jumble of different kinds of comfort, second-hand and new. A great place to spend the start of your Sunday with the papers and generally faff around in, was how it seemed to Sorrel.

Mullen lay on the couch in convalescent splendour. "Great to see you," he said. "My, don't you smell good."

"Well, it smelled good in the bottle," Sorrel said, "but I'm glad it travels. Joanna tells me you're in a lather. Are you?"

"On the nail," Mullen said. "A lather is what I'm in."

Sorrel found a chair and sat down. "What's it about?"

"You're going to like this," Mullen said. "Yesterday I had a phone call from Georg Frankl."

"Damn," Sorrel said instantly. "I thought that was all over and done with."

"It is," Mullen said. "Don't worry about that. Just let me tell it. Georg said that I would get something in the mail today and that I was to use it, then wished me luck and rang off. You may not know this, Sorrel, but I'm in hock to my bookie. In hock in a very bad way indeed."

"That doesn't tell me anything," Sorrel said. "Be specific."

"Several thousand," Mullen said unwillingly.

"More than ten?" Sorrel said.

"Fewer than ten," Mullen said, "but enough for them to set the leg-breakers on to me."

"Roberto," Sorrel said, her face alight and her eyes sparkling. "How deeply exciting."

"Maybe that's what I thought too, in a way," Mullen said, "until I got this hole shot in me. It leaves one feeling rather defenceless, I must admit."

"Of course it does," Sorrel said, "but you'll be better in a month or so."

"They don't wait until you're better, they want it now. In fact, they wanted it yesterday. I'm living on borrowed time," he said, with grim satisfaction.

"Gin, I think," Sorrel said to Joanna, as the import of Roberto's story reached her. Joanna gave her a gin and tonic and then settled on her side of the hearth rug.

"So where does Frankl come in?" Sorrel said.

"This came through the post today," Mullen said, and reached over to her with a hand holding two pieces of paper. One was a money order for a thousand pounds. The other had a message typed on it.

The message said: Brighton. Two-thirty. Nursery Handicap. Transbaikal.

"Ooof," was what Sorrel said. "Gosh, Roberto."

"Yes," he said. "Somehow Frankl must have discovered that I'm into racing."

"That man knows too much," Sorrel said, and for a space of a few seconds became pensive and autobiographical.

Emerging from this, she said: "What's the problem? Is it the horse?"

"No," Mullen said, spending a lot of time on the vowel. "I can make sense of the horse. It's taking his money. It's dirty money, after all. And if it's not dirty money, it belongs to the Government."

Sorrel chewed it over. "Don't be so pretty about it," she said. "You don't have those kind of morals and you know it. We're almost certain it was Taif shot you and Markish, and we know it was Taif who went off with Georg and Anna and all that loot.

You think there's blood on this thousand quid because Markish died, is that it?"

"Funnily enough, no," Mullen said. "I thought it was that, to start with, but it's not really. It's . . . it's as if Georg was sending me compensation for me damn near getting killed."

"Well, why shouldn't he?" Sorrel said. "It's rather a witty way of doing it, too. If someone was going to give you a present, what better present could you get right now than a bet that would clear you with the bookie and the stake to go with it? I take it the odds are enough to do that if Transwhatsit wins?"

"Transbaikal. Yeah," Mullen said, "and a goodish bit over. Georg could be onto a good thing. It's a six-furlong race and this two-year-old has been run at five furlongs and seven furlongs, right? Coming in 3–4, 2–3. I think the trainer knows he's a six-furlong sprinter, that's what I think. He's not entered him at six until he was ready. He's drawn inside at Brighton – well, you have to reckon that as a 4lb advantage. He likes the downhill start and the ground's got just the right amount of chop in it for him today, tacky but not too soft."

Sorrel said: "You've been talking to the stable jockey?"

"Hah," Mullen said. "Not directly. I'm not that daft. But I've been talking where it counts."

Joanna came in from the hearth rug. "The thing is, Sorrel, Roberto loves the bet. And he's only half-worried about taking money from Georg Frankl. The other half is that if he takes the money it gives Frankl a hold over him in the future, so the two half-worries make enough of a whole worry to put him off it."

"Do it," Sorrel said. "That's the first thing. If the horse wins for you, you're free and clear and you collect this afternoon, call the Office and say look, Frankl's sent me a thousand pounds."

"Would you do it?" Roberto said.

"No actually," Sorrel said, "but that's me. We're all good in some spots and weak in others. Simone told me how good you were to her. I'd not have been like that. And all through that shooting and kidnapping you were really brilliant. You don't need to be top of the class in everything. It's the bet of a lifetime for you and I think you have to do it."

"What if the horse comes in nowhere?" Joanna said.

242

"Then Roberto has an extra worry about whether Frankl's going to blackmail him one day," Sorrel said. "It just spiffies up the bet, that's all."

"Last day of the season at Brighton," Mullen said. "Never had a bet with so much edge to it, one way and another. Got to do it." He came up off the couch with the practised self-care of the experienced patient. "I'll do it. I have to cash the order myself. One of those gentle walks the doctor ordered."

"We'll all go, shall we?" Sorrel said. "I'll place the bet. Then there's no snail trail with your name on it."

"Deal," Mullen said. "Good thought."

"Also," Sorrel said, "I'm having useful thoughts about these leg-breakers."

"Bloody Starker," Mullen said. "I don't know how I'm going to get him off my back. I'll have to think of something."

"Who's Starker?" Sorrel said.

"Leg-breaker-in-chief," Joanna said. "I'm afraid Roberto punched him in the gut, and the deadline Starker gave is way past."

"We can't have this," Sorrel said, and thought. "Do you know, I have a sort of plan. You'll have to trust me, though, and you'll have to trust me that you can trust this other person to keep your Awful Secret about the money."

"What other person?" Mullen said.

"I'm not going to tell you, because I don't think you like him very much," Sorrel said. "Trust me?"

"I do," Joanna said.

"All right," Mullen said, contriving to appear suspicious and trusting at the same time.


"Mist?" said Mullen, back in the flat with the telly on. "Cancel? Don't cancel, don't cancel. Hold my hand everybody."

On the Sussex coast the mist was wafting in from the sea, and in the flat the atmosphere was pitched so high you could almost hear it crackle.

The stewards did not cancel. The electricity in the room dispersed for a moment and then came back with gathered force.

"He likes the ground," Mullen said.

"He looks rather small and ordinary," Joanna said.

"Wait and see," Mullen said. "Just you wait and see," as if he'd trained the horse himself.

Transbaikal came out of the chute and led them down the hill. Two furlongs on they took the left-hand bend and he vanished into the mist, leading the field by a clear three lengths.

"Christ, look at him go," Mullen said. "Georg Frankl, where have you been all my life?"

The camera at the finish came on screen. The horses came through the mist like the fastest ghosts ever captured on film.

"It is even he," Mullen said, sounding as cool as a cucumber. "He's got the race."

The girls, by contrast, were on their feet and yelling their heads off.

Transbaikal tore past the post. Sorrel and Joanna fell upon each other's necks and shook the floor jumping up and down.

Mullen lit a cigarette. His face lost the tension of months, and a smile came onto him that used every bit of bone, sinew and muscle between his chin and the top of his head.

"Hot damn," he said. "Hot ziggety damn."

"Gimme the betting slip," Sorrel said. "I'll go and collect."

"You won't be popular," Mullen said.

"There will," Sorrel said, "be no problem. When I come back, we'll set up a meet with your Mr Starker."

She left Joanna and Roberto with a look in their eyes.


Edward Raleigh was already there when she went into the appointed café in the King's Road. He was eating a croque-monsieur and drinking espresso and reading the *Independent,* looking tremendously at home.

"You like this sort of place," she said.

"Yes," he said, "my kind of place."

Sorrel ordered herself a cappuccino. "How do you think it will go?" she said.

"It will go just swell," he said. "You're carrying, aren't you?"

"Yes," she said.

"So am I," he said. "Not supposed to, but they'll know and it'll tell them something."

He was wearing a light tweed coat and a crew-neck sweater, a relaxed and unassuming fresh-faced man, having a good day with himself.

Starker and two men came in, looked around and sat down two tables away.

"Just let me do it," Raleigh said.

They waited while Starker and his cronies ordered beer. Bottled beer, not what they wanted. The beer came and Starker lifted the glass to his mouth.

Raleigh said, quiet but clear: "Over here, Starker."

Starker's massive shoulders pounced forward and the beer spilled on the table. He turned in his chair, wiping his mouth.

Raleigh had gone pink. Sorrel had begun to find this habit of his extremely endearing.

"Just you, Starker," Raleigh said. "Not your poor relations."

Gosh, Sorrel thought. She had been doing it for a while, but now she said with certainty to her ex-SAS tough-egg boyfriend in the Brigade, so long, dear man. Should she write or talk? Phone first, and see if he wanted to meet about it, be friends, that sort of who-knows-what-it-means-anyway thing. But it oiled troubled waters sometimes.

While she was speaking to herself like this she was watching Starker stand up and look them over.

"Give him the envelope," Raleigh said. "It doesn't matter if he sees what's in your bag."

Starker came to their table. "What's this?" he said. "Who are you?"

"This is pay-day," Raleigh said, "and never mind who I am."

"I don't like that kind of talk," Starker said, "not from nobody."

Raleigh blushed. "Eat shit," he said pleasantly.

He nodded at Sorrel, who opened her bag and took out the envelope. As she handed it to Starker she saw his eyes catch the automatic in the bag.

"Uh-huh," he said as he took the envelope, "what's this, then?"

245

"It's from Roberto Mullen," Raleigh said. "Clears what he owes you. Count it. Give her a receipt."

"It's late," Starker said. "He'll have to be made an example of."

"Mr Starker," Raleigh said, "we don't want you to make an example of Roberto Mullen. We don't even want you to let the air out of his tyres or jostle him on the pavement, or say anything to him you wouldn't say to your own mother."

Starker stood there, large and wicked written all over him, and counted the money with nimble fingers. He held a note up to the light and felt it, then put it back with the others.

"Who's we?" he said. "You and her?"

"Me and her," Raleigh said, "are just the tip of the iceberg. Do you believe me, Mr Starker, or am I going to have to spoil your life for you?"

Starker looked at Raleigh, and Raleigh looked at Starker. "I believe you," Starker said. "You're not much, you're no super-middleweight, but I believe you. Not a hair of Mullen's head, is that it?"

"That's it," Raleigh said.

Starker took a small pad out of his pocket and leaned down on the marble table top and wrote a receipt. He gave it to Sorrel. "All right?" he said.

"All right," she said.

"OK," Starker said. "Deal." He looked down at Raleigh with a rotten look on him. "But you eat shit too, you got that?"

"Don't hold your breath," Raleigh said. "Goodbye."

Starker went straight out into the King's Road and his buddies swallowed fast and went after him.

"That was about right, I think," Raleigh said. "What are you doing now?"

"I'm going to go home and have a bath," Sorrel said, "and then I'm going to take you out to dinner."

"All right," Raleigh said.

246

# 24

When he had finished his cheese, Seddall said to Mrs Lyon: "I'll come through to the kitchen and get my coffee in a mug. I want to drink it out the back and watch that great beast at work."

"In the fermyaird?" Mrs Lyon said. "Ye'll catch your death of cold."

"It's not that cold," Harry said.

"Then take the dug wi ye," Mrs Lyon said. "I'll no want him under my feet while I'm getting the room ready for Sorrel and her man, and efter that the dinner. Ye'll hae to take him under your wing the rest o' the day. He'll aye sit slavering at me when I'm getting dinner for folk, and he kens they're coming, he always does."

Seddall threw on a coat and, with the brown and white spaniel for company, kept his hands warm on the coffee mug while he watched the JCB dig out the hole that was going to be his swimming pool.

The contractor had been astonished. "You don't want us pouring concrete out there during the winter," he had said, "not with the frost we've been having. And there'll be more to come."

"I want the hole dug," Seddall said. "I want something happening now."

It was the truth. That was all there was to it. He wanted something happening now and it didn't have to be the hole for the swimming pool but it was all he could think of.

He wanted change. He wanted some making to take place: he was possessed by a need to move forward from the aftermath of events which had fouled his spirit and left him disoriented, filled with doubts and inhabited by questions he could not name, so that he could find no answers in him.

Seddall knew what he was going to do. He was going to hibernate here at Old Spring Farm and let Somerset, his native heath, do its work on him. His old home, a mile away, had gone up in flames, so this was his first winter at the farmhouse, a fact which had opened him to at least one survival instinct – the idea that he would set about making the house as he wanted it. This was not a thing to be done in a mad frenzy; one step at a time, while he grew used to the place and felt his way. But at least he knew he wanted a swimming pool, for he had taken to swimming as his exercise.

He watched the JCB digging out the ground under the roof of what had been the cow barn. The wooden barn would come down in the new year, but meanwhile it would stop the pit filling with rain or snow. He drank his coffee.

"What do you think of that, Bayard?" he said to the dog.

Not a hell of a lot, the dog said.

"I see," Harry said. "You're not into spectator sport. Come on, then, we'll go for a hike."

He put the mug on a windowsill, and the two of them went off under the cold sky, a shepherd's delight of a sky, its clouds reddened by the declining sun.

When they got back to the house in the early dark, the outside light over the back door showed the JCB at rest in the farmyard – "We'll put this down to grass next year, Bayard" – with a Peugeot estate parked beside it.

Once the door was open the dog shot out of sight, so that by the time Harry had shed his coat and made his way through to the front of the house, Bayard's first transports were over and he was sniffing Edward Raleigh's hand, while Sorrel brushed doghairs and slobber from her jeans and sweater.

"I hope you people are hungry," Harry said. "We've worked up an appetite, this beast and I. An early dinner would oblige."

"Starving," Sorrel kissed him. "And Mrs Lyon says we'll eat at seven if you're back in time, which you are."

"Great news," Seddall said. "Good to see you, Raleigh, though I think I'll call you Edward, now that you're one of the family."

At first glance Raleigh looked much the same as he had when Seddall first met him in France, but there was an indefinable change in him, and Seddall saw it. Although he could not define it to himself, he could express it: Raleigh had left school. Intuition told him this, and it was intuition which told him also that it was not to do with Sorrel but was a change in Raleigh's self, between the man and the world.

Harry mistrusted sudden change in a man, but time would tell.

They dined on Scotch broth and saddle of lamb and apple dumpling. When Seddall said to Mrs Lyon that she was laying it on a bit heavy, she said that the visitors had come all the way from London; she said it as if they had walked, or perhaps jogged, down to Somerset.

"Has Olivia decided where to take her holiday?" Sorrel asked over the lamb.

"To distinguish between Olivia's normal life and her travels," Harry said briskly, "I call them expeditions, not holidays. She is going to Outer Mongolia, to ride camels. She and two other women. They are even now scouring maps in Paris."

"You're not going with her?" Raleigh said.

With that, Seddall knew he was right about Raleigh. There had been a disagreeable resonance in that question: the bloody man was working, even here, as a guest in this house.

Seddall chewed on the meat in his mouth and gazed extensively at that fresh young face which he saw to be in its third stage of sophistication, taking Oxford as the first and employment as the second.

"You've a younger stomach than me," he said. "You've digested the treachery and the double-dealing and the rotten end Arkley made of a distinguished career in no time at all."

"It's a good bit more than no time at all," Raleigh said, and though he blushed, as was to be expected from him, Seddall knew that meant nothing. "But yes, I've digested it. You must have seen a lot worse than that in your time. It's part of the trade, isn't it?"

"Help yourself to some meat," Seddall said, "if you know how to carve a saddle of lamb, that is. I don't want it hacked about."

"Thanks," Raleigh said, and went to the serving table.

"Part of the trade," Harry said, and left it there, because he had felt an anger awake suddenly inside him and he knew it was an anger about life, not an anger that he ought to throw at Raleigh.

"Duncanson called Ted in for a talk, yesterday," Sorrel said. "Told him he didn't want him around any more. Asked what he'd think of going to Intelligence."

"You're going to MI6?" Seddall said.

"Yes," said Raleigh. "Got to clear my desk tomorrow. Shall I keep on carving?"

The response was positive. "I'll take lessons from Mrs Lyon," Sorrel said. "What do you think, Harry? About Ted moving to MI6?"

"Why not, if he likes the work?" Seddall said. "There are changes going on there now, which makes it a good time to join."

Raleigh went round the table distributing the results of his labours with the carving-knife.

"I like this room," Sorrel said. "I hope you're not going to change it too much."

"I'm not going to change it at all," Harry said. "Bar a lick of paint and some pictures as I come across them. I'm not even sure I'll get central heating, I like it like this."

By "like this" he meant a fire in the big fireplace with an electric radiator at the other end of the room, and the two windows shuttered against the cold. There was carpet over most of the stone floor, and plain furniture from local second-hand shops, gleaming from the vigorous polishing of Mrs Lyon. The whitewash on the walls was peeling, and even that felt comfortable.

"You'll want central heating as you grow older," Sorrel said.

"I'm growing older right now," Seddall said, "and I don't feel the need for it. I shouldn't have undertaken to eat all this. I'll have no space for the famous apple dumpling."

The apple dumpling was much reduced all the same, and they were three replete diners who sank into the upholstery of the drawing room and said thank you and goodnight to Mrs Lyon after she had delivered their coffees and a quiverful of Scottish apothegms.

"Now," Seddall said. "Tell me about Duncanson."

"I was writing my report," Raleigh said, "and asked Duncanson – no, just coffee for me, thanks – when I could come to see him to clarify some things that were not clear to me. Come at once, he said. He told me to bring a copy of the report as far as it had progressed."

When Raleigh went into his master's office, Duncanson had held out a hand and said: "Give." Raleigh gave him the report and the disc and Duncanson put them in a drawer of his desk.

"What are you not clear about?" Duncanson said.

"I'm not clear when we, when MI5, became aware that Arkley was involved in a scheme of his own."

"We didn't become aware," Duncanson said. "I did."

"How?" Raleigh said, and thought as he said it that he'd have done better to put the question less baldly. Later, he supposed he had been infected by the abrupt style of speech Duncanson was using.

"Next question," Duncanson said, and though he did not seem riled his manner was suddenly alarming: it was unnaturally low-key and unctuous, like a doctor visiting a seriously ill patient in hospital.

"I'm not clear," Raleigh said, "how the CBR consignment – the genuine CBR consignment – got back to the UK."

"Are you not?" Duncanson said, and sat silent, watching Raleigh in a markedly detached and objective way, before he spoke. "It was flown to France from Egypt in one of Arkley's MI6 aircraft," he said. "When Markish was shot . . ." – and here Duncanson hesitated as if seeking an appropriate form of words – "it seemed best to move in and withdraw it from that garden of his, discreetly, you know."

"I thought," Raleigh said, "Markish had that done before he died."

"No," Duncanson said.

"But Simone gave Harry Seddall a different account."

"That also seemed best at the time," Duncanson said. "It was not then apparent to me how much of this I would be able to keep secret."

"Secret?" Raleigh said.

Duncanson gave one of his ferocious grins. "Laddie," he said, "you've a lot to learn. Anything I know that no one else knows,

251

or anything MI5 knows that no other agency knows, is power in my hand."

"And Simone's story?" Raleigh said, tuning into the fact that there was some pleasure for Duncanson in his role of master of the craft instructing the apprentice.

"That was my script," Duncanson agreed. "We leaned on her a little."

"What with?" Raleigh said, playing the student eager to learn.

Duncanson shrugged, as if the question, too amateurish, had taken the savour out of the game, and said only: "Are you resolved of all your little doubts now?"

Raleigh found himself playing for time, while most of his attention was given to listening between the lines, as it were, trying to detect what was happening in this exchange, to catch what he was hearing from Duncanson that was not being said in words.

"I seem to have two doubts left," Raleigh said, inventing, however, the first of these. "For one thing, why was the money carried in those CBR containers?"

Duncanson deliberated, as if the question might be deeper than it seemed. "It seems rather obvious to me," he said. "If you're entrusting that amount of money to a man like Abd el Sudi, you tell him the boxes are carrying the plague virus, something like that, and that it is death to open them. So the boxes have to be the same as the others."

"Of course," Raleigh said. "It was just a niggle."

"Indeed," Duncanson said, regarding him deeply. "What else?"

"Simply, as to where the money came on the scene."

"Ah," Duncanson said. "Well, strange things happen at sea, but who knows, Raleigh, who knows?"


There was a long silence after that, Raleigh said, while they looked at each other. A curious thing happened. The silence went on too long, as if both of them were listening to what Duncanson had said – not for any particular cause but from some chance interaction between them – and once they had become aware of this listening, it grew of itself. The expression with which Duncanson faced Raleigh had altered, through indefinable stages, from one of impatient scorn to the retaliatory aggression of the powerful man accused.

"I wasn't accusing him of anything," Raleigh told Seddall, "but because of the way he was looking at me, I began to feel as if I was. And then, just like that, I was. I don't know what I was accusing him of. It was a thing that happened between us. Not what he had said, but the way he said it. As if he had been a part of it. And I was sitting there across the desk from him, asking myself how much of it all he actually had been part of. He could see it in me. He could see me wondering how far back towards the beginning of the whole business he was in it; not just following it, but in it. It was the strangest thing. Even now I don't suppose he was – in it with Arkley, I mean. And yet I don't know. I don't know."

Raleigh reorganized his legs to accommodate Bayard, who had toasted one side at the fire and now settled down to toast the other.

"What do you think, Harry?" Sorrel said.

"About Duncanson? About what went on?" Seddall nodded at Bayard. "Let sleeping dogs lie, I say. If Duncanson had things to hide, they'll be hidden now beyond discovery. Obviously, it was after that meeting he said he wanted you out of MI5?"

"That's right," Raleigh said. "First of all he told me he wanted no report from me, then he sent me off on leave, and then when I came back he sacked me. It's not quite like being sacked, though. He promised to get me well placed at MI6, which is what's happened. And I'd rather be at Six, so he's done me a favour."

Seddall knew now what it was he had sensed in Raleigh. The fellow would not only let this particular sleeping dog lie, he would stroke it if the occasion required. Duncanson, it seemed to him, had made a friend where he might have made an enemy.

Seddall thought he might as well test this proposition, although in fact he was thinking of what it would be like when his swimming pool was in being and asking himself what sort of garden he'd make out of the farmyard. The garden in front of the house had a good-sized lawn and was well-flowered. No point in simply repeating that. He brought his mind back to the present, with the foolish question he wanted to ask ready on his tongue.

"What of Georg Frankl?" he said. "It was commercial with him, from first to last? Is that Duncanson's view?"

"Lord, no," Raleigh said. "Mossad planted Anna on Arkley ages ago, which was a brilliant stroke on their part, you'll agree. And Frankl was certainly genuine when he came to us in the first place, though Duncanson thinks he may have wanted to be near Anna, and that he was in any case restless at Mossad. Very much a man of the world, Georg Frankl; not your dedicated Israeli. It was simply that when Georg and Anna found there was going to be money floating around they worked out how to get hold of it."

"What about Taif?" Sorrel said.

"Oh, Taif was a piece of luck for them," Raleigh said. "Anna heard about Taif from Arkley. Then, once Frankl decided he needed an extra player and that Taif might be just the man, all Anna had to do was toddle round to the hotel and ask him if he wanted to get rich. We think that's what happened."

"Yes, it makes sense," Seddall said, but he was hearing the flow of Duncanson's words in Raleigh's voice. He was in Duncanson's pocket all right; or would be while Duncanson's was the pocket to be in.

Not long after, Raleigh departed to take the first step in the next phase of his career. Seddall said his goodbye in the drawing room, and left it to Sorrel see him off. When she came back, Sacha the cat slipped into the room as the door was closing, jumped onto the couch and washed her face briefly, then stared into the fire.

Sorrel got herself a drink and sat on the floor. "Why does the cat turn up now?" she asked. "She's been out of sight all evening."

"Sacha's the cat that walks by itself," Seddall said, lying back stretched and somnolent in his armchair. "I never ask her where she's been."

"There's more to it than that," Sorrel said. "You know perfectly well what Sacha's like. She didn't take to our Edward."

"That's a bit whimsical," Seddall said. "And what's it matter who the cat likes or doesn't like?"

"Sacha's got an instinct," Sorrel said.

They were very much at home together: Seddall slumped in his chair, a day's growth on chin and jowl, his face relaxed into an expression of sardonic good humour – an expression almost smug, now that Raleigh had gone; Sorrel leaning against Sacha's chair, rueful and lovely, but full of health.

"Never mind Sacha," Seddall said. "You've got an instinct of your own."

Sorrel made a face.

"Do you like him?" Seddall asked her.

"Not so much as I did. I fancied him a lot, and I was right," she said, her eyes darting up at him, "but I don't like him as much as I did. Either I didn't see him, or he's changed."

"I'd say he's changing," Seddall said. "Doesn't mean he's a bad bloke."

"I think he's going to be," Sorrel said. "He's being seduced by the dirty side of Intelligence. I'm going off him, Harry. I'll have to tell him and get it done with."

He heaved himself up and went for the whisky bottle, charged her glass and his own, biffed her lightly on the face, and fell recumbent into his chair again.

"How are things with you?" she asked.

"You mean, how are things with Olivia?" he said. "How the hell do I know? She's never around. It's her idea of the perfect relationship. I'd never used the word relationship till I met Olivia. In short, my proud beauty, fuck the word relationship."

"Sounds bad," Sorrel said, and gave him that upward glance again, but this time it came at him as what Olivia might have called inappropriate.

"Sorrel," he said. "Don't do that. It takes me back."

She looked at him openly, the blue eyes very wide and candid-seeming. "That's nice," she said.

"Don't be a twit, Sorrel Blake," he said. "Two old lovers lonely in the storm, what bullshit that would be."

"People make their own weather," she said.

He looked at the fire and then at her, and she looked at him and then at the fire.

"Karl Marx," he said, "writing to the Paris Commune in 1870-something: 'Don't begin the past again'."

"You didn't used to be so pompous," Sorrel said, her face hot.

"Christ," he said, much shocked, "you're right about that. What have I been doing with myself?"

"I'm going to bed," Sorrel said. "If I leave my door open it means I'd like to see you."

She stood up, magnificent in anger, and the pull of her was electric and the look she gave him as she went out was indescribable.

"Hell's teeth," he said to himself. "Mongolia, yurts – Olivia, where art thou? I'm going for a walk," he said. "Who's coming?"

Bayard slept on, but Sacha came outside. It was a frosty night, stars and a cold, indifferent moon. He walked down the track and Sacha went through the hedge into the field, with him but not of him.

He came to a gate and leaned on it, his thoughts and feelings simply a tumult, no hope of understanding himself there. He saw the cat's black shape in the moonlight, flat to the ground, and made a deal with himself and watched and waited.

A cloud came from nowhere across the moon, but he had seen Sacha pounce and heard the squeal as she struck.

"You're a great animal," he said, and went back to the house.